SEP 1 3

W9-ATS-150

Cold Tuscan Stone

Books by David P. Wagner

Rick Montoya Italian Mysteries
Cold Tuscan Stone

Cold Tuscan Stone

A Rick Montoya Italian Mystery

David P. Wagner

Poisoned Pen Press

Copyright © 2013 by David P. Wagner

First Edition 2013

10 9 8 7 6 5 4 3 2 1

Library of Congress Catalog Card Number: 2013933484

ISBN: 9781464201905   Hardcover
       9781464201929   Trade Paperback

All rights reserved. No part of this publication may be repro-
duced, stored in, or introduced into a retrieval system, or
transmitted in any form, or by any means (electronic, mechanical, photocopying, recording, or otherwise) without the prior
written permission of both the copyright owner and the pub-
lisher of this book.

Poisoned Pen Press
6962 E. First Ave., Ste. 103
Scottsdale, AZ 85251
www.poisonedpenpress.com
info@poisonedpenpress.com

Printed in the United States of America

For Mary, without whose patience and support this book would not have been written

Chapter One

Fall's coldest day brought a damp chill that seeped through clothing and skin, but the bearded man was oblivious to the temperature. He crossed his arms over his chest, bent forward slightly, and focused on the figures before him. His breath came in small clouds of vapor, obscuring the scene that held his gaze. He could not tear his eyes away from the drama before him.

The funeral procession he watched followed the ancient traditions of Etruria, but timeless sorrow etched deeply into the faces of the family. Two powerful horses pulled the covered cart, heads bowed as if to honor the dead man inside. Their waving manes and pulsing muscles, so full of life, contrasted with the flat, tomb-shaped stones of the wall behind them. The wife, or perhaps an older daughter, followed on foot behind the cart with two children in tow, their eyes questioning her in silence. Behind their round faces her robe dragged on the ground, covering sandaled feet. She gripped the tiny hands and stared ahead, her face stiff with grief. The observer guessed the two small figures were the grandchildren of the deceased, not quite aware of what was going on, but sensing something dark. A lone, male rider, cloak flowing behind him, sat on a saddled horse at the head of the cortège. The steed strained forward against the reins, but the man's head was turned back toward the cart, his face reflecting the sadness of the woman. Was he her brother, and now the reluctant head of the family?

The watcher would never know. He breathed deeply and pulled at his carefully trimmed beard, hoping the gesture didn't betray his nervousness to the two men with him.

"Spectacular," he said. One arm reached out to touch the cold alabaster, its fingers running across the smooth faces of the two draft horses, down through the curled grooves of the milky manes, and pausing for a moment at the muscles of their shanks. His hand and eyes continued to caress the stone as he spoke. He almost whispered, as if he were standing before an altar in a church. "It looks like it was carved yesterday."

The two other men exchanged glances, and one of them spoke.

"The urn was discovered only recently, and it has been professionally cleaned with great care." The voice was clipped and businesslike. "Had it been exposed to the elements for more than two millennia, instead of buried in a tomb all that time, it would never have survived in this condition."

The three men stood in a half-lit basement room around the only piece of furniture in the space—a table on which the rectangular stone box sat. A heavy black cloth, which had covered the piece when they had entered the room, was now folded neatly on the side of the table. The damp chill of the Milanese streets outside had seeped into the house; only the lack of wind kept the temperature bearable. All three men kept on their heavy coats, not that there was anywhere to hang them. A musty smell, maybe of something stored there in the past, permeated the room, but the man intently inspecting the funerary urn was oblivious to all but the stone box before him.

"Volterra? Fourth century BC?" His eyes kept on the urn, examining the sides where the carving continued.

"Precisely." The two returned to silence as their visitor circled the box. The collector had made his desires known weeks earlier—put in his order, as it were—and they had delivered. Now it was time to let the Etruscan urn itself make the final sale.

Minutes passed before the man turned from the ancient stone to the two men who had been waiting patiently. "The cover?"

"This is the way it came to us. The lid must have been lost or destroyed at some point."

The first man ran his hand along the top edge and peered inside. "That makes it considerably less desirable."

"The price reflects that."

"Your price does seem reasonable…but I should like a few days to decide. It is not a small sum. Perhaps I could take a few photographs to help me—"

When the potential buyer lifted a small camera from his coat pocket the larger of the other two stepped forward and held up his hand.

"No." He spoke a touch too firmly. Then he added, in a less menacing tone, "I'm sure you will understand that photographing this piece is impossible. Under the circumstances."

"Yes, I understand completely." He slipped the camera back into his pocket. "As to the tomb where it was found. Where was it located?"

The two associates exchanged glances, as if to decide who would reply. The shorter one finally said, "I'm afraid we can only say that it was in Tuscany, in the area around Volterra." He glanced again at his companion. "We are not told the exact location."

The man pretended that the answer satisfied him. "Yes, of course."

After a few more minutes of examination, the urn was covered with the cloth again and the three walked to the door. The buyer opened it and headed up the shadowed stairs toward the street. The larger man turned to his colleague and shook his head quickly. The other nodded agreement before following their visitor up the stairs. At the top, a metal door creaked open. The three stepped outside into a fog that almost obscured the building across the narrow alley. The short man pulled out a key and noisily closed the deadbolt on the door before turning to the client. Thirty meters away, where the alley began, cars crept slowly through the fog, their lights on but dimmed. The

Milanese knew fog well and treated it with respect. The three walked in silence out to the street where they stopped.

"I will be in contact by the end of the week. I know you need an answer."

The two dealers smiled stiffly and nodded. No handshake was offered, so the buyer hurried off toward the center of town while a tram rumbled past him on its tracks, making the sidewalk vibrate under his feet. They watched him until one tapped the other on the arm and jerked his head back toward the passage. By the time the tram was passing the alley, the key was back in its metal door.

Chapter Two

It just doesn't seem possible.

Rick Montoya settled back into the soft back of the chair, stretched his long legs so that his tooled leather boots were visible, and faced the official sitting behind the heavy wooden desk. The office had to be one of the choice rooms in the ministry, its windows overlooking the orange tiled roofs of central Rome. In the distance the large tricolor flag of Italy fluttered slowly over the presidential palace, silhouetted by one of the seven hills. If this were a hotel, the view alone would make the room worth hundreds of Euros a night, with or without breakfast. The man behind the desk spoke into the phone as he smiled at Rick.

"Two coffees please, Marta."

Was this really Beppo Rinaldi? Rick had run into Beppo on the Via del Corso just after moving to Rome six month earlier, but they hadn't much time to talk. The two exchanged business cards and promised to meet and relive their high school days on the basketball team. When Beppo called a few days ago, Rick had all but forgotten the encounter.

Rick, along with everyone else in their class at the American Overseas School of Rome, always assumed that Beppo Rinaldi would go into the family business. Beppo was a Roman, after all, one of a minority in the school where most students either had one American parent or were the kids of diplomats working at the foreign embassies. With his American foreign service father and a Roman mother, Rick fell into both categories. Beppo, however, was the scion of rich local parents who thought fluent English and an American high school education would serve their son well in international business.

But Beppo had surprised Rick by saying that instead of joining his father's company, he was working at the Ministry of Culture. That career shift was startling enough, but now what fully amazed Rick was the section of the ministry where his friend sat. Beppo, the goofy kid whose claim to fame in school was a lucky winning shot in a basketball game, was now investigating stolen antiquities. Rick shook his head and returned the smile as Beppo put down the phone.

"Beppo, I can't believe you're working here. I—"

"You thought I'd be working for my father? I thought I would too, but when I started my university studies I got interested in art history. Loved it. One thing led to another, and before I knew it here I was. Not bad, huh?" He glanced up at the painted ceiling of the room. The *palazzo* had once housed a religious school, and a well-funded one at that. The Jesuits had spared no expense on the decoration of this part of the building, but Rick suspected the classrooms were more spartan. "And your translation business, Rick, I trust it is prospering?"

The question prompted Rick to straighten his tie. Lunch with an Italian meant coat and tie, and in his short time back in the city Rick had spent much of his earnings, perhaps too much, on an Italian wardrobe. So while not dressed as well as Beppo, he didn't look like an American tourist. Only his cowboy boots gave a hint of his New Mexico roots, but he told his Roman friends that he wore them for their comfort. Which was just what he'd told his drinking buddies in Albuquerque when they'd noticed his Bruno Magli loafers. Today he'd almost put on a pair of light brown wing tips to go with charcoal gray slacks and a blue blazer, all three recent acquisitions, but instead convinced himself that the well-shined boots worked just fine. A dark blue shirt and solid red tie completed the wardrobe. You can never go wrong, his father always told him, with a solid red tie.

"Thankfully, yes, Beppo, the translating business is doing well. It's still just me and my computer, but I may have to hire a secretary soon and even get a real office instead of working out of my apartment." He scanned the room while shaking his head in disbelief. "It won't be as sumptuous as this, of course. So, where do you want to eat?"

Beppo leaned forward, elbows on the desk. He folded his hands under his chin, showing more forehead between eyes and hairline than Rick remembered from school days. They say that nobody changes much from high school, but Rick was starting to notice some differences beyond the tailored suit and the receding hair. Beppo's expression could be serious.

"Rick, before we go to lunch to talk about the good old days at AOSR, there's something I want to discuss with you. Something to do with my work. I think you could be of considerable help, if you accept my proposition."

Just as I suspected, Rick thought, there had to be something more than a reunion afoot. Rick had split his life between Italy and New Mexico, so he'd spent enough time in Rome to think like a local. *Cosa c'è dietro?* 'What's behind it?' the cynical Roman would ask himself in even the most innocuous situation. More often than not, such ingrained skepticism served the *romani* well. But Beppo could be a positive contact for his business, and his workload of the moment would not keep him from taking on more business, not by a longshot. Translations for Beppo would be a great way to get his foot in the door at the ministry, and could lead to other government work around the capitol.

"As long as it doesn't take too long. I'm hungry."

Beppo gazed at his friend for a few moments with a weary expression that Rick did not remember seeing in school. "Not that long. Let me show you something." He got up from the desk and walked behind Rick's chair. Having been dazzled by the window views of the city, Rick had not noticed a table near the door which held a large object covered by a black cloth. Beppo carefully pulled off the cloth, revealing a highly-decorated stone box. The sides were carved in relief, covered with figures in action. It was a battle scene, soldiers wielding spears and shields, wearing armor and helmets. Centered in the rectangular front panel, in the middle of the fray, a charioteer commanded his two horses. In contrast to the chaos of the war panels, a carved human figure covered the lid of the urn, an aged man reclining on a sofa, his wrinkled head held up by a hand cupped under his chin. He could have been sitting for a portrait while enjoying an ancient banquet.

At Beppo's nod, Rick reached out, running his palms over the carvings, feeling the stone reliefs with his fingertips. "Etruscan? I was a language major in college so it's not a period I have studied. No doubt you have."

Beppo stared as if seeing the stone for the first time. He kept his eyes on the piece as he spoke.

"Often the Etruscan are described as mysterious, but that's mainly because serious study of them started relatively recently and so much is still unknown about their civilization. Historians spent more time on the Romans, who absorbed Etruscan territory into their empire. And only in the last century has the Etruscan language finally been deciphered, which has led to many more discoveries about them. And as you might expect, much of the scholarship has been done in Tuscany, since most of the cities in the Etruscan federation are found there. This urn was found in western Tuscany."

He glanced at Rick and then returned his gaze to the stone. "It is a fairly typical Etruscan burial urn from the fourth century BC. It held the ashes of a wealthy person, though likely not very prominent politically, given the urn's size. The figures on the front and sides are myths or perhaps an important battle, but they're typical, and likely had nothing to do with the life of the man whose ashes were placed inside." He carefully placed a hand on the stone head and ran his fingers over its features. "However, the image of the man himself is accurate. The Romans raised portraiture, especially in sculpture, to levels never seen before and rarely repeated since. They probably learned their early skills from the Etruscans. This figure of the deceased is an excellent example of how Etruscan artists captured the real person in their work. They don't romanticize the subject, as you can see."

Rick glanced at his friend's face and grinned. "Where is the Beppo I remember, the guy in the back of the class, always quiet? You sound like a professor."

A brief smile flitted across what had been a serious face, contemplating the carving. "Sorry, Rick, I love this stuff. But let me tell you what has happened." He glanced away from the urn to Rick. "And how you might help us save some of these beautiful objects."

This didn't sound like a translation job.

"Several urns from this period, like this one, have suddenly appeared on the market. Their sale is illegal, of course. Anything discovered in a dig is the property of the Italian state, but you know the sale of stolen or looted artifacts is big business. It's what keeps our office busy." He walked back to the desk as he talked while Rick returned to his chair. "We think that a new tomb has been discovered, and not by reputable archeologists. These pieces have begun turning up in the usual places, and we are doing our best to track down the sources. It hasn't been easy. Oh, thank you, Marta."

A woman had arrived with a round tray bearing two plastic cups, four packets of sugar, and a pair of tiny wooden sticks. She put the tray on the edge of the desk and disappeared. Both men reached forward, took a packet, and tore open their sugar.

"Not very elegant, I'm afraid. If you call on the minister you get real cups and silverware, but not here."

"No problem, Beppo." Rick stirred his espresso. "How do you know about the urns showing up on the market?"

Beppo drank his coffee in one gulp and threw the cup into a wastebasket. "We have our contacts, of course. The office got word that one was on sale in Milano last week, and we sent one of our undercover men there." He was speaking rapidly now, and gesturing with thick-fingered hands with perfectly manicured fingernails. "Unfortunately the sellers got cold feet at the last minute and disappeared with the urn, but not before our guy had a chance to see it. He swears the piece was genuine."

"It could have been fake?"

"There's a large market in fakes. That isn't our priority. Such things are usually handled by the regular police. We're after the real thing, like that one over there."

"That's stolen?"

"It was."

Rick was curious about how it had turned up in Beppo's office, but clearly his friend would say no more.

"These latest urns have all been from Volterra, Rick. Without boring you with details, I'll say that the type of material, the carving quality, and the iconography all indicate they must have been found in a tomb near that city. So we'll concentrate our efforts on Volterra. Once pieces leave the country, it is far more difficult to get them back. I received word this morning that one may have surfaced in Bulgaria. That is very disturbing."

"But what do I have to do with it?"

Beppo shifted away from the desk, his jacket opening to show the brightly colored silk tie and tailored shirt. A foulard which matched the tie was casually but carefully tucked into the jacket pocket. His elegant wardrobe indicated that working for the ministry hadn't cut Beppo off from the profits of the family business.

"The other day I remembered your connections."

Rick was puzzled. Connections? His Italian uncle, the policeman? But how would Beppo have remembered that from high school?

"What do you mean?"

"Well, your connection with New Mexico."

Rick blinked.

"Let me explain." Beppo opened a drawer and pulled out a small card which he passed across the desk. After reading it, Rick became even more confused.

"A commercial art gallery in Santa Fe? I've been there, but now I'm completely lost." He handed the card back.

"Rick, stolen antiquities appear in the Santa Fe art market, mostly from South America, but there is the occasional piece from Italy. We have worked with this dealer in the past, and they have always been very cooperative. I called them yesterday and they agreed to help us again for this case."

"Still not with you, Beppo."

"Simply put, Rick, we'd like you go to Volterra and pose as a buyer for the gallery."

"Me?" Not what Rick had imagined. Not even close. A few documents translated, some interpreting for a visiting English speaker, but not undercover work.

"It would be like this: You are a friend of the American gallery owner, and since he knows you are now living in Rome, he's asked you to go up to Tuscany to look into some possible purchases to export back to New Mexico. The gallery's interested in alabaster pieces, as well as a few fine works of art, especially sculpture in the classical and Etruscan style. All legitimate, of course. You would also carefully leak the news that you might be in the market for some *genuine* artifacts. Volterra being a relatively small town, the word would get out and you would be approached by the men who have found the tomb with these urns. At least that's what I think will happen." Beppo settled back in the chair and watched his friend's reaction.

Rick immediately thought of his Uncle Piero. Wouldn't he love this? As the favorite nephew, Rick was the only one in the family Piero ever talked to about his work. Rick ate it up, but his mother didn't, worried her brother was trying to steer her only son into a police career. Much too dangerous a profession for an Italian mother to accept without a fight. When Rick dined with his uncle after moving to Rome, always at the same restaurant, the subject was inevitably the crime of the moment. Overhearing snippets of conversation, the waiters at first assumed Rick was a younger police colleague. But when the true relationship became known, they noticed how similar the two men at the corner table were. It went beyond physical traits—lanky frames, kind eyes—to their gestures, the serious way they always studied the menu, and the even more serious way they both studied any attractive woman who entered the room. When Rick wrote his weekly email to his mother he never failed to mention seeing his uncle, though without the details. She may have gotten the idea that the two met at Mass.

"I don't know, Beppo. I'd have to think about it. Do you really believe it could work?"

"I sure as hell hope so, since it was my idea and I managed to sell it to my boss." His smile was forced. "Not that my reputation within the *ministero* is anything you should consider before making your decision. But we must move as quickly as possible, and naturally you'll have to get some detailed briefings here at the ministry before you drive up to Volterra. So do think about it, though please, not forever."

Rick was thinking, all right. What first came into his head was finally visiting Volterra. In all the years he had spent in Italy as a kid he had never been to this famous hill town in western Tuscany. Rick's father, the New Mexican, loved to explore new places in Italy but his job at the embassy didn't allow that much time off. And Rick's mother, the Italian, usually insisted that those precious vacation days be used to visit her family around the peninsula. There was an aunt in Tuscany, but she lived in the south east part of the region. Volterra, in the west, was always on the "to visit" list for the Montoya family. Going undercover for the Italian government would certainly make him an unorthodox tourist. How would it work? As if reading Rick's mind, Beppo spoke.

"We, of course, would pick up all your expenses, and would also be in contact with the police in Volterra to keep an eye on you." Rick's eyes widened slightly and Beppo added quickly, "We don't expect any trouble. It is our experience that these traffickers avoid violence at all costs. It would just be a precaution."

Beppo stood and straightened his jacket.

"How about some lunch? I have a favorite place a few blocks away, and their specialty is Roman artichokes. It's on me, by the way." He reached into another drawer and pulled out a book, passing it to Rick. "This is an excellent volume on the Etruscans. Pallottino is still considered the best, and I'd like you to have it even if you decide not to take up this offer."

"Thanks, Beppo." He flipped through the pages and came to a photograph of a funerary urn like the one on the table behind him. He turned more pages and found the she wolf is the prized piece in Rome's Capitoline Museum. Even he knew that the two figures of the infants Romulus and Remus were added in the middle ages, but that did not detract from the artistry of the Etruscan wolf.

"Something else, Rick, that hardly needs mentioning, but I must." Rick looked up from the pages and saw that Beppo's serious look had returned. It was becoming standard. "What I have told you here should not be shared. Except with your uncle, of course."

So Beppo did remember that Uncle Piero was a policeman. Or had he done a background check and found out? Probably better not to ask. Something else came to mind. "Beppo, did you ever meet a girl at the university here named Erica Pedana? Art history, specializing in the Mannerists? She's a professor now at *La Sapienza*."

Beppo squinted in thought. "A relative, Rick?"

"No, a friend. She's from Rome."

The big smile that Rick remembered from high school returned to Beppo's face. "I got my *laurea* at Padova, Rick, not here in Rome, so I don't know her. But if you're asking if you can let her in on this business, I would rather you did not." He rubbed the back of his neck with his hand, seeming to realize how serious he'd sounded, and forced a laugh that was not convincing. "And the ministry will not pay to have her accompany you to Volterra."

Rick looked at his friend and tried to understand why, whenever the old Beppo tried to emerge, he was pushed back inside by the ministry bureaucrat.

"Speaking of the university," said Beppo, "that reminds me." He took one of his cards from a small stand on the desk, wrote something on it, and passed it to Rick. "I had some classes with this guy in Padova. We were not close friends, and I have to admit that he was a bit strange, but it might be useful for you to meet him when you get to Volterra. He's the curator of the Etruscan museum there."

Rick studied the card.

"You mean *if* I go to Volterra."

"Of course that's what I meant." He moved from behind the desk and gestured toward the office door, like a good host. "I haven't seen Zerbino since we left the university, but he'll remember me. You can tell him I work in the ministry, but please don't get into specifics." He buttoned his jacket. "*Andiamo a mangiare.* By the way, Rick, do you remember that game our senior year, when we played the team from the base in Aviano?" The old Beppo was trying hard. "Do you remember how tall those guys were?"

"Beppo, I am amazed you took this long to bring the subject up."

"And do you remember how the game ended?" He was grinning as he opened the office door.

When they got to the elevator Rick was wondering how he would keep this from Erica. How could he just pop off to Volterra without explaining why? Beppo's words, if Rick remembered correctly, were that he'd rather Rick did not tell her. "Rather not." The door was clearly ajar. And when it was all over, whose bad side would he rather be on, Beppo's or Erica's? Not much of a decision there.

He was also thinking about Beppo's mention that the Volterra police would be keeping an eye on him. Not that any problems were expected. It would be just as a precaution. Don't even give it another thought.

◇◇◇

"Aren't you going to drink your Campari?" asked Rick.

Erica pondered the question as if it dealt with something deeper than the red liquid in her glass. Rick watched and waited. Once again—the curse of the professional translator—he remembered the meaning of her name in English. *Heather.* How appropriate was that? Beautiful at first look, as well as second and third looks, but a bit prickly when you get past the blossoms. That description could be used with quite a few Roman women he'd met since moving here, women who weren't named Erica. Must be something in the water.

Erica's long wool coat was draped over the extra chair at their table. A leather attaché case rested on the seat, next to a large shopping bag with the name Fratelli Rosetti, a shoe store a few blocks away. While Rick was talking, she had leaned forward on her elbows, her chin resting on clasped hands, the sleeves of her silk sweater pushed up to show a gold bracelet on one wrist, contrasting with a dark blue Swatch on the other. She brushed back her dark brown hair, perhaps the better to hear Rick's story, revealing large gold hoops swinging from her ears. Her knees, covered by a plaid skirt, touched his under the small table.

When they had first met in the late summer a few months earlier, her outfit was just as fashionable. They found themselves looking into the windows of a shoe store, and since the men's and women's shoes were on opposite sides of the entrance, they unconsciously backed into each other. Awkward *scusi*s were exchanged, a conversation started, and two hours later they were still chatting over empty coffee cups. She talked of growing up in Rome, studying art at the university, and a gallery internship in the exciting city of New York. He told her of his bi-cultural family, living in various parts of the world, and now trying to start the translation business in Rome. He also used diplomatic skills learned from his father to point out that New York was not considered by the people of New Mexico to be the real America.

Now they sat in the same bar as that first day, a place that had become their regular meeting spot. It was about halfway between their two apartments, though Erica once pointed out that it was a few minutes closer to hers. It wasn't, but why start another argument? The atmosphere at Mimmo's was that of dozens of coffee bars in downtown Rome, the same neon glare bouncing off the stainless steel machines, the sweet brown smell of espresso, and the thud of metal against wood as wet coffee grounds were loudly discarded to make room for the next order. They always sat at the same table near the window, but their eyes seldom glanced out at the piazza.

Erica listened to the highly edited account of Beppo's proposal without comment and barely touched the *aperitivo* in the glass in front of her. The bar was beginning to thin out now, its other clients drifting off to their homes after a quick drink and a bit of gossip with co-workers following a day at the office. Many of them were staffers from the nearby Parliament offices, their passes dangling from tri-color ribbons around their necks. She finally picked up the small glass and took a sip of the Campari as he drained the last drop of espresso from his small cup.

"Are you going to do it, Ricky?"

"What do you think?"

She covered his hand with hers and her head moved closer. "I would never presume to influence your decision." She paused. "But knowing you, I'm sure it would be difficult to keep you away from Volterra."

She does know me, he thought. "You didn't answer the question."

"Ricky, of course you should go. It's your civic duty." He was about to smile when he realized she was serious. Her next comment confirmed it. "Italy is unique in the world for our historical and artistic patrimony. If you can help in some small way to preserve it, you must take the opportunity to do so. Did I ever tell you about my grandmother?"

He shook his head in reply, not understanding what her grandmother would have to do with all this.

"Just before she died—I was a little girl—she and I were in the church our family has gone to for generations. As we were walking out that day, Nonna stopped and pointed to an empty space above the altar of one of the side chapels. The wall, she said, once held a small painting of the Madonna in a gilt frame. The painting had the most beautiful face she had ever seen, and she often prayed before it. One day during the war, just hours before you Americans liberated the city, she was kneeling in that chapel praying for the safety of her family, when a German soldier burst into the church, brushed past her, and ripped the painting off the wall. She was still frozen on her knees when she heard the door to the church slam and a truck grind into gear outside. The painting has never been recovered." She paused, stuck in the memory. "I sometimes wonder if Nonna's story helped push me toward art history."

He rarely saw this side of her. More often than not their conversations about her work got stuck on faculty intrigues, apathetic students, or the lack of outside consulting opportunities. But a few times, and only a few, her passion broke through, showing why she had picked art history as her life work. He savored the moment as she took another drink of the Campari. Her serious look brightened.

"You've been to Volterra, haven't you, Ricky?"

Did she know the answer? "I'm ashamed to say that I have not."

"Well, that settles it. Fascinating town. Etruscan artifacts, Roman ruins, medieval buildings. It has everything." She tilted her head and looked at Rick's face. "You've already accepted, haven't you?" Rick shrugged, caught, and she squeezed his hand, still underneath hers. "I wish I could go with you, Ricky."

He felt a pang which hinted that their relationship could be more serious than he wanted to acknowledge. "I do, too."

"Maybe I can adjust a few things on my class schedule and get away for a couple days." Her hand remained over his. "They have some wonderful Mannerist paintings in the museum there that I haven't seen in years. Does your friend Beppo really want you to leave so soon?"

"Yes. He thinks that every day increases the chance of losing more of these priceless funerary urns. I suppose he's right. But could you get away? What are you looking for?"

Erica had begun rooting through her case, and now she pulled out her agenda and began to flip through it pages. Almost every professional in Italy used a leather-bound notebook which held everything from a calendar to telephone numbers, and included paper and pen for writing notes. The electronic devices were catching on, but agendas were still holding their own.

"I just remembered, there was a *compagna* of mine at the university who is an art dealer in Volterra. Donatella Minotti. Call and give her my best regards." She found the name and phone number and wrote them on a paper torn from the book. "We had various classes together the first few years at the university. When we chose our specialties, she went for Etruscan art and I opted for Mannerism." Still holding the paper, she lifted her brows. "Perhaps I shouldn't give you her name. She's extremely attractive."

First Beppo and now Erica. Everyone knows someone in Volterra. He pulled the paper from her fingers, folded it, and tucked it into his jacket pocket.

"She couldn't be more attractive than you, *cara*. And she's probably married with ten kids by now."

"Not Donatella." She looked at him with a curious smile. "You know, Ricky, I'll try to rearrange my schedule. I would hate to think of you spending those nights up in a strange city all by yourself."

The desire to change her schedule said more about this Donatella woman than Erica realized, thought Rick. He dropped some coins on the table and helped her with her coat, taking in the fragrance of her perfume. It was Jicky, as he had discovered recently at her apartment, a scent that was new to him. Curiously, he had never focused on such things back in Albuquerque. It must be part of the acculturation process, starting to notice a woman's perfume.

"New shoes?" Rick picked up the paper bag and held it out.

"They didn't have the pair I wanted so I had to settle for these. Why do they put shoes in the window if they don't have them in all sizes?"

"It's a hard life here in Rome." As soon as the words came out he knew he'd made a mistake. Her glare confirmed it.

"Are you going to start on that again?" Erica shook her head slowly. She pulled the shopping bag from his hand and slipped her leather case over her shoulder. "I get it, Ricky. We Romans just don't appreciate what we have. Didn't your girlfriends in America ever complain about anything?"

She had a point. A girl he was dating before leaving for Italy came to mind, eerily enough also a professor of art history, Latin American art, not Italian Mannerism. She had railed against all manner of injustice, mostly what she considered the major issues facing society like hunger and climate change. How could two women have the same interests and yet be so different? And how could Erica one minute wax passionately about the Italian cultural heritage and in the next complain that a shoe store didn't have her size? One thing, though, she wasn't boring.

Fortunately the storm passed quickly, as it usually did. She took his hand as they walked to the door and out into the street.

"Erica, one thing Beppo said to me is that this whole business in Volterra is, well, very confidential."

"But you told me anyway."

He shrugged. "It would have been hard to disappear for a few days without telling you where I'd gone. And if I can't trust you…"

Erica remained silent and appeared to be deep in thought. A light wind was blowing through the piazza, and she let go of his hand to pull her white silk scarf closer around her neck. He waited for her reaction.

"It will be colder in Volterra," she said. "Ancient hill towns always feel colder. It must be all the stone."

"I'll bring an extra sweater," said Rick.

She studied his eyes and kissed him lightly on the cheek. The softer Erica had reappeared. "Be careful, Ricky. And call me."

"Yes ma'am," he answered in English, with a smile that was not returned. She turned and walked across the piazza in the direction of her apartment. Even with the wool coat he could trace her slim figure, accentuated by heels which American women would deem highly impractical on the cobble stones of Rome's historic center. But they served their purpose, thought Rick, as she disappeared around the corner.

Chapter Three

Commissario Carlo Conti walked across the central piazza of Volterra toward his office, the cool fall air keeping him alert after the quarter-liter of red wine enjoyed with lunch. In his younger days it would have been like drinking a glass of mineral water, but in recent years he had noticed that even a small amount of alcohol would have its effect. He still consumed his regular *quarto* of wine with each meal, but only occasionally did he finish it with a *digestivo*. And grappa was out of the question.

Once again he found himself thinking of retirement. There was no getting around it, the idea of returning to the village where he was born and raised was more appealing as each day passed. He chuckled as he remembered the schoolboy whose only dream was getting out and moving to the largest city he could find. But now the hilltop town of San Giorgio had everything he needed in life. How ironic. The boredom that drove him away those many years ago now would welcome and comfort. Though she would never say it, Gemma too was ready for the move. He smiled as he thought of the only woman in his life; he could not have asked for a finer wife. His colleagues often told him how fortunate he was, and he always agreed. She had put up with so much over the years because of his police work: long hours alone, fears for his safety, his bad moods when the job was not going well. He often made a point of showing his appreciation, but he knew it was never enough. His friends were predicting, half in jest, that having him around all day might ruin the marriage for Gemma. But he would be sure to spend a good deal of time in the square at San Giorgio playing bocce. Was not his cousin Mario already retired and into such a daily routine? It would be easy to fall into it himself. Some gardening, an occasional visit to the beach, the grandchildren driving down from Rome to be spoiled. Yes, that could be a very pleasant retirement indeed.

"Commissario." The policeman at the desk acknowledged his arrival as the door behind Conti swung shut and he walked down the hall to his office. The building was centuries old, but it smelled the same as every police station he had ever worked in throughout Italy. *It must be in the disinfectant the cleaning staff uses*, he thought. It probably all comes from the same manufacturing plant in the south. The odor pulled him back from San Giorgio to Volterra.

The office, though one of the best in the building, was not at all large and certainly not luxurious. They didn't build many large rooms in the Middle Ages, but they did build them too solidly to allow knocking down walls, not that Conti had wished for a bigger office. There were two windows. One, near his desk, had a panoramic view of the piazza, while the other at the far side of a table overlooked a narrow alley. The table had six chairs on each side and one at either end, large enough for Conti to hold meetings with his staff. They were infrequent. He hated meetings. His desk, in front of which stood two uncomfortable chairs, was squeezed into one end of the room. On poles behind the desk chair hung the requisite flags of Italy and of the *Polizia dello Stato*. Between them on the wall, a framed photograph of President of the Republic. Except for the view of Volterra from the windows, it could be the office of any police commissioner in Italy. He sat down and opened a file that had been placed in the center of his desk. Ten minutes later, after reading all its contents, he closed it and picked up the phone.

"Is Detective LoGuercio here? Ask him to come to my office."

A few moments later there was a knock and the door opened. "Yes, Commissario."

The two were about the same height, but the slight bend in Conti's posture made Detective Paolo LoGuercio an inch or two taller. The baggy cut of the commissario's suit added to the illusion, contrasting with the detective's fitted clothing. An observer would note immediately that the two were of different generations, but their outward appearance was not the only clue. More striking was the deferential manner of the younger man toward his superior, obvious in his demeanor from the moment he entered the room. Was it sincere respect for the older man or was LoGuercio simply performing the ritual dance of any Italian bureaucrat, doing what was needed to continue his climb up the ranks?

"Sit down, LoGuercio. How are you settling in?"

"Very well, sir." He paused, hoping the older man would speak, but after no response he continued. "I found an apartment outside the walls which is very comfortable, and have managed to see a bit of the city that I probably wouldn't visit in connection with my work. You know, the churches and the museums."

"The city is fascinating. Is that why you requested this assignment? Are you interested in such things?"

The detective coughed nervously. "Probably no more than anyone else. But it's a good way to get to know a new place."

"I imagine so. And the museums and churches here are very different from those in Sicily." The younger man seemed eager to change the subject from his own interests and previous work assignment. Conti sensed this, and before LoGuercio could answer, tapped his fingers on the file. "Do you know about this anonymous tip we got last week?"

"I'm not sure, sir. I heard something about fake Etruscan objects."

"That's the one. The phone call led us to a shed in a wooded area outside of town. Inside were boxes of carvings which looked like they were ready to be shipped somewhere. We asked an Etruscan expert from the museum to check them out and he said they were fakes, though good enough fakes to fool a lot of buyers."

"Who owns the property?" LoGuercio sat back slightly, adjusting the crease on his trousers.

"Some woman who lives in Florence inherited it years ago and has been sitting on it with the idea of selling it some day. She didn't even know there was a shed there. That's what she said, and her story seems credible since she's a school teacher, not the type you would expect to be involved in anything illegal. At least you would hope not."

"Somebody was using the shed to keep a stash."

"It appears so."

"Why the tip, Sir?"

Conti glanced up and then returned his gaze to the papers on his desk. "Good question, LoGuercio. My guess is that someone involved in the scheme was not happy. Not getting a big enough cut, had a fight with the boss, felt some remorse about a life a crime. Who knows? Now that we have the objects, the criminals will probably disappear, at least for the moment." Conti looked at the detective, as if trying to make a decision. He slowly pushed the file to one side of the desk. "LoGuercio, I have a project for you."

The detective visibly perked up. Since arriving in Volterra two weeks earlier his main assignment had been to learn how the office functioned. He was bored with reading reports and learning the routine. He was ready for real police work.

"Would you like me to assist you with this investigation?" He tried not to show too much excitement in his voice.

Conti handed over the file. "Possibly, when I decide where we should go with it. In the meantime all I want you to do is read the file and return it to me." He smiled when he saw the detective's reaction to the prospect of more reading. "But I do need you for a case in which we've been peripherally involved for several months." He pulled another file from the stack. "It now appears that Volterra may become the focus of this investigation, though not in the way I had expected."

Detective LoGuercio leaned forward, puzzled but interested, forgetting how hard the chair felt. His supervisor continued.

"You may be just the person to work on this, given your interest in things artistic." The younger man shifted uncomfortably in his seat at this comment, and the commissario added, "Didn't you work on an art theft case in Palermo?"

LoGuercio was not surprised that the commissario knew about that detail of his record. The old boy network would have offered up everything about him well before he arrived in Tuscany. How deeply had the man dug into his background?

"Yes, sir. Is that what this case is about?"

"Not exactly the same, but it involves stolen objects that the Ministry of Culture considers of value. Real Etruscan objects, not fakes like the carvings we found in the shed. The art cops in Rome are coordinating the investigation. I trust you know about that office."

The detective took a breath. "I have heard about them, yes, sir."

"Well, our crack art police have come up with a scheme to find the source of some stolen Etruscan antiquities that could be from this area. I still can't believe it, but what they want to do is send some American up here to pose as an art buyer." He shook his head slowly. "This is insanity, of course. Not only will it come to nothing, we have been asked to watch over this amateur." He looked up from the file into the face of the detective. "That's where you come in. LoGuercio, did you hear me?"

The younger man had such a strange look on his face that it surprised Commissario Conti. He expected that LoGuercio would not to be very excited about the assignment of tailing someone. He would have felt the same way; nothing could be more boring. But everyone has to do this kind of work when starting out.

"Yes, sir, I heard you." LoGuercio composed himself. "When is he arriving in Volterra?"

"I don't know yet, but it will be soon. Apparently the ministry is giving him a briefing today, so they will tell me after that. Or perhaps they will come to their senses and change their minds. I'll let you know." He stared down again at the file. "I think it might be better if you don't meet him. He will be easier to watch if he doesn't know his watcher. Get someone to help you. DeMarzo is pretty good, use him. I expect the American will arrive in the next day or so. I don't need to tell you that anything regarding this case should be kept strictly with those of us who are working on it. The art cops were very specific about that."

Conti looked back down at the papers and detective LoGuercio immediately understood that the meeting had ended. He rose from the chair and left the room, clutching the file. After the door closed the man at the desk got up and went to the window, staring down at the square. Then he turned and extended a cupped right hand in front of his squint before swinging the arm behind his back and slowly rolling the imaginary bocce ball toward the wall.

◇◇◇

The room where Rick got his briefing must have been intended as a storage space for the priests who built the palazzo. It was smaller than Beppo's office, featured none of the ornate ceiling decorations found throughout the rest of the building, and had not a single window. The rectangular florescent lamp that hung over the table could have come from a pool hall, but worked perfectly for the billiard-sized table it illuminated. On one wall hung a whiteboard, on another a map so old that it included Nice as part of Italy. There was no other decoration, unless one included the institutional furniture. Rick sat on one side of the table facing Beppo and a ministry colleague named Roberta Liscio. On Rick's left, at the end of the table, sat a man introduced only as Signor Vetri. He was of indeterminate age, and wore a dark brown suit with a matching tie. Unlike the woman, who had smiled pleasantly when she shook Rick's hand, Vetri had merely nodded at the American visitor and taken his seat.

Signora Liscio, the administrative person, spoke first, explaining how Rick would pick up his rental car, the hotel where he would be staying in Volterra, and how he would use the ministry-issued credit card to cover his expenses. Not that this would obviate the need to keep a careful record of expenses, she emphasized. When she slid the card across the table the look on her face gave the impression she was signing away her firstborn child. The floor then belonged to Beppo, who began by passing a single sheet of paper to Rick.

"These are the three people you will approach in Volterra, Rick. We decided to make it a short list even though there are others who could be considered possible suspects, but these three are by far the most likely to be involved in this operation."

Beppo didn't notice that Rick had stiffened slightly when he glanced down at the paper.

"The first name, Antonio Landi, is outwardly a pillar of the Volterra business community. His store, Galleria Landi, draws tourists seeking the alabaster objects for which Volterra is famous. He has exported large quantities of alabaster over the years, all overtly legitimate, but we have our suspicions. In the past few years we think he may have included some small Etruscan objects among his exports, though we've been unable to catch him in the act. He very well could have moved from small pieces to larger ones. What may be important for you, Rick, is that Landi knows everyone in town, including, we believe, its shadier elements. If he is not involved with the burial urns himself he may well know who is, and we assume he would be glad to serve as an intermediary." Beppo pulled a passport-sized photo from the file and passed it to Rick. Landi's angular features looked like someone who would be found in a police lineup; not that Rick had ever seen one, except in movies.

Rick took out a pen and put a check next to Landi's name and address. Signora Liscio listened carefully as Beppo had talked, and Rick guessed she was not normally included in this aspect of the ministry's work. Vetri, in contrast, settled back in his chair and studied the lamp.

"The second name on the list is a certain Rino Polpetto, who runs an import-export business. The fiscal police have never been able to pin anything on him, though they have had their suspicions about some of his exports, and we also have suspected him of some irregular dealings with antiques. Unfortunately he covers his activities well."

"Or he's just an honest businessman," said Rick as he studied the second photo. The man could not have been more different from Landi; his face was round and his smile wide.

"We try not to waste our time with honest people here, Rick." Beppo took back the second photo and passed a third. It was the one Rick was waiting to see.

"Donatella Minotti. As you can see, Rick, it should not be much of a chore for you to make contact with her." Signora Liscio shook her head at the comment, unnoticed by Rick, who was studying the picture. "She is an art dealer, and her sales include everything from paintings to sculpture, with the occasional Etruscan piece."

"She has a gallery?" Rick continued to look at the picture. It was another passport photo, but despite its small size her beauty was obvious, as well as her faint look of annoyance.

"She did for a few years, but now has built up enough of a professional reputation to sell directly to clients from her villa. Those clients have included a few people who we have been watching in connection with other cases. That is why she is on the list."

"So she could be clean?" Rick hoped his voice did not betray his thoughts. If Donatella Minotti were involved in this, it could prove very awkward indeed for his relationship with Erica.

"All three could be clean, or all could be involved in something illicit. What we hope is that one of them is selling these burial urns, or will at least help you flush out the people who are selling them." Rick slid Donatella's photo back across the table and Beppo continued. "The best way for you to approach these people would be in a very low-key way, establishing yourself as a credible buyer. When you think you have that credibility—and exactly when will be your call—you can drop a few hints that you're also interested in a few pieces of genuine Etruscan art, very unique pieces, that sort of thing."

"So I shouldn't ask if they have any Etruscan burial urns in the back?"

Beppo looked at the other two people at the table, whose frowns were evident. "You will have to excuse my friend's American sense of humor. He can't help himself." He turned to Rick. "It doesn't matter which of these three you contact first, but on arriving in Volterra you must call on the local police chief, Commissario Carlo Conti. He knows you are coming, but we haven't given him many of the details."

From his uncle, Rick had heard stories of turf battles between Italy's many and varied law enforcement entities. "So Commissario Conti is managing to contain his enthusiasm about my presence in Volterra?"

"You could say that. This may be an opportunity to use some of those diplomatic skills you've picked up from your father."

"They're in the genes, Beppo."

The meeting went on for another ten minutes. Beppo shared a few more details about the three contacts; Signora Liscio gave Rick a map of the city, pointing out the location of Conti's office; but Signor Vetri continued to remain silent.

After Rick had turned in his pass and left from the ministry building, he stood for a few moments in front of its stone entrance and looked again at the list. There appeared to be a one-in-three chance that Donatella Minotti was involved in just the kind of illegal activity that so appalled Erica. He folded the paper and slipped it into his jacket pocket where he felt the card Beppo had given him the day before. The name on the card, Arnolfo Zerbino, had not come up once during the briefing. Was it possible, Rick wondered, that the silent Signor Vetri didn't know of Beppo's acquaintance with the museum curator? And that Beppo didn't want the man to know?

◇◇◇

Unlike Detective LoGuercio, Sergeant DeMarzo was pleased with the prospect of tailing the American. It would allow him to dress as a civilian and get away from the statistical reports that had burdened him the past week. Not to mention being out in the fresh air rather than sitting in his cubicle. And watching some American tourist, how hard could that be? LoGuercio was pleased with DeMarzo's enthusiasm, and impressed with his questions, which indicated he'd been on such jobs in the past. Also, he knew the city better than a transfer who'd only been in Volterra a few weeks. With that in mind, LoGuercio decided that it might be a good idea to get out and walk around the city himself, before the American arrived. And he needed to make a phone call. He left DeMarzo at the cubicle, picked up his coat in his office, and walked out the main entrance into the piazza.

A moment later LoGuercio stood in the very middle of the square, now starting to fill with locals crossing it between afternoon appointments around the city. He looked up at the stone façade of the building he had just left, its roofline broken by a lone set of pigeons. He wasn't sure which window was Conti's office, but had a pretty good idea. There were no faces visible from any of the windows; no doubt everyone was diligently working at their desks, including the commissario. He recalled his brief meeting with Conti and wondered if the man was always such a charmer. Shaking his head and smiling, he reached into his jacket pocket and pulled out his mobile phone. It was answered after the third ring.

"You won't believe this," he said into the phone. "I've been assigned to work on a case of stolen Etruscan artifacts."

Chapter Four

Knowing that Signora Liscio at the ministry would never forgive him if he lost his *autostrada* receipt, Rick pulled it from his pocket and used it to mark the page in Beppo's book. While pondering the latest factoid he'd learned about the Etruscans, he signaled the waiter to bring *il conto*. The restaurant, one large rectangular room with a high ceiling, was starting to fill up as the normal lunch hour crowd arrived. Most of the diners were locals; this was not the time of the year when tourists would be passing through Saline di Volterra. Only a few kilometers from Volterra itself, Saline is a small town named for salt mines still in operation a couple millennia after their discovery. He looked at the tiny bowl of salt on the table and wondered if it was the local stuff.

The morning drive up the coast had given Rick more of an appetite than usual. As the commuters were entering the city in the opposite direction, he'd started up the Via Aurelia, the ancient road that climbs past the Vatican before winding down to the sea as it heads north. Fortunately for the suspension of his rental car, its surface had been repaved since construction in the third century BC. After enjoying the Mediterranean views, he passed Piombino and turned inland, along the Cecina River lined with browned vineyards, up to Saline.

Rick had ordered a pasta with wild boar sauce, a local specialty, and was not disappointed. The ribbons of pasta had gone directly from the rolling pin and cutting board to the boiling water, then tossed in the dark, meaty sauce. Perfection. When they'd discussed a second course, the waiter had mentioned that a fresh basket of porcini mushrooms had appeared that morning in the kitchen. Rick had not hesitated, and they arrived at his table grilled to perfection with a light brushing of the local olive oil.

He took his last sip of espresso, paid the bill, and walked out to his rental car, a silver Alfa with a diesel engine that clacked softly. As he reached into his coat pocket for the keys they rattled against his small GPS. It had saved his rear end while climbing in the Sangre de Cristo mountains earlier in the year, one of his last hikes before moving to Rome, so it had become a good luck charm. But he'd also brought it with the hope of doing some hiking around the Tuscan countryside on this trip—probably not a realistic hope, given his undercover assignment. Hiking trails were not among the topics that had come up during his briefing at the ministry the previous day.

A moment after the Alfa's engine came to life, he left the town of Saline and began the final slow climb up to Volterra. As he had learned from Beppo's book, the Etruscans built their towns on hilltops, and Volterra was considered one of the best examples of such ancient fortified cities. It was already visible high in the distance, its gray stone walls contrasting with the browns of the autumn earth below it. As he turned into the first of the wide curves that cut back and forth through the open fields, Rick thought that from this distance the city likely looked the same as it had five hundred or even a thousand years earlier. A few clouds were forming above it, just as they did over the mountain on Albuquerque's east side, often covering the peak and bringing spectacular thunderstorms. Did Volterra enjoy those natural light shows too? Perhaps there was a niche in New Mexico for telling the future from the shape and size of lightning bolts, like the Etruscan *fulguriators* he had just read about in the book. There were certainly enough palm readers around the University of New Mexico, so why not lightning readers? He downshifted into third as the road steepened.

When he came to the thick walls of the city he bore to the left. The blocks at this lowest level were the original Etruscan. He kept his eyes on the road, but knew there would be a higher part of the wall with stone added by the Romans, and on top of that the Medieval. Italy: always layers upon layers. He followed the wall around a bend to the narrow gate at the very northern part of the old town. Despite the signs saying local traffic only, he drove in, and immediately found his hotel on the left side of the narrow street. When he parked and got inside, the woman at the desk seemed more worried about his car parked in front than getting him checked in.

"You can leave your bag here," she said frowning as she took his passport. "Just back up a few meters and the entrance to our parking garage is right there; you can't miss it. The police get very annoyed when there are cars parked on this street."

It would not be good, Rick thought, to begin his first meeting with Commissario Conti by asking him to fix a parking ticket. He left his bag and went outside to the car, following the woman's orders to the letter and finding a parking space at the far end of the hotel's dimly lit garage. When he returned to the reception desk, she passed him his room key and passport and pointed him toward the elevator, a forced smile on her face indicating that she needed to get back to her computer. What did hotel desk clerks do all day before computers?

The room was small, as expected in a hotel that a few centuries earlier had been a convent. It had a modern bathroom, added recently and probably not even dreamed of by the nuns who had lived here long before the latest renovation. They also would have been surprised to see a large swimming pool in the courtyard outside the window, now drained for the winter. Rick looked out and tried to imagine the sisters sunning themselves there in the summer, a swarthy pool boy bringing them towels and drinks with little umbrellas. He pushed the thought from his mind and opened his laptop to check his mail. The nuns likely didn't have wireless Internet either. There were a few messages from clients, including a request for a three-page translation job that would be easy enough to do quickly and send back electronically. He would have something to toil on when not catching grave robbers.

Rick checked the time on his cell phone. Still more than three hours until his six o'clock meeting with the policeman. If he remembered correctly, the top name on Beppo's list, the owner of a tourist shop, was located close to the police station. Of course in a town this size, everything was *a misura di uomo*, within walking distance of everything else. It was Tuscany. Protocol indicated that he should meet Conti before starting his rounds, but why waste a few hours? It shouldn't matter to the policeman. Rick finished unpacking, changed out of his comfortable driving jeans and sweater into something more respectable, and slipped on his overcoat.

As he folded the sweater, he remembered his promise to Erica to pack an extra one for the cold, and back out came his phone. He punched a couple of buttons and put it to his ear. After a few rings Erica's voicemail kicked in and he debated whether to leave a message. "*Ciao, bella, sono arrivato.*" He hesitated and added, "—the hotel is perfect, thanks for the recommendation. *A presto.*" When he hit the off button he again checked the time. She shouldn't be in class at this hour; was she still annoyed? What would be the term in Italian for "drama queen"? *Diva* is too easy, he thought, there must be something more nuanced. It annoyed him, a professional translator, that nothing came to mind.

A moment later he left the elevator, dropped his key at the front desk, and walked toward the entrance doors. The same woman stood behind the desk, and as the key thumped down she looked up quickly and smiled before returning to her screen. He pulled out his town map, studied it to confirm his bearings, and pushed through the glass door to descend onto the cobblestones of the Via San Lino. The guidebook said it was named for a local priest who had done well in the church hierarchy, though not well enough to become a household name outside of Volterra.

There was no sidewalk. When the street was set up centuries earlier the only non-pedestrian traffic was horses and carts, and everyone shared the relatively narrow space that ran in front of the stone houses. These days, except for the occasional mini-bus or other public vehicle, the street was used only by people on foot, but at this hour most of the locals were still at home having lunch or taking the Italian version of the siesta. They would emerge, rested and sated, by midafternoon. Inside the walls only residents were given passes to drive the narrow streets, and they were smart enough to use their cars only when needed, which was mostly to get from their parking garages out of town and back.

Even without cars to dodge, as he was used to doing in Rome, Rick walked close to the buildings to protect himself from the chill wind. It had been calm when he drove into the town, but the clouds that now covered the sky had brought breezes with them. Rick closed two of the buttons on his coat. The street began an incline on its way up to the main square of the city where the tourist shops are found, including Galleria Landi. But at this point Via San Lino is still part of a neighborhood, with a few small stores on the ground floor of the narrow stone structures, none more than four stories high, most of them two. Some shops had been converted to parking garages for the apartments above, but there were enough businesses to keep the street's residents from having to walk too far to find the basics. He passed a small grocery, then a hardware store with so much stuff stacked up or hanging from the ceiling that it was a wonder any customers could fit inside. An old woman in a shop selling yarns did not look up from her knitting needles as he walked past her window. The smell of coffee was pushed by a small fan out of a tiny bar, probably to lure passersby like Rick. He was tempted, but still could taste his post-lunch espresso. The street forked just as Signora Liscio's map had indicated and he bent to the left. A few hundred meters later he emerged into the Piazza dei Priori, the heart of Volterra. Erica was right, it was a magnificent space.

The feel was medieval, beginning with the city hall on his right, its harsh stone softened somewhat by rows of coats of arms affixed to it over the centuries by rulers and prominent families. Decorative pieces of wrought iron stuck out from the façade at intervals, ready to hold flags, or perhaps torches, for town celebrations. His eye moved up past the arched windows to a large clock, and then to the tower above it. An impressive building indeed. He knew from the Tuscany guidebook, a gift from his mother, that it was the oldest town hall in Tuscany still in use, and it looked it.

To the left, on the corner, was the *commissariato* where Rick would meet Conti in a few hours. It too had a stone tower to add to its imposing bulk, but unlike the town hall a cluster of antennas grew out of its crown, hinting at the profession of its present occupants. Clearly it was the less inviting building of the two, but of course that was the idea. Rick glanced back at the clock on city hall, recalculated his schedule, and walked out of the piazza.

A block later he reached Volterra's main shopping street where its stores were beginning to open after the midday break. He passed two men chatting about the weather as they noisily cranked up the metal grates in front of their businesses, one selling shoes, the other jewelry and watches. *There must be more shoe stores in Italy than restaurants*, he thought, *with jewelry stores a close second.* Two women emerged from a coffee bar and Rick was hit again with the strong aroma of its espresso machines. This time, though only for an instant, he actually considered a quick shot of caffeine, then kept on walking until he reached the address at the top of his list. Climbing two steps, he entered Galleria Landi.

Soft indirect light filled the store, highlighting the glass shelves holding all manner of alabaster carvings. The light brought out the opaque colors of the alabaster, while it gave the thinner pieces of stone, such as bowls and plates, a dull glow. On one side ranged displays of large sculpture: human figures, trees, and animals. Rick recognized copies of famous works including a small replica of Michelangelo's Pietá from St. Peter's Basilica. And of course the ubiquitous Tower of Pisa. He wondered how many foreign tourists would buy such bulky pieces of art to jam into their suitcases. And since some of them weighed hundreds of pounds, how many tourists would pay the freight to ship them home? Farther along the wall stood smaller items such as floor and table lamps, their alabaster shades casting a warm tone from the bulbs underneath. The right side of the store interested Rick in his role as buyer, its shelves crowded with copies of Etruscan pieces either in alabaster or metal. There were various stone panels decorated with human and mythological figures, as well as bronze geese and salamanders. Ceramic vases in various shapes and sizes, looking to Rick as much Greek as Etruscan, covered a long shelf, battle scenes filling their dark red surfaces. It wasn't Costco, but he found the amount of inventory a bit overwhelming.

In the middle of the room the jewelry collections glittered, mostly Etruscan in their style. Their glass cases formed a rect-angle enclosing a smiling young woman dressed in a crisp white blouse and blue skirt. She patiently watched Rick walk around the room before asking if she could be of any assistance.

"My compliments on your merchandise. It is an excellent collection. I trust most of it is from local artisans?"

The woman was pleased not only with the compliment, but also the fluent Italian in which it was paid. He still wore his casual shoes from the trip, and even though Timberlands were widely sold in Italy, she had decided he was an American. Footwear, for many Italians, was the surest test of foreignness. That, and the way one walked. "Yes, most of the work is done locally. Are you Italian?"

"I'm from America," Rick answered, not wanting to compli-cate things with another explanation of his dual citizenship. "My interest is in purchasing some items in quantity for an establish-ment back in the United States." He pulled out one of Beppo's cards from the Santa Fe gallery and passed it to her. She looked at it and reached down to press a button below the counter.

"I'm sure that Signor Landi, the owner, would be pleased to talk with you, Mr....?"

"Montoya, Riccardo Montoya." He took the card back, wrote his name and cell number on it, and returned it to her.

As he introduced himself, a frowning man appeared from the rear of the shop, but his face changed to a smile when he saw the look on his employee's face. It was clear that the button was usually used for problem situations. Rick assumed that disgruntled customers would be the most extreme problem that the owner normally dealt with.

"Signor Landi, may I present Mr. Montoya from America, who may be interested in some quantity purchases." The man read the card which was passed to him and shook Rick's hand.

"Welcome to Galleria Landi, Signor Montoya. How may I be of assistance?"

The smile was thin, like in the photo Rick had seen in the ministry, but now he could see that it matched not just the man's face but also the rest of his body. He was dressed in a heavy wool suit which was slightly too large for his frame, as if he had recently lost weight. Accentuating the gaunt lines of his face was a narrow beard and moustache that could have been painted on the man's pale skin. The yellow teeth, as well as Landi's voice, indicated that he had been a smoker all his adult life, and likely earlier.

"I am living in Rome, and a friend who runs this gallery back in Santa Fe asked me to look into possible purchases here in Tuscany. He thinks that the Etruscan style would be of interest to his clients."

"Excellent," said Landi. "What sort of pieces do you think would be appropriate? As you can see we have various lines." He held up his hands and looked around the shop to prove his point.

Rick was ready with his answer. Beppo had impressed on him the need to go slowly. The idea at this point was to build up credibility and give the impression that he was a serious buyer. Rick explained that Tuscan art could sell well in a certain niche of the Santa Fe tourist market. Tuscan style homes already enjoyed great popularity in Santa Fe and throughout the Southwest United States, so Tuscan decoration would make perfect sense. The gallery was especially interested in things Etruscan, so Volterra became a logical place to start. No need to talk about prices at this point, now he just wanted to see what was available and be sure it could be found in reasonable quantities. He lowered his voice and told Signor Landi that high quality and timely delivery were very important to the gallery owners. The Italian nodded his head in understanding, the stained teeth all too visible.

They walked around the shop while Landi talked about the various pieces. Yes, we have a large stock of these goblets, and those miniature *stele* are easy to turn out. The alabaster eggs come in various sizes and would certainly be easy to ship without risk of damage. Those bronze lizards are very popular with American tourists, but perhaps you are looking for something more upscale?

Rick listened, nodding at the appropriate moments, while he studied the man. He wondered how his uncle the policeman would have sized up Landi, and what characteristics would have made an impression, positive or negative. The exterior was not important, you couldn't deduce anything about the man by his looks, since he didn't appear any different from hundreds of people that Rick had met in Italy, all of them honest people. Same with Landi's smoking. The habit was not illegal, though the way the government was moving these days, it soon could be. Landi behaved as expected of a businessman in this situation: ingratiating, with frequent glances to check Rick's reactions. The man wanted the sale, and this could be a big one for him. One would conclude that the shop was his main business and only business, not a front for an illegal operation which brought in the big money. After about twenty minutes Rick said that he had really taken too much of Signor Landi's precious time, perhaps he could return another day. Better not to appear too eager.

"But of course, Signor Montoya, you may return whenever you wish. I think it would also be of interest to you if—ah, Orlando, you have arrived at the perfect time."

Rick turned to see a small man peeling off his leather gloves as he entered the store. He wore a camel hair overcoat that extended below his knees and his neck was protected by a long red scarf. Stuffing his gloves in his pockets, he pulled off a wool cap to reveal a mostly bald head. Did the man fear losing most of his body's heat through the top of the head? One thing for sure: this man disliked cold weather. Landi introduced him to Rick as Orlando Canopo, his assistant and the manager of the workshop that produced much of the store's stock. Beaming, he told Canopo of Rick's reason for the trip to Volterra, then turned back to his visitor.

"He is quite an artisan himself, Signor Montoya, but Canopo was meant for better things than just carving alabaster."

Canopo glanced at his boss with a pleased look on his face.

"I was just about to suggest to our visitor, Orlando, that he visit our workshop. If he sees the excellent craftsmen working there he will appreciate the quality of our products even more." Landi turned to Rick. "If you have time now, I'm sure Orlando would be glad to accompany you."

Rick glanced at a clock on the wall as the two men waited for his reply. Like almost everything else in the store, it was made of alabaster, but with bronze numbers and hands.

"I have an appointment at six, at…nearby. Would there be time?"

"I think there would," answered Canopo in a deeper voice than Rick expected, even given the man's somewhat diminutive size, "but if you run late, you can return when it would be convenient. It's only a few blocks from here." There was a slight accent that was not Tuscan. Somewhere in the south.

The store owner grinned, shifted his eyes between the two men and rubbed his hands together as if he were about to sit down to a steaming bowl of pasta. "Excellent, now you won't have to take off your coat, Orlando." There was a private joke here that would not be shared. Landi shook hands with Rick. "I look forward to seeing you again, Signor Montoya. Tomorrow?"

"It has been my pleasure, Signor Landi." He wondered how much nicotine smell had passed to his fingers. "Yes, tomorrow. *A domani.*"

Landi watched the two men leave the store and then pulled Rick's card from his jacket pocket, studying it carefully. He ran his fingers over the paper, as if testing its fiber content, before placing it in a small drawer next to the cash register. The girl, who had been standing silently in a corner of the shop, watched her boss with an expressionless face. He glanced at her, walked to the back of the shop, and disappeared through the door. She stood for a few moments before returning to her place among the jewelry.

Outside, Rick and Canopo walked down the street, now filled with afternoon shoppers. A light wind brushed their faces.

"Perhaps something to warm us up, Signor Montoya? The workshop can get quite drafty."

"That sounds like an excellent idea. It is getting chilly."

"I won't have to put my gloves back on just yet."

As they entered the bar, conversation stayed on the weather. Canopo was born in Sicily, and though he'd been living in Volterra for fifteen years, he still was not used to the cold winters of Tuscany. He asked Rick if he had spent any time in Sicily, and looked at the American in sadness when the reply was negative. Their espressos arrived with a pair of clinks as they were set onto saucers, and the barman splashed a shot of grappa into Canopo's cup without asking. Rick declined the liquor and stirred a spoonful of sugar into his coffee. Canopo drained his in one gulp before patting a paper napkin to his lips.

"So, Signor Montoya, you are interested in the art of the land of the Etruscans."

Rick sipped his espresso and thought that it was almost as if Canopo knew of his real mission in Volterra. Perhaps this would be the man to field his hints when the time came, when he had established some trust and his credentials as a real buyer were accepted. Or with both Canopo and Landi.

"The pieces I saw in the shop were very beautiful. Americans are always impressed by Italian design and workmanship, but the Etruscan angle adds an additional fascination to the work."

"And an additional profit to be made?" The cognac seemed to have warmed up Canopo in more ways than one.

"I suppose you could say that," Rick answered.

"You have been to Volterra before, I trust? From your fluent Italian I assume you have been to most parts of the country. Except Sicily, of course." The last sentence was said with either regret or reproach, Rick was not sure which.

"No, this is my first visit."

"Ah," was Canopo's simple reaction. "In many ways it is not very different from my native island. There are good people and bad people. The Tuscans claim to be above all the rest of us, but in truth they have the same vices as everyone else in Italy, those vices are simply dressed in more elegant attire." He had been staring at his empty cup and now looked at Rick. "You have a rare gift, Signor Montoya, of getting people to talk freely."

"This is the first time I've been accused of that, Signor Canopo."

Canopo narrowed his eyes as he looked at Rick's face. "But it's true, I sense such things." The smile returned. "I also sense that you won't take my comments the wrong way. I am very happy here, I have a wonderful family and Signor Landi has treated me well. All this despite the wretched cold of this city." He glanced at his watch, as if to remind them both of Rick's other appointment. As he did, Rick pulled back his coat to reach into his pants pocket.

"Don't take out your money, Signor Montoya; it is of no value here."

Rick thanked him for the coffee as they walked through the glass doors. They stepped into the street and Canopo gestured to the right with his hand.

"The shop is in this direction, I think you will—"

Rick had been looking down the street where Canopo was pointing, but now glanced at the man's face. The smile had gone and what was remained was either annoyance or concern.

"Please excuse me for just a moment." Canopo's voice sounded a bit higher than it had inside. Without waiting for a reply he left Rick standing and strode quickly across the street toward a shoe store. Like all such establishments in Italy, the shoes were displayed along a glass corridor which lead to the entrance. This is a strange time to buy a pair of shoes, thought Rick, but then noticed a man standing close to the shop door. Because of the angle, he could see only the man's left shoulder and his left arm inside the pocket of his coat. This limited view was soon blocked completely by Canopo, who stared through the glass, avoiding eye contact with the other man as the two talked. Before Canopo turned, Rick looked away so the two would not see him watching them, and he was checking the watches of a jewelry store when Canopo reached him.

"Signor Montoya, I am mortified. Something has come up and I will have to show you the workshop tomorrow. I pray you will forgive me."

"Of course, of course, I understand completely. It may have been a bit tight for me to get to my appointment anyway.

"You are very kind. Until tomorrow then." Canopo pumped Rick's hand and scuttled down the street, pulling his hat down over his head as he went. Rick watched him for a few seconds, then turned to see what had happened to the other man, but he was nowhere to be seen. Must have gone into the shoe store.

There was still more than an hour until Rick's appointment with Commissario Conti, enough time to wander the ancient streets of Volterra. He felt a tinge of guilt at engaging in some tourism on the ministry's dime and time, but it quickly passed as he walked in the opposite direction from Canopo. At the corner the street dropped steeply toward the west wall. If he descended he would have to climb back up, so he opted for a left turn, bringing him out in a small square. It was the *capolinea* for provincial bus routes from outlining towns. Two busses were parked at the curb, one with its motor running softly, while their drivers stood on the sidewalk talking. Rick continued along the street which narrowed as it became cobblestone and started a soft incline.

At the end of the street he walked through a gate and found himself in a park. Not a small park with a bit of grass but an immense open green area surrounded by tall trees. In Italy, where there's grass there are kids, and despite the chill and deepening dusk a small pack of young boys kicked a soccer ball in the middle of the field. Near Rick on wooden benches women sat next to empty strollers, chatting while keeping an eye on their toddlers scratching around for bugs in the dirt. The greenery formed a sharp contrast to the gray stone of the narrow streets a few hundred meters behind him. Rick raised his eyes, drawn to the view at the far end of the park. The walls of a huge castle rose high, a perfect backdrop for the set for a Disney movie. Strange that he hadn't remembered anything about castle tours in his guidebook, since castles had been a passion of his since childhood. When he had moved back to Rome, one of his first tourist visits was a return to the Castel Sant' Angelo, with its long history and great views over the Tiber. He remembered standing on its battlements as a kid while his father recounted the story of Pope Clement VII watching in helpless horror as foreign mercenaries sacked the city below. Volterra's castle ramparts would have wonderful views of the valley, and while it didn't date back to the emperor Hadrian like Castel Sant' Angelo, there had to be some fascinating history in its stones. He made a mental note to find out. It looked like a keeper for sure.

◇◇◇

The wind was picking up now, bending left and right to follow the curves of the narrow stone streets. After leaving the American, Canopo walked in short, brisk steps, keeping his eyes to the ground as he thought about the upcoming meeting. Normally they met inside, where it was warm. Why would he pick this spot, possibly the coldest place in Volterra? He pulled his scarf tighter around his neck and stuffed his bare hands back in his pockets, better than putting on his gloves. He turned left and started down the street which ran along the top of the wall. As he had dreaded, the wind blew even more strongly there. It tore up from the ruins after whipping trees in the distance, picking up speed through the stone columns of the Roman theater. To add to the chill a cover of black clouds had started closing off the last few rays of sunlight, though it was not quite dark enough to cause the street lights to go on. It was no surprise that no one was in sight. Anybody with a brain would be inside at this time of day, likely with a warm drink. The thought of another shot of grappa made him smile, but his mood sank to match the temperature when he saw the expression on the face of the large man standing by the wall.

"I came as quickly as I could." Canopo joined the tall, silent figure. He looked up at the man's face, waiting for him to speak.

The man remained silent, gazing out over the ruins below, his slight frown showing concern or distraction. A long leather coat was his only concession to the cold wind that raced along the street. Canopo decided that sheer size must keep the man from noticing the temperature, like a bear hunkered down in a frozen forest. He wore no hat. His gloveless hands were placed on the edge of the wall as if he were about to make a speech to an invisible crowd gathered below. There was no offer of a hand-shake, or any other acknowledgement that a shivering Canopo now stood a few feet from him.

"Canopo," he finally said. Was it a statement or a question? He continued after a pause. "*Mio caro* Canopo, we've had a prob-lem. The police have discovered our storage shed and confiscated everything." Canopo tried not to show fear, but he could not prevent taking a short breath. The man continued. "So we've lost most of our stock. This will set us back months....Come over here so I don't have to raise my voice."

Canopo scanned the empty street. "But there's no one—"

"Come here."

Canopo found himself standing next to the man, both of them now blankly staring at the stones far below their eyes. There was still enough light to make out the structures laid out by the Romans, those remnants that had not been carted off over the centuries. A wide arc of stone seats lay between them and a tower of Corinthian columns, all that was left of the theater's stage. Only the outline of its semicircle was visible, cut into the side of the hill. Grass that grew among the stones was turning brown in the fall cold, matching leaves which had blown into small piles around the stage. Far off to the left a few cars were leaving a large parking area, one of several such spaces found outside the walls of what had always been and still was a pedestrian city. Canopo watched their red tail lights disappear around the distant edge of the wall.

"What are we to think?" The man continued to focus on the stones below.

"I don't understand." Canopo's voice faltered.

"It seems very unlikely that the cops just stumbled on it, *mio caro* Canopo. And there were only a few of us who knew its location. We have no reason to suspect the other members of the organization, so it has come down to one of us." He shifted his eyes from the stones to Canopo. "I know that *I* never told anyone about the shed." He swung around, and his finger shot out to punch Canopo in the chest three times, one for each word. "That leaves you."

"I never said anything to the police or anyone else, I swear." Despite the wintry air, he could feel himself beginning to sweat. "Why would I do it? What would be in it for me?"

"Money? You should be doing pretty well. You get a regular salary from the store, you're paid well for our little operation, and now it seems you're on the police payroll as well. Whatever the reasons, it doesn't matter now." He lifted his head and glanced quickly up and down the street.

"What are you—" Canopo's voice froze.

Abruptly the man reached down and seized Canopo under his arms. The strong hands pressed in, squeezing a groaning breath from Canopo's lungs as he stared up in shock. An instant later he realized that his feet were no longer touching the stone pavement. He pulled his hands from his pockets as he felt himself being lifted above the top of the wall. Canopo's fingers clawed at the face, trying to hold fast to something, anything, that could save him. Suddenly all he felt was the frozen air rushing past him. He was cursing the cold when he hit the stone.

◇◇◇

"Did you see that, Herb?"

"What should I be seeing, Shirley, I'm opening the car?" The man in a Nike jacket glanced up and saw a strange look on his wife's face. "What is it?"

"A man, at least I think it was a man, just fell from the top of the wall, way over there."

He squinted through his glasses. "Are you sure? It's pretty dark."

"I'm not sure. No, I am sure. What else could it have been?"

"Somebody throwing a sack of garbage? It is Italy, you know. They throw garbage all over the place. Remember Naples last week? This isn't Davenport."

"Herb, nobody would be throwing garbage down on the Roman ruins."

"I wouldn't count on it." He opened the passenger door of the rental car. "Come on, Shirley, I don't want to be on these roads when it's too dark. They're dangerous enough with these Italian drivers."

◇◇◇

His walk through the quiet streets of the historic center surrounded Rick with the richness of Volterra's culture. He regretted that Erica wasn't with him now, explaining all the art and architecture, putting everything in context as only a good art history professor can. He rounded the corner and entered the city's main square, deserted except for a few people scurrying across its stone pavement. A strong gust of wind swirled through the piazza like a New Mexico dust devil, causing Rick to pull up his collar and hurry toward the police station. After mounting some steps, he entered the building and found himself in a large, bleak waiting room. It was flanked on one side by a classic, long, scuffed reception desk which must be a requirement in police stations worldwide. This one, at least, was wood, perhaps in deference to the age of the building. Various men and women, some in uniform, walked through the room looking busy. Rick approached the desk and asked for Commissario Conti. The uniformed man took his name and added it to a list on a clip board in front of him.

"The Commissario has been detained." He pointed to the equally long and scuffed bench at one side of the room. "He has asked you to please wait," he added, before going back to his papers.

The bench was hard, and became even harder the longer Rick sat. Fortunately he was not bored; the people circulating through the room kept up his interest, including several sitting with him on the bench. He thought of Grandma Montoya who loved people watching: give her a place to sit where people streamed by and she could not be happier. Periodically a policeman would appear to call out a name, and when someone popped up from the bench he would lead them through the doors into the heart of the building. Feeding the cycle, others came through the main doors to check in at the desk and take their place on the bench until their turn came. Many carried papers, and Rick supposed that they were working their way through the Italian bureaucracy to get some permit or perhaps pay a fine. He tried to analyze the people who sat with him, concluding that they were not wealthy or well connected. Anyone with money would have found some way to avoid the bureaucracy, or at the very least to skip waiting in line. It was not unlike encounters with the state bureaucracy in New Mexico, but here the language was Italian, not Spanish.

He checked his phone, saw that he had been sitting for a half hour, and wondered if he should inquire at the desk about Conti. Just at that moment the desk sergeant answered the phone. When he heard the voice his body stiffened slightly and he glanced over at Rick while nodding at the unseeing person on the other end of the line. After hanging up he looked back at Rick and smiled, again nodding slightly.

Twenty minutes later Rick was the only occupant of the bench, like the worst player on the basketball team. He glanced up and saw a man in his sixties appear at the doorway and walk to the desk. The color of his baggy suit matched his thinning hair, and he walked as if his feet hurt. Must be another pensioner needing a permit of one sort or another. The sergeant, now on his feet, silently pointed to Rick with his chin and the new arrival strode to the bench. Rick stood up and shook the man's hand.

"Signor Montoya? Conti. *Piacere.* I very much regret that you have been kept waiting. Unfortunately it could not be avoided. Please come to my office." Already annoyed by the wait, Rick was now disturbed by the thin smile on the Commissario's face as they shook hands. Was Conti late on purpose, to show who was in charge? If the man got his enjoyment from such games, this could become a tedious exercise. Rick murmured an answer about not minding the wait and followed the man through the door, then along a wide corridor with doors off it at regular intervals. At its end was Conti's office. The policeman motioned Rick to sit in a chair in front of the desk. Rick was expecting to be offered a coffee, but no offer was forthcoming.

"An unfortunate accident delayed me, Signor Montoya." Conti settled into his institutional metal chair, leaning back with a slight squeak. "A man jumped to his death from a high wall at the north side of the city." He looked at Rick as if waiting for him to answer.

"I'm sorry to hear that," Rick said, for lack of anything more profound.

Conti continued to gaze at Rick for several seconds before speaking again. "Signor Montoya, I spoke to the man's employer." Another pause. "It seems that you were the last person to see the dead man before his fall."

"Canopo?" Rick immediately remembered the encounter outside the shoe shop and the man rushing off down the street.

"That is correct. Signor Landi said that you had left his store to visit their workshop. We checked, and apparently neither of you arrived there. Can you tell me what happened?" Conti eased his chair back and folded his hands over his stomach, but kept his eyes on Rick. The chair gave another squeak.

"We were together only briefly," Rick began, trying to recall the details while gathering his thoughts. But they were difficult to gather. He had spent barely ten minutes with Canopo, but in that time they had somehow connected, like two strangers in a foreign land. "After we left the shop we went into a bar on the street and had coffee. As we were leaving he stopped to talk to someone, and—"

"Who was that person?"

"I have no idea. It was a man, I'm sure of that."

"Did you hear any of the conversation?"

"No, Commissario, Canopo stepped away from me and spoke to him at the entrance to a shoe store. When he finished the conversation and came back, he asked to postpone the visit to the workshop until tomorrow, since something had come up. Then he rushed off."

"What did the man look like?"

"I didn't really see much of him. He mostly had his back to me, and was inside the entrance to the shop."

"Did Canopo leave with this man?"

"No, after he gave me his excuses and hurried off, I didn't see the other man."

"Which way did Canopo go?"

"Down the street, away from the shop, I think that would be—"

"I know. It would be toward where his body was found. What did you talk to him about?"

"Nothing of any importance. The weather. He complained about the cold, being from Sicily, I remember that. And a bit about my purchasing Etruscan artifacts." Conti's eyebrow raised. "Well, not artifacts, just Etruscan art that the store sells."

"Did he appear upset? Disturbed by anything?"

"Not at all. He was very friendly and talkative in the bar. But after he talked to this man, he seemed in a hurry. Nothing more than that. I assumed it was something to do with his work." Rick's chair was as hard as the bench, and he shifted in it to gain a bit of comfort. "There is something else I remember he said when we were in the bar." Conti leaned forward slightly, but waited for Rick to continue. "He compared the Sicilians and the Tuscans, saying there are good and bad people in both places. Said the Tuscans can be just as bad but think they're better, something like that. I found it strange."

Conti's face showed puzzlement. Was he wondering if Rick was making this all up? He nodded and swiveled in his chair, stretching out his legs, all the while keeping his eyes on Rick. "Where did you go after he walked away?"

"I had an hour or so to kill before our appointment," Rick answered, immediately regretting his choice of words. "So I walked around the center of town for a while before coming here. My last stop before coming here was the big park."

"The archeological park, the highest point of the city."

"It seemed that way. If I have time during my stay I want to explore that castle. It is very impressive."

Conti frowned and then his mouth turned upward to form that half smile Rick had seen in the waiting room. "Obviously you are not aware, Signor Montoya. That castle is a federal prison." This was the first change in the man's expression since they had sat down. "Did you talk to anyone as you walked the streets?"

Rick understood the inference of the question but he tried not to show it. "I spoke to no one. Do you suspect foul play, Commissario?"

Conti hesitated before answering. "It does seem strange that the man would take his own life. And thanks to the cold weather, the streets of the city were deserted, including, it appears, those near the scene of the accident. So we have no witnesses to the fall, though we are still trying to find anyone who might have been in the area. I had hoped you could be of help." He noticed Rick's expression and added, "Of course what you told me will help in completing the picture." He bent forward and placed his forearms on the desk. "But you have not come here to discuss the death of someone you just met. We should be talking about your undercover work, should we not?"

Rick detected an edge of sarcasm in the man's voice when he said the word "undercover." Beppo had told him that the local police would not be happy about the ministry's encroachment on their turf, so Conti's tone was to be expected. Rick thought about how his father would have reacted, and he opted for the diplomatic.

"Commissario, I know that the ministry very much appreciates your cooperation in this matter. And I will be keeping you apprised of my progress and look forward to your suggestions." Conti's expression did not waver. So much for diplomacy. Rick pulled his leather notebook from his pocket, opened it and reviewed the local people who Beppo had given him to contact. Conti listened carefully but without comment, until Rick mentioned Arnolfo Zerbino, the museum curator.

"Zerbino? The ministry doesn't think he could have anything to do with this, do they?"

"No, no, I didn't mean to give that impression, Commissario, his will be more a personal contact. Beppo, that is, Signor Rinaldi, knew the man when they both studied at the university. He thought Zerbino would be someone I would enjoy meeting."

"That is reassuring. Dr. Zerbino has been helpful to us in the past with cases of missing artifacts. That was before the ministry got involved." The sarcasm again. "Well, Signor Montoya, it appears that you are off to a good start, despite this unfortunate incident. We are at your disposal for any support you might need, and I look forward to hearing of your progress. You have my telephone number and now you know where I can be found."

He held up one finger and tapped his cheek in thought. "In that regard, it might be better if in the future you do not come into the building through the main doors used by the public. We don't want to give your new business associates the impression that you are cozy with the police, in case they may be keeping an eye on you. I will have one of my men show you a back entrance and get you cleared to use it from now on." He was about to rise from his chair when Rick spoke.

"Commissario, who do you think is behind these stolen artifacts?"

The policeman eased back into his chair, reminding himself that although Rick spoke Italian without an accent, he was very much an American. Italians rarely asked such direct questions, instead priding themselves in the use of subtlety and nuance. He sat for a few moments in thought before answering, slowly and deliberately, as if talking to a child.

"Signor Montoya, I know the ministry is convinced that these items have come from this area, and been discovered recently, but I am not. The people living around Volterra have been raiding Etruscan tombs for centuries. Who can be sure that these pieces are not from the secret collection of some noble Italian family, fallen on hard times and in need of cash? And that is only one possibility. So I am skeptical. But that does not mean that I wish you anything but the greatest success in your endeavor."

The thin smile that had greeted Rick in the waiting room earlier returned to Conti's lips, and Rick sensed that the meeting was over. Both men rose to their feet and Conti came around to the front of the desk. "You are staying at the San Lino, I understand? It is a fine hotel."

◇◇◇

After Rick left the room with one of Conti's men, the commissario returned to his chair and stared at the window for a few moments before picking up his phone. "Ask Detective LoGuercio to come in."

The young detective, in another well-tailored dark suit, appeared almost instantly, as if he expected to be called. And indeed he had, having walked past Rick when he was sitting at the bench in the waiting room. Conti was looking through his files and nodded at the detective before continuing to study the papers.

"The American was just in here, so you and DeMarzo should start the surveillance."

"Already done, sir. I noticed Montoya in the lobby and told DeMarzo to follow him. He just called me to say that he was leaving through the back entrance."

Impressed, Conti looked up at the man and nodded. "Very good, very good. I don't think he will give DeMarzo any trouble, but if by any chance there is a problem, you should have someone else ready to assist." He noticed the look on the detective's face. "But you had probably already thought of that."

LoGuercio, who was still standing, shifted nervously. "As a matter of fact, I did, sir. And we also have a contact in the hotel to help us track his movements."

This elicited another nod from the commissario. "You impress me, LoGuercio, I am pleased that you have the situation totally under control." He couldn't help himself and added, "It allows me to go back to more serious police work."

LoGuercio hesitated before speaking. "The suicide, sir? I just heard about it."

Conti frowned and looked down at the file. News always traveled quickly around the building, and it was not every day that the police in Volterra investigated a death.

"Suicide is what we assumed when the body was found, but the more I've learned about this man and his final movements, the less it seems likely that he would take his own life. In Sicily didn't you have deaths that first looked like suicides, but turned out to be murders?" He looked up at the detective who was staring at the wall. "LoGuercio?"

"Sorry, sir. Yes, that happened on occasion in Palermo." He added, "Sir, if you are busy with this suicide case, perhaps I could get more involved with the fake artifacts investigation we talked about a few days ago. When I'm not following Montoya, of course. I went over the file as you requested." He studied Conti's face.

"I appreciate your enthusiasm, LoGuercio, but for the moment that case is well covered. I will continue to keep you in mind."

"Thank you, sir."

When he was alone again, Conti stared at the papers on his desk without reading them. He tried to organize his thoughts as they bounced from stolen relics to deadly falls and back. After a few minutes he pushed the papers into their file and again picked up his phone.

"Gemma dear, I'm leaving now. *Buta la pasta.*"

Chapter Five

Rick surveyed the long table, wondering when it was that Italian hotels began laying out such a spread of breakfast foods for their clients. He remembered staying in Italian hotels as a kid when the fare was simple and brought to the table; bread, *caffè latte*, butter, and some jam. Sometimes too many choices was not a good thing, especially when the one choosing was not quite awake, which was the case this morning. He had stayed up late getting some work done on his computer, plus a bit of Facebook updating with New Mexico, but no emails to his parents. He would tell his mother about this trip when he got back to Rome, putting it in a very benign light. "Finally got to see Volterra," that kind of thing. So today he'd slept in until seven thirty, not like him at all. At his fraternity at UNM he was always the first one up, and unlike all his friends, without exception, he loved eight o'clock classes. *I must be getting old*, he thought.

He put his newspaper and room key down on an empty table, ordered a caffè latte from the waitress, and walked to the buffet. Small metal pitchers of hot coffee and milk were awaiting him when he returned to the table carrying a plate of rolls, butter, and jam, along with a yogurt. Good service, and his favorite flavor of yogurt. Why didn't they make bran yogurt in the States? Probably someone did some outrageously expensive market research and decided against it. Strange, one would expect that all the health food nuts would love it. He certainly knew enough of them in Albuquerque. While pondering this he poured equal amounts of the two liquids into his cup, their aroma hitting his nostrils as they mixed. After adding sugar he took a sip and spread out the newspaper, his eyes going immediately to a story below the fold.

LOCAL MAN PLUNGES TO HIS DEATH.

In the photo, two men with their backs to the camera looked down at a large rectangle of cloth on the ground. One, who appeared to be Conti, leaned against a chunk of marble, its gray surface contrasting with the bright white of the sheet covering Canopo's body. Rick stared at the photo and remembered other times he had encountered death. His Italian grandmother died when he was in college, and two years ago his father's oldest brother had fallen from a horse and never recovered. So death was not new to him. But those were old people, and dying was to be expected. Canopo should not have died.

He returned to the story and took a sharp deep breath when he reached a sentence in the final paragraph. *It has been revealed that the last person to see the victim alive was an American art dealer who is in Volterra on business.* Without thinking he looked quickly around the room to see if anyone was looking at him, but everyone seemed more interested in their coffee.

He shook his head, opened up the paper, and forced himself to read more local news. A political crisis in the Tuscan regional government mirrored the situation in the national parliament. There were rumors that a local soccer star was in negotiations with a team in Milan. The city tourist bureau announced the summer's cultural events, including July concerts in the main square. He folded the paper and pulled back the cover of the yoghurt, trying to put the death of Canopo out of his head.

It was not a good start to the morning, but he brought his thoughts back to the day's schedule. He would have to return to Landi's shop. Beppo had put the man at the top of Rick's list, apparently convinced that he could be involved in the ring, or at least be close enough to the action to point Rick in the direction of the actual tomb robbers. But given the death of Landi's employee, it might be politic not to show up immediately this morning. Instead, Rick would continue down the list of Beppo's names. He pondered the second person on the list, Donatella Minotti. When her name came up in the ministry briefing he had failed to tell Beppo that the woman was Erica's college friend. Nor had he told Erica afterward about Donatella's appearance on the list. If Donatella was just an honest art dealer, as Erica believed, it wouldn't be an issue with either Beppo or Erica. Under the opposite scenario it could be difficult, to say the least, if Donatella turned out to be involved in trafficking. But no use worrying about it now. Rino Polpetto, the exporter, was the third name. Rick decided to drop in on him after breakfast, but first he would call Donatella.

◇◇◇

"Signora Minotti? My name is Riccardo Montoya, I am visiting from Rome."

There was hesitation on the other end of the line. Perhaps she noticed a slight Roman accent and was puzzled since the name was not Italian. "Yes, Signor Montoya, how can I be of assistance?" Rick went through his routine, and she listened to it patiently. "Possible purchases for a gallery in America? Yes, I would be pleased to talk with you." There was another pause. Had she seen the story in the paper? It was almost impossible to get a sense of the woman over the phone, without the gestures, body language, and facial expressions which define Italian personalities. Her voice revealed almost nothing, which he decided was intentional.

"I also bring greetings from a mutual friend, Erica Pedana."

"Ah, Erica…but I don't understand. You work for a gallery in America but you speak perfect Italian and know Erica."

"Well, I actually live and work in Rome, but have connections with the gallery from my time in New Mexico."

"So you are not an art dealer?" The term was not one he had used when explaining the reason for the call; she must have gotten it from the newspaper story.

"No, not really. My friends in Santa Fe knew I was in Italy and asked me to help them out. My regular job is a translator and interpreter."

She digested this information. "I see. Well, I look forward to meeting you in person, Riccardo." The switch to his first name was noticeable. It was the Erica connection, no doubt about it. Again he felt a tinge of guilt that he had not told Erica about her friend's inclusion on Beppo's list. It was like the guilt he'd felt when telling Erica about the whole scheme, despite Beppo's request not to. But the pangs of conscience were more than neutralized by his enjoyment of all the intrigue. The longer he spent in Italy, it appeared, the more his Italian side was taking over.

"Would this afternoon work for you?" she said. "Unfortunately I'm very busy this morning."

Rick agreed, got directions to her villa outside of town, and said good-bye. He rose from his seat in the hotel lobby, dropped his key through the slot in the reception desk, and walked out into the street. As the door closed behind him, a man sitting at the opposite side of the lobby folded his newspaper, stood, and walked toward the door. The woman at the desk glanced up and watched him leave.

◇◇◇

Without realizing it, Rick had passed the office of Rino Polpetto during his stroll around the town the previous afternoon. The street was on a slight incline, sloping just enough to disturb the symmetry of the houses; all were a bit lower on one side, but their doorways were level. He was not good at estimating the ages of buildings, but from the look of their rough façades Rick thought that everything on this street must have dated from at least the 15th century. A historical plaque on one large and ornately decorated palazzo confirmed this. But like most of the other buildings on the street, the one which housed Polpetto's office was not grand enough to merit special recognition by the local historical society. There were four offices inside, each displaying a polished brass name plate next to the outside door. From the names it was impossible to know what business was carried out in the other three offices, not that Rick cared. He pressed the button under one of the plates:

POLPETTO
IMPORT-EXPORT
SECOND FLOOR

A buzzer unlocked the door with a loud click. He pushed it open and walked into a narrow hallway lit by a single bulb in the ceiling, letting the door close behind him with a soft thud. The building smelled musty, though a glance around did not reveal much dirt. Probably not sufficient traffic to track it in. The bulb cast enough light to find the stairway, but when he got up to the next floor he could barely make out the name plates on the two office doors. He found the right one, and his knock was rewarded with another click. Facing him in the small waiting room was a single desk, behind which sat a woman who stared at Rick through thick glasses. Her eyewear caught Rick's attention. The glasses were bright red and had points on the sides, reminding him of a character in a cartoon. Dangly plastic earrings matched the vivid color of the glasses, set against blond hair. She wore it medium length in a style that he suspected was vaguely out of fashion. The woman was not unattractive and, unlike most Italians her age, wore very little makeup. Perhaps the glasses added enough color to her face. The desk hid the lower part of her body, and a thick sweater did the same for what showed above the waist.

Two chairs were pushed against the wall opposite the desk, a small table between them. The only decoration on the walls, if it could be called that, was a digital clock above the table. A lone window across from the chairs gave the room its light, since a fixture in the ceiling was not turned on. He could not be sure if his appearance was a welcome break to a boring morning or an annoying interruption to the woman's normal routine. Her tone of voice didn't help him decide.

"May I help you?"

"My name is Montoya. I would like to see Dr. Polpetto." As he spoke he noticed that the only item on her desk, except for the telephone and a thin lap top computer, was the morning newspaper, neatly folded and placed at an angle.

"I'm sorry, Dr. Polpetto is not in this morning. Was he expecting you?" She said it as if she knew the answer.

"No, I arrived in Volterra only yesterday. Perhaps I could make an appointment to see him? I'm interested in buying some local art work to send to America, and have been told that he could possibly be of assistance."

She adjusted the glasses, which did not appear to need adjustment, and her face changed slightly. Not quite a smile, but close. Was it because he was now a business opportunity, not a distraction, or did she connect him with the newspaper story of Canopo's death? Perhaps a bit of both.

"I'm sure Dr. Polpetto would be pleased to see you. But may I inquire as to what kind of art are you interested in purchasing, Signor Montoya? I would not want to waste your time, or that of Dr. Polpetto, if it is not something he could help you with." This time, yes, the mouth did form a smile, though a bit forced.

"Etruscan pieces, primarily. In various price ranges." He stayed purposely vague.

Her expression did not change, but she nodded. "Yes, he has done considerable business in Etruscan art. Tomorrow morning, at about this time?" Since everything about her said precision, her use of the word "about" surprised him. She reached into a drawer and pulled out a large leather book, opening it to a page marked with a red ribbon. Rick could see that the calendar did not have any entries for the week. He nodded and passed over a card from the Santa Fe gallery on which he had written his name and cell phone number.

"I'm staying at the San Lino, but probably the cell phone is the best way to reach me if there is a problem with the time."

She stared at the card for a moment, then opened another drawer to take out a pen, which she used to write his name in the book. When she finished, she closed the book and returned the pen to the drawer. The card remained centered on the desk surface. Everything had its place.

"Until tomorrow," she said, finally with a real smile, though not a very convincing one. When Rick closed the door behind him and started carefully down the dark stairway, the secretary began dialing the phone while looking at the card in front of her.

◇◇◇

Commissario Conti drove up to the small house on a two lane road about a kilometer outside the walls of Volterra, his second visit in less than twelve hours. Canopo's residence was about what he had expected, given the location in an area that was not quite rural but offered more space than the cramped neighborhoods in town. The square two-story building stood by itself, a low wall separating its small yard from a bus stop almost directly in front of the wall's gate. A scrawny tree, doing its best to survive the car and bus fumes, was the yard's only adornment. A hill started immediately behind the house, its incline covered with bushes and a few small trees. Conti pulled the key out of the ignition and reluctantly unwound his frame from the seat. He never got used to talking with the relatives of crime victims. Perhaps that was why he chose to come without a driver this time, so that he could be alone on the way back and let himself mentally unwind. He put this task on the growing list of those he would not miss in retirement.

Last night the widow had accepted the news with a calm that Conti had seen few times in the past. The tears had followed later, no doubt, after his departure. He tried to compare it to similar heartbreaking occasions over the years. In Calabria the reaction was always the same, a total breakdown, making any questioning impossible, at least until a few days passed. Here in Tuscany the women were stronger, if that could be a fair description. Certainly less emotive.

He was about to ring the bell a second time when a girl about six years old opened the door and peered out. A voice came from the rear of the house.

"Ask who it is, Angela."

When the girl continued to stare silently up at Conti, he called out himself. "Commissario Conti, Signora Canopo. I called earlier." As he finished his sentence the door was pulled back and a short woman dressed in black took the hand of the child and motioned him inside.

"Of course, Commissario. Please come in."

The widow, in her early thirties, appeared to have aged several years since the night before. No doubt a lack of sleep made her voice low and scratchy, and she seemed to be slightly bent. She led the policeman down a long hallway to the kitchen at the back of the house, its windows looking out on the scrub of the hill. The room was clean and neat; she was either a meticulous housekeeper or cleaning was her way of dealing with the crisis. A small double-chambered espresso pot was on the stove. After sending her daughter into the other room she sat down and motioned him to another chair at the table. "Can I offer you a coffee, Commissario?"

"Thank you, that is very kind, but I just had some back at the office." Was she relieved? He had the sense she wanted to get the interview over with as quickly as possible. "Let me again extend my deepest condolences. Do you have other family here in Volterra?"

She sat stiffly, her hands clasped in the folds of the black dress. "I am from Lardarello, but my brother lives here in Volterra with his wife. She spent the night with us and will be back this afternoon. They have offered to take me in, since I can't afford the rent of this house now that…" She took a short breath and pressed on. "Now that Orlando is gone." Conti was about to speak when she said, "Commissario, my husband would never have taken his own life."

He had expected her to say it, but was surprised by the steel in her voice. It made it easier to reply. "You seem sure."

She straightened her shoulders. "I am very sure. He lived for Angela, and we were planning to have more children. We were putting away money for a house, a larger one for the expanded family. We looked at the newspaper every day to see if anything new had come on the market. He had so much to look forward to, it just doesn't make sense that he would give it all up." She looked down at the table and added, "And Orlando was very religious. He knew the church's position on suicide." She fell back in her chair, breathing heavily, finishing a speech which she had probably been practicing during the night.

"I must tell, you, Signora, that the police on the scene came to the conclusion that your husband's death was by suicide." Noticing the drained look on her face, he quickly added, "But as the officer in charge of the case, and after learning about your husband, I found it doubtful. I am proceeding under the assumption that there was foul play." Her expression immediately changed. "May I ask you some questions, Signora?"

"Of course, of course." The hands rose from the lap and were placed in front of her on the table, clasped tightly as if to keep them from trembling.

"Had you noticed any change in your husband in the weeks before his death? Had there been anything different in his routine?"

She stiffened, perhaps expecting the question but hoping it would not come. "He had seemed preoccupied recently. I thought it was simply worry about getting a down payment for our house. There had been one for sale about a month ago that we could not bid on because we didn't have enough saved, and I think he didn't want another to slip away. He had been working late at the shop almost every evening, to earn more money for that first payment, and he would come home very tired. The long days were certainly wearing on him. He could not spend as much time as he wanted with Angela, and that was hard for him. It was also hard for her." Her eyes glanced toward the other room where her daughter was playing.

"Do you know of anyone who would have wanted to harm your husband? Were there any old enemies?"

"Commissario, I thought about that most of the night, and I could not come up with a single name. He was not the kind of man to make enemies. Or close friends, for that matter, but of course here in Tuscany, Sicilians are looked on as foreigners." She looked at Conti, perhaps trying to place his accent. "Orlando's life was his family and his work. He was a very skillful artisan, and he hoped to move up in the business, but you have learned that already from his boss, I suppose."

"Not yet. My contact with Signor Landi yesterday was short, but I will be talking with him again. I called on you first." They looked up to see the little girl standing in the doorway, staring at the policeman in silence. Conti stood up. "I should be on my way, Signora Canopo. If you don't mind I will call you if I think of any other questions."

"Of course, Commissario, anything that I can do to help."

She walked him back down the hall to the front door under the gaze of Angela and opened it, shaking his hand weakly.

"Please find out the truth, Commissario."

He murmured that he would try, and walked out to his car. As he pulled out into the street he saw that she was still at the door watching him, her daughter's small hand holding tightly to her skirt. He decided that instead of driving back to the office he would return to the crime scene, now convinced, at least in his gut, that a murder had indeed been committed.

The dark blue police car wound along the streets north of the city and parked next to the archeological area below the tall north wall of Volterra's center. He stepped out from the driver's seat and was recognized immediately by the security guard who waved him past the gate. He walked slowly through the stone ruins, looking up at the wall where a group of school children were staring down, some of them pointing. Did they know about the recent death here or were they interested in Roman history? The climb up the steps was more tiring for him than the evening before. The adrenalin always seemed to flow on the first visit to a crime scene, and then the work faded back into the tedious. The yellow tape had been removed along with the body, but Conti remembered exactly the place where Canopo's crumpled figure had lain the previous night and he climbed up to it. Somehow being here might help make some sense of what he knew so far in the case, as if the ghost of the fallen man could speak to him. He sat down on a slab of stone and stared at the spot before looking up at the top of the wall. The children, thankfully, had gone.

Why would Canopo have been up there? From the point on Via Matteotti where the man had left Montoya, the fastest route to anywhere in town would certainly not have included the isolated street that ran above the ruins. No, this must have been his destination, and his final one, it turned out. On a cold day in the late afternoon, the only reason not to meet indoors would have been to avoid being seen or heard. No chat over coffee at a bar where there would be witnesses. If Conti could only find out who it was he'd met, or the reason for the encounter. He looked down again at the patch of ground, more convinced than ever that the case was homicide. If Canopo was pushed or thrown from the wall above, it would likely have taken more than one man, despite the victim's small stature. Had they planned to do him in from the start, or had the conversation turned ugly and precipitated the murder?

Conti was getting nowhere, only coming up with more scenarios and more questions. But that was always the case early in an investigation. He got up from the stone seat and once more looked down at the ground. It was a sad place to end your days on earth, but was there anywhere of which that could not be said? After crossing himself slowly, he walked down through the rows of ancient seats, across the stage, and back out to the gate. He barely acknowledged the wave of the guard before getting into his car.

◇◇◇

Rick held up a hand to signal that he didn't want to interrupt. Landi nodded in understanding and went back to his customers, two people who Rick decided were Germans. There was something about those long, belted raincoats that said German tourist, they were not something Italians wore. Nor did tourists of other nationalities, for that matter. Living in Rome, Rick was becoming adept at one of the local pastimes, guessing the nationalities of the city's visitors. Landi was dressed more somberly than the previous day, in a dark suit and blue tie. The look could be the rotation from his closet, or he might be showing some respect for his deceased employee. His yellowed teeth showed prominently as he spoke to the Germans, carefully pausing between words for the benefit of nonnative speakers.

There was another customer in the shop, and he was being helped by the young woman who had greeted Rick the previous day. She was dressed, as the previous day, in white blouse and dark skirt, the uniform of the Italian shop girl, but her face was not the same. In place of the smile was a dull gaze, and her eyes were reddened either from crying or lack of sleep. She had taken the loss harder than her boss, but had still come to work. When she saw Rick she gave him a quick sad look and returned to her client.

While he waited, Rick studied a shelf of flat alabaster panels decorated with classical motifs. Each sat on a small wire stand, like ones which held the antique plates decorating a sideboard in his grandparents' home in New Mexico. He took one in his hand and decided it weighed about five pounds, perhaps too much for tourists to buy in any large numbers unless they didn't mind paying extra at airport check-in. Or were driving home to somewhere in Europe. The scene on this panel was a god with helmet and shield, sitting on a throne surrounded by what looked like warriors. Thanks to Beppo's book, Rick knew that the Etruscans shared much of their mythology with the Greeks, but since he didn't know much Greek mythology to begin with, it didn't help to understand this design.

"Those panels are very popular with tourists."

Rick turned and greeted Landi, whose German clients were walking toward the door carrying a large paper bag marked with the tasteful logo of Galleria Landi.

"I was shocked to hear of Canopo's accident, Signor Landi." Rick could not decide if actual condolences were in order for the dead man's employer. "It must have been terrible news for you."

"Yes, yes, we are all stunned." He clasped his hands together and held them to his mouth, almost the caricature of mourning, before dropping them to his sides. "When the police appeared here last night, I did not understand at first. I assumed that Orlando was with you at the workshop, but when I called there—at the request of the Commissario, of course—I was told that you never appeared." Landi paused and looked at Rick, waiting for a comment.

"Just outside the shop," Rick said, "he spoke to someone on the street. Then he told me he would have to show me the shop tomorrow. That is, today. And he rushed off." That was probably about as much as Conti would want him to say.

Landi digested the words for a few seconds, shaking his head slowly. "What could that have been about? He certainly didn't tell me of any possible appointments. I don't suppose he told you who the man was." Rick shook his head. "Well, life must go on," said Landi, his wiry smile returning. "Do you have time for a visit to our workshop now? I think that Graziella can handle the store for the moment, and my wife is in the back if she needs help. Shall we?"

"By all means."

It did not appear that Landi was suffering in his grief.

◇◇◇

Powdered stone dust floated through the air and covered everything, its dull white softened by the light of the florescent lamps hanging from the ceiling. Large blocks of stone lay scattered around the floor, like some of the ruins Rick knew well in Rome. Finished sculpture stood on the shelves, and unfinished pieces were clamped firmly on the wooden tables. Five men wearing long coats and folded paper hats stood at work stations around the shop, but only the nearest of them looked up when Landi and Rick entered. The others were too intent on their labors. In the dusty haze of the room there was little to distinguish the workers from their work; had it not been for their movement, the men could well have been mistaken for crudely carved gray statues.

The sound of machinery had been audible on the street, but now it was so loud that Landi had to raise his voice to be heard. The main culprit was a large lathe at one side of the room which was shaving a trunk of alabaster about three feet long. Landi shouted that the piece would be sliced into thick discs which would then be carefully made into bowls or dishes. He pulled a flat plate from a nearby shelf to demonstrate the nearly-finished product. It was already thin but would be made even thinner, he said, allowing light to shine through it. They moved to a heavy wooden table where another worker was chipping away with a small chisel at a cherub about two feet tall. An assortment of other chisels in various sizes and angles were loosely arranged on the table, their wood grips shiny from years of use. The man held the tool in his right hand and slid it over the pointed index finger of his left, like a small pool cue, softly grinding the alabaster to open a space between two of the angel's toes.

Landi did not identify the first two workers, but the man at the third table was introduced as Signor Malandro, the foreman of the shop. Rick saw that the coat he wore was a different color, a light blue in contrast to the dirty white on the other men, no doubt to indicate his foreman status. Even in the smallest of work groups rank was important. Otherwise the foreman didn't appear much different from the others, though the blue of his coat showed more dust. The man's hands were thick and rough, the hair under the newsprint hat a dark gray, though it could have been stone dust rather than natural color.

Malandro's unshaven face and hollow eyes took stock of the visitor with a long stare before he turned silently back to his table. Rick wondered for an instant if the man knew he was the last to see Canopo alive, and was somehow holding him responsible. Malandro was carefully making marks with a thick pencil on a large block of stone, but it was too early in the process for Rick to even guess what form this piece would eventually take. Landi, with a louder shout, asked his foreman to give the workers a break. Putting down his pencil, he walked over to each of the workers, tapped them on the shoulder and signaled with a chop of the hand to stop working. They were soon seated at various wooden stools, half of them lighting cigarettes. All sat silently, but only Malandro watched the two men who had interrupted their work routine.

"There, that will allow us to talk," said Landi in a relieved tone. He went on to describe the work in the various corners of the room. This shop, he said, specialized in more traditional styles, the kind of sculpture turned out by Volterra's artisans for thousands of years. Bowls, human figures, vases. Designs were mostly classical to appeal to buyers who wanted something with a clear Italian look to it. Other shops turned out nontraditional alabaster art, both practical and whimsical, but since Rick had mentioned Etruscan-style items, he wanted to bring him here. Was his assumption correct?

"Yes it was," Rick replied. "This is certainly the kind of thing that would interest the gallery. How much of it is done by hand, and how much by machine? Handmade pieces would certainly be more attractive to our customers." Rick thought how easy it was to slip into his role, and he was enjoying the challenge.

"Well, as you can see it is a combination of both, but when it gets to the final stages, it is mostly by hand. We save time, and of course expense, by using machines to get the stone into the general shape required, but then it is small drills and a lot of old-fashioned chisels which create the final contours. We can use sanding machines up to a certain point, but in the end handrubbing is the only way to bring out the brilliant shine from a perfect piece of alabaster."

He walked with Rick to a corner table holding a rectangular slab whose surface was decorated with classical figures in bas-relief. Two women in diaphanous gowns danced under a tree, while a hoofed satyr sitting between them played a double flute. The scene was framed by garlands of leaves and fruit.

"This work started from a piece of alabaster cut to size using that large mechanical saw over there. Then its figures were shaped with small electric drills, but mostly the worker used chisels whose design and function have not changed for centuries. Many of the techniques go back to pre-Roman times."

Rick turned his eyes from the stone to his host. Landi had an expectant smile on his face, spoiled somewhat by the row of yellow teeth. No doubt he was hoping for at least a pro forma compliment about the merchandise, or perhaps something about a firm sales order. But instead Rick went to a new topic. It was time.

"Signor Landi, your mention of ancient art brings up something else of interest to me. While these pieces could be appropriate for our normal customers, we also have very affluent collectors in our city who are, might I say, looking for something exceptional, even extraordinary. They see a beautiful work of art in a museum and want to own such genuine art themselves. When they purchase rare works they often keep them locked away in a private room, for safety and for the joy of owning something unique. If you know of any items like that on the local market, my associates in America could be interested. Obviously the gallery would show our appreciation to you if we were pointed in the right direction."

Landi's face went serious as he took in Rick's words. Did he get the message? And if he did, was he the right person to do anything about it? Rick was beginning to doubt it when the man began to nod slowly.

"I think I may know someone who could be of help. Let me make a phone call when I get back to the store." He was smiling again as he turned to the men who sat near where they stood. "Dino, our thanks, we will let you get back to work." The foreman nodded sullenly and got up, followed by the other craftsmen who put out their cigarettes and shuffled to their tables. The air, which was now almost clear, would soon be filled with dust again.

Back in the street, Landi brushed off his clothes with rough slaps. "No matter how careful I am when I go in there, I always come out covered. I don't understand how the men stand it. At least Malandro, who you met there, will start to get a break from the shop. I haven't told him yet, but he will likely be replacing Canopo, splitting his time between the store and the workshop."

He's going to have to clean up quite a bit before he's put out in front of the tourists, Rick thought. At that moment his cell phone rang, and he pulled it out of his coat pocket. Not a number he recognized, but a local one. He looked at Landi.

"Please take your call, Signor Montoya, I really should be getting back to the store anyway."

They shook hands and Landi stepped quickly down the street.

"Montoya."

"Signor Montoya, this is Commissario Conti. I need to see you right away. Are you close to my office?"

Chapter Six

Rick's first entry into the back of the building went without a hitch. He didn't even have to show an identification before being waved past the policeman. Conti was so anxious to get Rick to his office quickly that he must have alerted security. As Rick stopped to get his bearings, a man who had entered the building just behind him brushed past and hurried down a corridor. Unlike the others milling around inside the entrance, the man did not have a uniform. Rick found the stairway that took him up to Conti's floor.

"Signor Montoya, thank you for getting here so quickly." Conti had come to his feet when Rick entered, and now shook his hand before motioning him to the chair in front of the desk and sitting back down. The smile today seemed more genuine. Was the policeman more accepting of Rick's assignment? Would that be the reason for the call? He settled into the same chair as the previous evening, noticing that the seat was just as hard, and looked at Conti.

"Of course, Commissario. Has something come up regarding my activities here in Volterra?"

"No, not directly. I am in need of your help on another matter, one that you are aware of because of your…" He searched for the right words. "Your connection with the subject of my investigation. I am referring to the Canopo case."

"But Commissario, I already told you everything yesterday. Certainly there could not—"

Conti held up his hands. "No, no, I fear I have not made myself clear. Your involvement in the…the accident, is not in question. What I need is your professional assistance."

Rick shifted in the chair, wishing it had some kind of cushion. "I don't understand."

"Signor Montoya, there were two American tourists who witnessed Canopo's plunge from the wall. When they returned to their hotel they told their hotel manager about it, and he, fortunately, called us. When I did a check on you yesterday, purely routine, of course, I found that you are a professional translator. Alas, my English is almost non-existent, so I thought that—"

"Of course, I would be pleased to be of assistance." Rick smiled.

Conti returned the smile, which this time did not seem forced. "There is something else that I found out about you, Signor Montoya."

Now what?

"You did not mention to me that your uncle is quite a high-level policeman in Rome. Most Italians would have immediately brought up such a family connection when finding themselves in a difficult situation with law enforcement authorities, as you had yesterday. It is obvious to me now that you are American, or mostly American."

Perhaps Conti had a point; it had never entered Rick's mind to mention Uncle Piero. He made a mental note: *Montoya, next time you're a suspect in an Italian murder investigation, act more Italian.* "It didn't seem relevant, Commissario."

"Of course it didn't." Conti actually chuckled as he rose from his desk, a first in Rick's presence. "I believe they are in the waiting room, but please stay seated. I think I have enough English at least to greet them and bring them here." He motioned to the other end of the office. "We will sit at the table."

When he found himself alone, Rick got up, walked to the window of the office and looked down on the piazza. A group of tourists were staring back at him, probably thinking he was a cop if they somehow knew this was the city's police station. Would Conti have left him here by himself, with the papers on the desk, if he didn't know about Uncle Piero? He knew Conti hadn't actually talked to his uncle, or Rick would have had a call from Rome immediately after the two had spoken. But it was clear that whatever Conti's source about Rick's family, the man was now more comfortable around him. As he pondered this development, he heard Conti's voice in the hallway.

"Is this door," he said in English, and pair of seniors entered the office ahead of him. They were dressed for comfort, including running shoes, white for him, black for her. Both wore zippered wind-breakers, good for warmth as well as protection against anything but a heavy rain. Very practical. They had probably researched weather history for Tuscany before leaving on the trip, and packed accordingly.

"I present Mister Montoya, my colleague." Rick was considering the use of the term "colleague" when Conti turned to him and switched to Italian. "Signor Montoya, this is Signor and Signora Rudabeck, they are from Iowa." He pronounced it ee-OH-wah.

As he shook hands with Rick, Mr. Rudabeck spoke.

"WE DON'T SPEAK ANY ITALIAN."

Rick had witnessed this before, especially with Americans: if you just talk louder, the person will understand your English. Translation through volume.

"You don't need to shout, Mr. Rudabeck, I'm an American. The Commissario has asked me to help with his interview since his English is, well, somewhat rusty."

"See, Herb, I knew they would have someone who speaks English. Where you from, Mr. Montoya?"

The classic question from an American tourist. "I live in Rome now, but went to school in New Mexico."

"We've been to Phoenix," Herb said in a normal voice, relaxed after hearing Rick's English. "We're from just outside Davenport. On the river."

Rick was deciding how to reply to the Phoenix reference when a look from Conti indicated it was time to get to the business at hand. The couple was invited to sit at the conference table at the other side of the room. Rick and Conti took the chairs opposite them. Coffee was offered to the Rudabecks and they politely declined. Conti said to Rick that what he needed was simply a description of what they saw, and the couple was ready when Rick relayed the question in English. As they spoke, Rick kept his eyes on their faces and gave a running translation into Conti's ear. Thanks to his work, the routine was second nature to him.

"I'm the one who saw the accident, Herb, so let me tell him. We were coming back to our car in the parking lot. We have a rental car, we picked it up in Florence."

"They don't need to know about the rental car, Shirley."

She ignored the comment. "It was just getting dark, and my husband was putting the key into the lock to open the door. I was looking up at that moment, back toward the town, and that was when I saw the man falling off the wall. I didn't hear anything, but it may have been too far away. Do people usually scream when they fall, like in the movies?" From the look on her face, she was beginning to understand it had not been a movie.

"I don't know, Mrs. Rudabeck," answered Rick. "Did you see anyone up on the wall after he fell?"

"I'm not sure. It was dark, like I said, and I think my eyes naturally followed the man as he fell. If there was anyone up there, he might have left before I looked back up. I did look up at the top of the wall, I know that, because I remember thinking how long a drop it was. But I can't recall seeing anyone."

"We had just walked along that very street when the sun was starting to go down, about an hour before that," added her husband, who seemed oblivious to his wife's growing emotion. "Looked down at the Roman ruins. It's a long way to fall."

So the length of the fall was well established.

Conti relayed a few more questions, trying to find out what else, if anything, the tourists had seen. When it became clear to him that they had nothing more to add which could be of any help, he stood up and gave the couple an appreciative bow.

"I thank you very much." Conti hesitated, trying to think of something else to say in his limited English, and repeated, "I thank you very much."

"You're very welcome, officer." Mr. Rudabeck turned to Rick. "And thank you for your help, Mr. Montoya. We'll be telling this story to our friends when we get back to Davenport, that's for sure. It's even better than what happened to Shirley on the bus in Florence."

The bus incident did not appear to be something Shirley wanted recounted. She quickly stuck out her hand to Rick. "Be sure to look us up if you come through Davenport. We're in the phone book." She turned to Conti and took his hand in both of hers. "That poor man," she said to the silent policeman.

Rick volunteered to see the couple to the building's front entrance, much to Conti's relief. When he returned, the commissario was sitting at his desk looking at papers in a file, and Rick took the seat facing him.

"Was that helpful, Commissario?" He knew the answer, and Conti confirmed it.

"Not helpful, but necessary. It confirms what we knew already, which is always a good thing, but didn't give us anything new. Now if she had seen someone above…"

Conti's voice trailed off. Rick watched the man's eyes, which were pointed at the papers in front of him.

"You think it was murder, Commissario." It was not a question. Conti looked at Rick, hesitating a moment before speaking.

"You are the nephew of a colleague, so perhaps you have discussed some of his cases with him. I suppose it would not be a problem if I shared my thoughts with you, since you are involved, so to speak, with the case. I trust your discretion." The introduction sounded to Rick that Conti was talking to himself and not the person he faced. "Yes, Signor Montoya, I believe it was murder." He pressed a finger to the papers. "The initial autopsy report points in that direction, though I suspected foul play almost immediately. It did not make sense that the man would have taken his own life, and my conversation with the widow convinced me even more that he didn't commit suicide."

"What did the autopsy indicate?"

Conti pulled a paper from the file and placed it on top. "Two items of interest. There were some fresh bruises on the body which likely were not caused by the impact of the fall, indicating that he had been held or pulled."

"To get him to the edge and over."

"Exactly. And there were traces of skin under the fingernails of one hand, meaning that he had scratched someone. This and the bruises seem to point to a struggle. A short one, perhaps, but a struggle none the less."

"So someone wrestled him to the edge and pushed him over. Or more than one person."

Conti smiled. "You think like a detective, Signor Montoya. Yes, one or more persons." He closed the file with a quick hand motion. "And your situation? Is there anything new there?"

Rick wanted to continue talking about the murder, but respected Conti's wish to change the subject. Canopo's death would come up again.

"I trust you saw the paper this morning, Commissario?"

"Yes, you are now famous. Be assured that it was not I nor my men who told the reporter about you being the last one to see Canopo alive. But at least your name did not appear in the story."

"It might as well have, there aren't that many American art dealers in town. I suspect that Landi, or someone in his shop, told the newspaper about me. I should have asked him that when I saw him this morning." Rick recounted the meeting with the shop owner, and the hint he dropped with the man about items of special interest.

"Do you think Landi understood?"

"I'm not sure, Commissario. But he did say he was going to call someone. We'll have to wait and see."

Conti's face said that he was still annoyed, or bored, by the whole artifacts business. Or perhaps it was simply that his mind was on the murder. "Where are you going next?"

"This morning I stopped by the office of the exporter, Polpetto, but he can't see me until tomorrow morning. I have an appointment with Signora Minotti late this afternoon. So after lunch I thought I would drop by the museum to meet Dr. Zerbino."

"I would ask you to give him my regards, but obviously that would not be appropriate."

"No, Commissario, it wouldn't."

They stood up and Rick noticed, for the first time, that Conti was wearing the same rumpled suit as the previous day. He could not be sure of the tie.

◇◇◇

"*Ciao Beppo, a presto.*"

Rick snapped his cell phone closed and looked down at the plate of pasta that had just been put before him; cheese tortellini with a thick meat ragú, the perfect dish for a cold day. Beppo had been pleased with the update, but didn't seem especially anxious to hear about the details. The call might have caught him at the wrong time, when he was busy with other cases or dealing with the annoying office politics of the ministry—what Italian government office was immune to infighting? Bureaucracy may have been invented by the French but Machiavelli was an Italian. Or maybe Beppo was in the middle of his lunch, and like most Romans considered the *pranzo* a sacred part of the day, if possible enjoyed without interruptions from less important issues. Since Beppo had seemed in a hurry, Rick had not even brought up the murder case. Now he wondered if he should have mentioned it, even though it had nothing directly to do with his ministry work in Volterra. He'd leave it for the next call. Rick pulled the Etruscan book from his coat and spread it open above the plate.

The tortellini, an ample bread basket, and the quarter liter of red wine were filling enough to keep him from following the pasta with a main course. Instead he had a small green salad and asked for a few more slices of bread. He watched as the waiter mixed the oil and vinegar in a spoon before tossing it with the leaves. No choice of dressings here. He had been one of the last people to enter the restaurant and now he was likely to be close to the last to leave. Only two other tables were still occupied. One held a group of East European tourists who had just ordered another round of grappa, and were clearly developing a taste for the stuff. For Rick, drinking it was like sipping kerosene, albeit a very high quality kerosene. At the other table, in a corner, sat an older man across from a girl in her early twenties, an empty wine bottle between them. Rick had caught her looking in his direction earlier when the conversation between them had stalled. *Isn't that precious*, he thought with an inward smile, the man is taking his niece out to lunch. Family is so, so important to Italians. Rick raised his hand to catch the eye of the waiter.

"*Il conto, per favore.*"

The cool air of the street felt good on his face, and he took in a deep breath. The lunch had fortified him well, and he was ready to take on Beppo's university colleague. Rick had not met many museum directors in his life, in fact he hadn't met any, but his guess was that like any other profession they could be dull or charming, or somewhere in between. It would be just his luck that Zerbino was more the former.

He consulted his town map before starting to work his way through various streets until he turned onto the wide Via Gramsci. Every town in Italy had a street named for one of the founders of the Italian Communist Party, and Volterra was not going to be an exception. The party was now virtually defunct, or more accurately it had morphed into a new political entity with many of the same characters but a different name. Change to insure survival had been both an individual and institutional tradition in Italy for thousands of years. As Rick knew from the book, the Etruscans had managed to survive by being drawn into the growing Roman empire. The more things change…

"Signor Montoya."

The woman came out of a store and was walking toward him. He didn't recognize the voice, but when he saw the red glasses he knew immediately who it was. She was not behind a desk this time, so he could tell her shape below her waist. The legs, anyway, and the ankle-high leather boots for Volterra's stone streets. Still no view of the skirt; a long purple coat nicely covered it. That's assuming she's wearing one, he thought naughtily. They shook hands.

"On your way to your next appointment, Signor Montoya?"

"You have an advantage on me that you know my name, but I don't know yours."

The smile was not forced this time, she seemed a different person out of the office. "Claretta. Claretta Angelini."

He offered a slight bow. "*Un piacere*, Signora Angelini. Yes, I am off to another appointment." That was enough information for her.

"I hope that you will have time to see some of Volterra. There is not another city like it in Tuscany. Or Italy, for that matter." She had been moving her hands in a circle to make her point, and now, as if noticing the temperature, she put them into the pockets of her coat. Rick wondered how long she would be able to keep them there. "The civic museum, is just around the corner over there." Out came one of the hands to indicate direction. "It has some wonderful works of art."

"I have been told that, and plan on seeing it."

She was still intently studying his face when she pulled up her sleeve and checked her watch, its large face almost covering her wrist. It was edged with red enamel to match her glasses. "You must be going to your appointment, Signor Montoya. I have not yet tracked down Signor Polpetto, he is off on one of his trips, but I am very sure that the appointment tomorrow will be agreeable." It sounded like it was her decision. She looked up at him with a questioning face. "Are you in contact with other exporters, Signor Montoya? I imagine that we are not the only ones you will be seeing in the city."

Rick found it curious that she said "we" rather than "Signor Polpetto," as if she considered herself an equal partner. "There are various businesses on my list, yes."

"Volterra is a small city, but it offers many possibilities." She was back to studying him, and her eyes had a certain probing quality that had been absent in the office. He recalled the story in the paper and pictured her unfolding it from that corner on the desk after he left the office, re-reading the account of Canopo's death. Then carefully refolding it and putting it back in its place on the desk. And now she wanted to bring up the murder, if she could get up the courage. He waited and smiled.

"*Bene*, Signor Montoya, it was a pleasure to see you." She held out her hand for Rick to take. "*A domani.*"

She either didn't have the courage, or something caused her to avoid the topic. Or perhaps he imagined the whole scenario. "*A domani*, Signora Angelini."

Rick watched her return to the store and noticed it was either an art gallery, an antiques shop, or a combination of the two. The window was crammed with dusty figurines, marble busts and small paintings, its clutter the opposite of Polpetto's outer office. Was this a branch of the man's business or was the secretary just out for a walk?

He continued up the street past a small park before coming to the stone façade of the *Museo Etrusco Guarnacci*. As he did, a man walking his bicycle behind him stopped to lean it against a light pole, taking a cigarette from a pack in his pocket and lighting it. Rick's city guide book said the museum was named for its founder and benefactor Mario Guarnacci, a local intellectual and early student of the Etruscans. Guarnacci donated his collection of artifacts and books to the city in 1761, forming the core holdings of the institution. To that core collection were added items owned by another prominent Etruscanologist, Pietro Franceschini, thereby making it one of the finest Etruscan museums in the country. Better to know the basics before meeting with the museum's curator, Rick thought, you don't want to look bad in front of Beppo's college friend. And you never know, there could be a quiz. He walked up the steps and through the doors.

For such an old institution, the museum's entrance facilities were surprisingly modern. A glass-enclosed ticket booth covered much of the right wall, with two women sitting inside at small computer screens. Ahead, past the turnstiles, he could see all the way down the hall, past rooms which opened on either side, to the windows far in the back. In the middle of the hall a harried teacher was doing her best to herd a group of grade school students into one of the side rooms, without much success. The children were more interested in talking to each other than following her directions, and in a building with little to muffle the sound, their high voices bounced from wall to wall. Just past the ticket booth were the glass cases of a small shop, now a fixture in most museums, or at least any that wanted some extra income. Rick could see Etruscan reproductions in various sizes, similar to those at Galleria Landi, under the glass and on shelves behind the counter. Three of the kids had strayed over to the shop and were squatting down, peering at the bronze ducks behind the glass. One looked over to see the frowning teacher striding toward them, nudged the other two, and within seconds they had scurried back to the group.

Rick walked to the ticket booth and asked to see Dr. Arnolfo Zerbino. The woman looked over her half glasses at him and hesitated for a moment before inquiring as to whether or not he was expected. Rick made a mental note that if he ever had a secretary, he would tell her never, ever, to ask a visitor if he was expected. He said he was not, but passed his own translation service business card under the glass and asked if she would tell Zerbino that he was a friend of Dr. Giuseppe Rinaldi. Better not to use Beppo's nickname. Who knows how friendly the two had really been? The woman looked at the card, picked up the phone, and after a short conversation hung up and asked him to wait. As he was turning away, she said something to her colleague that Rick could not hear. The two women laughed and returned to their computer screens. Rick took a seat on a bench. He was becoming an authority on wooden seating—could there be a market for a tourist guide to Volterra's benches?

Five minutes later a large man emerged from the elevator. He was dressed in a three-piece tweed suit that had a definite English cut. A large girth under the vest, half glasses at the end of his nose, and a shiny bald head framed by tufts of hair on either side gave the impression that he had just stepped out of a London club. All that was lacking was a walrus moustache. Even his shoes, oxblood wing tips, supported the image. His face showed a mixture of annoyance and curiosity, and Rick again wondered if the man was that close with Beppo at the university. The image of the two of them downing ale together at some pub in Padova was difficult to conjure up, despite the man's British demeanor and Beppo's high school persona. Zerbino pushed through the low exit gate, and Rick rose from the bench for the confrontation.

"Signor Montoya?"

Rick stepped forward and shook his hand. "My pleasure, Dr. Zerbino." The curator seemed increasingly perplexed, waiting for some explanation. His eyes fixed for an instant on Rick's cowboy boots, then bounced back up to his face. "I am an American living in Rome. Dr. Rinaldi, Beppo, is a very good friend, and when I told him I was going to visit Volterra he insisted that I come by to bring you his regards. But I know you are busy, so I'll let you get back to your work."

This seemed to bring the Italian out of his puzzled state, and his face changed to almost a smile. "Absolutely not, I remember Beppo well and it is a pleasure to meet you. The last I heard of Beppo was that he's at the Cultural Ministry."

"That's correct. I'm not sure what part he works in." *Not a complete lie*, Rick told himself, *I don't know the real name of the office.*

"If you have time, I would be glad to give you a tour of the museum."

"That's very kind of you, *dottore*, but I'm sure you—"

"Nonsense, it will be my pleasure." His eye was caught by some movement inside the booth, and both men saw one of the women holding her hand to her ear. "Ah, that's right. I'm afraid you'll have to turn off your cell phone and leave it here. We are having some issues with our remote security system." He took Rick's phone and slid it under the glass, taking a plastic number in return which he passed to Rick. "So tell me, what brings you to the city? Pure tourism, I trust." He glanced at the woman behind the glass who immediately clicked open the turnstile so that the two could enter the museum proper. A freebie, thought Rick. Another of the perks of knowing someone from the culture ministry.

"Well, some tourism of course, but I'm mainly here to scout out possible business opportunities." He explained the connection with a Santa Fe art gallery and its request that Rick look into buying some art for them while in Italy. He added that art sales was not his profession and briefly described the translation and interpreting business. Rick assumed that the curator would warm up somewhat, but instead the man's disposition did not change. He sensed that Zerbino had made the decision to carry out an obligation to a former university colleague who just happened to be working at the ministry. One never knew when an extra contact in the government cultural bureaucracy could come in handy. "One hand washes the other" was a classic Italian phrase. So he would be polite, but not much more than necessary.

The curator took Rick into the first room of the museum's ground floor and launched into what seemed almost like a canned discourse: a short explanation of the Etruscans, helped by various maps and panels on the walls, after which they moved toward the middle of the floor where the space was divided into numerous smaller rooms. He could have been speaking to anyone, his eyes barely met those of his guest, darting instead from one ancient object to the next as he rattled on. Zerbino knew his Etruscans, that would be expected from the museum curator; what seemed out of place was the disinterested tone. Perhaps that's the way the guy is all the time. Rick would try to remember to ask Beppo.

Zerbino unbuttoned the suit jacket and hooked his thumbs in the small pockets of his vest before going on. "The Guarnacci donation, the core of which you see in these rooms, includes one of the finest collections of Etruscan funerary urns in the world, more than six hundred in number, which are divided in the museum by theme. As you can see, those in this room are decorated with animal motifs." He stood in the middle of the small room whose shelves were covered with urns similar in size to the one Rick had seen in Beppo's office in Rome. While Zerbino continued to talk, Rick walked closer to the shelves and examined a few of them, frequently glancing back at the curator so as not to appear rude. The urns were decorated with animals, mostly wild and some more ferocious than others. All were still as vibrant as when their carvers had put chisel to stone more than two millennia earlier. The next room's urns had a more poignant theme, the voyage from this world to the next. Clearly it was a popular thematic choice; it was the first of four rooms whose urns depicted the transition to the afterlife, always using modes of transportation well known to the Etruscans. Here were horses carrying the deceased, in the next room they traveled in covered wagons pulled by oxen, and in another the chariot was used.

"There certainly are, well, a lot of urns," said Rick as they entered a sixth room whose walls were once again lined with shelves. Zerbino emitted the sigh of the *cognoscenti* forced to mingle with the *ignoranti*, but managed a benevolent smile.

"It can be a bit overwhelming, Signor Montoya. But for Etruscan specialists, each one is a treasure. We hate to part with them, even for a short time, but as you can see I occasionally lend pieces to other museums for special exhibits, under the assumption that they will reciprocate when called upon. We also allow serious academics to take them from the shelves for study and analysis." He pointed to a small card propped up on one of the shelves. It was clear that the missing urn must have been displayed there for decades, its base had left a light, rectangular spot on the wood. Rick had noticed a few other such cards in the previous rooms. If Beppo's plan were to pay off, would the recovered urns be displayed in one of these rooms? Probably not, there were enough museums in Rome which would love to get their hands on such treasures.

Zerbino continued his lecture. "The urns in these next rooms deal with stories from Greek mythology. The religion of the Etruscans was of course very close to the Greeks, and they shared much of their mythological tradition. Yes, Renata?"

The last question was directed to an earnest young woman with glasses who had approached as he was talking, and she curtly told him that his appointment had arrived. Zerbino turned to Rick.

"I'm terribly sorry, but I really must not keep this person waiting. Please take your time in seeing the rest of the museum; it is at your disposal. And I hope you will give my warm greetings to Beppo. I trust he is well."

"He is, and I will certainly give him your regards. Thank you for your time."

Zerbino gave a stiff hand to Rick and hurried out of the room, followed closely by his secretary.

Rick knew the trick well, it was one his father still used to perfection in his diplomatic work. You tell your secretary to come and get you after a specified time, allowing an escape if the situation requires it. But at least Zerbino had given Rick about twenty minutes of his time and had told him a bit more about those wacky and mysterious Etruscans. To begin with, they sure liked funerary urns. Rick walked along the shelves that lined the room, his eyes moving from one urn to the next. He came to a space and read the card that stood in the place of the missing piece. It had the date, a scribbled set of initials, and the notation that it was on loan to a museum in Germany. He continued to walk around the room, thinking how similar these urns were to the one he had seen in Beppo's office in Rome.

Rick was not close to becoming an Etruscan scholar, but he was convinced after wandering these rooms that Beppo's urn was from Volterra. He was also starting to understand why Erica had opted for the Mannerists over the Etruscans, not that those were her only two choices. At that point he came to another card, telling him that the urn that had been in that spot was now undergoing restoration. Into the next room he strolled. Amazing: more funerary urns.

He instinctively reached to his pocket to check the time, but realized his cell phone was at the front desk. Perhaps it was time to start wearing a watch again. Fortunately a bored museum guard sitting in a corner was able to give him the time, and he saw he still had a couple hours before his appointment with Donatella. He walked up the stairs, passed a large statue of the museum's benefactor sitting in his ecclesiastical robes, and began to work his way through the rooms of the second floor. Here the institution seemed to be reluctantly changing its image from one of a 19th century museum to a modern one. Some rooms still had the old wood and glass cases filled with small artifacts and even smaller cards identifying them, while others had their pieces featured in a more dramatic display, with hidden spots and back lighting. As sometimes happened to him in museums, even the best ones, everything was starting to look the same, but he wanted to see what his guidebook described as the most famous work in the building. When he got to it, he found it displayed in a position of honor in the center of the room, enclosed in a softly-lit glass case. The boy, his straight arms stiffly at attention, was all legs and body, wire thin and tall. It looked as if the sculptor had created a normal body, and then begun to pull on the clay, slowly elongating the figure, and could not bring himself to stop. The result was a haunting, almost snake-like bronze sculpture which stared at Rick with a faint smirk. Try to figure this one out, it seemed to be saying in a voice that echoed back almost two and a half millennia.

There wasn't anything that could top that. Rick walked briskly through the next rooms and perused the Greek items on the top floor before taking the elevator back down to the *piano terra*. The woman pulled his cell phone from one of the cubby holes behind her desk and exchanged it for the plastic number. When he left the building he brought the phone back to life, turned right, and headed down the street toward the hotel. The man with the bicycle followed in the same direction.

◇◇◇

The car drove slowly down the narrow street, the strolling pedestrians moving even more slowly to the sides when they saw it was a police vehicle. It was a small show of defiance to the authorities that involved little risk, and Conti was used to it whenever he drove through a *zona pedonale*. Landi's shop was a short walk from the police station, but he thought a demonstration of force, even if it was only the dark blue armored Fiat, might help get some answers. The sergeant parked in front of the shop and Conti got out and stepped into Galleria Landi, watched by the people on the street. He knew that customers would hesitate to come into the shop while a police car parked in front. The girl behind the counter was clearly uncomfortable with the appearance of the commissario, but he could not tell if her discomfort was due to his car's effect on business or something else. His appearance, he knew from experience, often brought out the worst fears in people, especially when he was a reminder of someone's death.

Conti had talked to her the night of the murder, and was convinced she had told him everything she knew. It was Landi he now wanted to talk with, and he could see from her face that she sensed it. But the face today was different. In their previous encounter it has shown shock, disbelief, even some anger; all the usual emotions that appear immediately after getting jolting news. Today the news had sunk in, and her eyes showed sorrow and fear. Canopo had apparently been a friend as well as a colleague, and she had passed the night with little sleep.

"Signor Landi is not here at the moment, Commissario. He is…"

Conti waited a few seconds and said, "Yes, Signorina? He is where?"

"At the workshop. He's been spending more time there since…"

She couldn't seem to finish her sentences today, so he helped. "Since Canopo's death. I would certainly expect that without a workshop manager, Signor Landi would have to spend more time over there." He spoke with as gentle a voice as he could; no use getting the girl more upset than she already was. "I'll go there. Sorry to have bothered you."

"No bother at all, Commissario." She smiled for the first time.

As Conti walked toward the door he noticed a stone carving of a reclining figure, on one of the many shelves. He picked it up and looked back at the girl, who was stuffing a tissue into her skirt pocket.

"Those are very popular with the tourists," she said before he could speak, apparently getting her tongue back. "The figure represents a deceased person at a banquet, and the pedestal on which the man reclines is the cover of his own funerary urn." He studied it from various angles "It is of course smaller than the original," she added, "but very realistic for a copy, don't you think?"

He nodded, replaced it on the shelf and walked out to the car.

"To Landi's workshop," he said to the driver. "You remember where it is."

Conti settled into the seat and tried to remember where he had seen a similar piece. In the window of one of the many other tourist shops around town, no doubt. They drove from the totally pedestrian center of the city to an outer band with a few cars, soon pulling up in front of the tall doors of the workshop.

The large room had not changed from his last visit: the same layer of dust on the floor and the same sullen stares on the faces of the workers. Also the same noise, though some of the machines were being turned off as he walked in. From the look on Landi's face it was evident that the girl had called ahead. He wore a long white coat, to protect his suit from the dust of the room, and he rubbed his hands together in an attempt to get them clean.

"Commissario. So good to see you."

Conti ignored the lie and shook Landi's offered hand.

"I just wanted to ask you some more questions, Signor Landi, if it is not inconvenient."

"My time is yours." He looked around for a place for them to sit, but stone dust covered the few vacant chairs. "Would you like to go outside where there is less—"

"Here is fine, I only have a few questions." Conti moved to a corner to get out of the earshot of the workers who now turned their eyes back to the tables. "Did Canopo act differently in the days or hours just before his death?"

"As I told you before, Commissario—"

"Signor Landi, you don't have to preface your answers with 'as I told you before,' just be indulgent to an old policeman and answer the questions to the best of your ability." He looked at his watch, an old trick he used to make people answer quickly without doing too much thinking. *The policeman is in a hurry.*

"Of course, of course, I'm sorry." Landi looked over at the men who appeared not to have heard the exchange. "Well, Canopo was a very intense worker. Not overly serious, mind you, he was always in a good mood, but he took everything seriously. He worked even harder after his daughter was born, no doubt wanting to do the best for her, and it was then that I thought he could become something more than just a skilled craftsman. Over the last few years he lived up to my expectations and was doing very well for himself." He gave Conti a worried look, as if expecting another dressing down. "I hope I haven't strayed from your question, Commissario."

"No, not at all. Go on."

"That's all, really. I didn't notice anything different in his behavior in the days before his death."

"What was his normal work schedule?"

"The workshop opens early and closes at five every day, so after the workmen left he would usually come to the store and stay until it closed at seven."

"Weekends?"

"Saturday he was at the store, this place is closed on weekends."

"Any travel, business or otherwise?"

"I do any needed business travel, Commissario. Wait, I did send him up to Florence a couple months ago to check on a client. Not much to it, it was a way to break him in, to give him experience with another part of the business. He did fine."

"I'll need the names of whoever he saw up in Florence. And you have no idea who the man could be who stopped him on the street that day?"

"As…I mean, no, Commissario, I have no clue. I didn't know that much about his personal life, other than his immediate family. Perhaps it was some relative who appeared. He was from Sicily, was he not?"

Right, thought Conti, let's blame the mafia.

"Who's in charge of the workshop now? When you're not here."

"That would be Malandro. I think you spoke with him the last time."

"I did. Will Signor Malandro be getting a raise with his new responsibility?"

Landi glanced at the foreman, who was working at a far table, and turned back to Conti. "Yes, I suppose I will give him a higher salary. If I understand what you're implying, Commissario—"

"I'm not implying anything, Signor Landi, I'm just trying to get some questions answered." Conti knew that Malandro and the other men had given the same alibi for the time of the murder: they were working here in the shop. It made sense, given their normal work schedule. But perhaps it was time to check those alibis more carefully, questioning the men again, one by one.

Back in the car, Conti pulled out his cell phone. "Sergeant, this is Commissario Conti. Is there any word on Canopo's bank statements?…I know what they told us…No, don't bother, I'll have to call the bank myself when I get back.…Yes, yes, I'm on my way."

They always want to know when I'm coming back to the station, thought Conti, and let out a small chuckle.

"Sir?" asked the driver.

"Nothing Sergeant," he said. "I was just wondering if after I retire Signora Conti will always want to know when I'm coming home."

The driver kept his eyes on the street and said nothing.

Conti put the phone in his pocket and glanced out the window at a patch of hills visible in the distance at the far end of a side street. Suddenly he remembered where he had seen that Etruscan reclining figure he had picked up from the shelf at Galleria Landi. It was in that shed with the other fake antiquities.

◇◇◇

Villa Gloria, the country residence of Donatella Minotti, was about a twenty minute drive from Volterra. Rick steered his rental car through the narrow one-way streets before squeezing through the north gate and starting around the city's wall to the west. The Roman ruins appeared on his left. How many hours had it been since Canopo's life was ended there? It seemed like a week, but in fact the time could be measured in hours. Would Commissario Conti come up with the murderer, assuming he was correct that the death wasn't suicide? He seemed like an intelligent policeman, but as his uncle Piero had told him many times, luck plays a part in any criminal investigation. Would Conti get lucky? He slowed down as the car in front of him turned into the parking lot below the wall. Perhaps it was Herb and Shirley, returning for a bit more excitement before jetting back to Iowa.

He had almost made a complete loop, but just before coming to the Porta San Francesco, near his hotel, Rick took a sharp right turn and drove down the hill to the north. The road clung to a contorted finger of high ground that dropped off steeply on either side, slowly descending from the city's high promontory. It was easy to see why the Etruscans chose this spot to build the city. There were just a few ways to reach the hill, all of them difficult, and with its thick walls the town became virtually impregnable. The road cut sharply left and right as it worked its way down, passing a few buildings perched on small patches of flat land overlooking the deep gorges. Short, scrubby trees and sharp rocks were the dominant features of the area, giving it a wild and timeless look, but the harshness of the surroundings softened as the car descended to flatter land. He was coming into the valley of the Era River whose waters started near Volterra and flowed north before merging with the Arno and passing through Pisa to the sea.

The clouds that hung earlier over Volterra had thinned to only a few white wisps, and the temperature was warming as the afternoon progressed, creating a perfect fall day. This was a section of Tuscany that saw relatively little tourism. The map on the seat next to Rick showed mostly open land with few towns. Here the local economy was almost exclusively tied to agriculture, though at this time of year the earth was starting its long, rejuvenating sleep. The only movement he noticed in the brown fields was a lone pheasant hunter carrying a shotgun, following his dog through the dried stalks of corn, their ears long since harvested.

The road he took after leaving the city was the main route to Pisa, but now Rick slowed the car to make a left turn and head west. The directions Donatella had given him were clear, there was no need for the map nor the trusty GPS which was still in the pocket of his overcoat in the back seat. A few minutes later he turned onto a dirt road, passing a sign which announced that he was entering private property. No mention of welcome. Ahead he could see the outline of a high stone wall which came in off the hill at the left and disappeared in the distance on the right. When he got closer he could see that the wall's even line was broken by a heavy steel gate topped on one side by a small camera trained on the road. Another sign appeared whose very large letters warned of even larger dogs on the property, with an appropriately vicious canine portrait, no doubt for the benefit of the illiterate. Good security.

Rick stopped at a small metal box on a pole, opened his window and pressed a red button. A voice crackled something from the box, and the gate slowly opened to allow the car to enter. It was another minute before the villa appeared through the trees. There was no sign of any dogs, big or small; perhaps the signs lied.

Outside the wall, several hundred meters down the dirt road from the gate, the driver of a dark blue car stopped and turned off his engine.

The lightly rust-colored stucco of the villa walls reminded Rick of buildings in the Southwest, but the similarity ended with its color. If most Americans tried to picture the typical Tuscan villa, it would be something close to Villa Gloria. Its two-storey main structure was topped by a slightly-pitched-terra cotta roof shading the narrow balcony above the entrance door. The villa's rectangular upper windows had green wooden shutters; not the fake ones found in colonial-style houses in America, but shutters which actually swung open and shut on iron hinges. Framing the wide front door was a stone arch which looked like it had been recycled from an even older structure. Atop the main building was a small windowed cube like on a caboose, built to provide a panoramic view of the countryside. Had someone been up there watching his approach? No need, with the security camera. A wing that's architecture mirrored the main building was built out to the right, forming a protective wall to the front patio along with some well-trimmed hedges. Rick parked the car in a gravel area at the end of the driveway and started up a stone path which led to the patio. All the parts of the villa came together perfectly, making the building warm and inviting. The same could not be said of the person who answered the door.

Rick was not used to looking up at people, especially with his boots on, but this man had him beat by several inches. Not just tall, but large. His black clothing added to the bulk, nearly filling the narrow doorway and making Rick glad that his arrival was expected. The servant's head, topped by hair the color of shoe polish, sat on a thick neck which, thankfully, did not have bolts protruding from its sides.

"Signor Montoya." The words were said as a statement of fact, as if the man was confirming Rick's presence to himself rather than welcoming a guest to the villa. The voice was like the sound Rick's car tires had made on the gravel driveway. "This way, please."

After a small atrium they entered the living room, its walls a deep red and covered with paintings, each one lit by a small lamp, as in a museum. Rick's first thought was that they were for sale; the woman is an art dealer, after all. If not, it would seem a bit pretentious. The only other time he'd seen the little lights was on some of the paintings in the American ambassador's residence in Rome, and even that seemed a bit too much. He checked out the low ceiling which was supported by wooden beams, probably the originals, but you never know. Italian building restoration was an art, but on the other hand, even the newest of building could be made to look ancient. He was about to give closer attention to the paintings, almost all of them brightly colored outdoor scenes, when the man spoke.

"Signora Minotti will see you in a moment. May I get you something to drink?"

When Rick declined the man disappeared without a word, making the room feel larger. He stood in the center and studied the furnishings, which were not different from those in many apartments he'd seen in Rome, except for the number of paintings. A large Persian carpet in the center of the tile floor held a low rustic table spread with art magazines in English and Italian. Facing the table, a leather sofa flanked one side, three modern chairs made of chrome and leather the other. Rick tried unsuccessfully to remember the chairs' designer, someone Scandinavian, then walked to the wall to examine one of the larger paintings. The scene showed a man and a woman in peasant clothing walking along a river bank holding hands. It was not the figures which dominated the painting, but rather the strong colors of the trees framing them. Rick leaned forward to study the thick brushwork of the leaves.

"I am a great lover of the Italian impressionists. Unfortunately they do not get the credit they deserve. Even the more educated collectors blindly prefer their French counterparts."

"Signora Minotti, I didn't hear you come in."

"Please call me Donatella."

If this visit had been purely business, without his Erica connection, would Donatella have dispensed so quickly with the formalities? The soft smile went with her voice and body, but that was where the softness stopped. There was something in her manner, despite the feminine exterior, that said "tough." Make that a very feminine exterior. She lowered herself to the sofa and gestured for him to take a seat on one of the chairs. Strange, she had said two sentences and he'd come to the conclusion that she was not the kind of woman he'd want to negotiate a real business deal with. Fortunately his role as an art buyer was just that, a role.

Erica was correct, Donatella was certainly attractive. And as would be expected of a passport photo, the image he'd seen at the ministry briefing did not do her justice. She slipped off the pair of black loafers, leaned her knees to one side, and tucked her bare feet under the designer jeans. It struck him as an almost girlish gesture, perhaps done on purpose, like she'd been told by someone to soften her manner. Brushing the dark hair from her eyes, she pushed up the sleeves of her wool sweater as if to indicate that the business part of the encounter should begin. But even the most serious of meetings had to start with the necessary social exchanges. This was Italy, after all.

"Dario said you didn't want any refreshment. Can I change your mind?"

Somehow the man's name fit. "Thank you, no."

"And how is the lovely Erica? Doing well, I trust." Too much emphasis on the word lovely.

"She is, thank you, and she sends her warmest regards." The comment did not, he noted, change the smile on Donatella's face. Had there been a rivalry? "She is hoping to change her schedule to come up and join me." The smile tightened. The rivalry was still there.

"That would be wonderful, I would love to see her. So, tell me about this business of yours." So much for a discussion of Erica, Rick thought, and just when it was starting to be fun.

He explained his buying venture while Donatella settled deeper into the cushions. She interrupted him a few times to ask questions, but mostly let him talk. By the end of his explanation she was nodding and smiling more than when he began. This time genuine smiles.

"There may be something I can help you with, Riccardo. I deal mainly in traditional Etruscan motifs, though not the smaller pieces you might see in the tourist shops like bronze geese and lizards. My clients are interested in one-of-a-kind larger pieces. Ones that look like they have been taken from a tomb."

If the comment was made to get a reaction from him, it worked.

"Donatella, that may be just what would interest the gallery. Is it possible to see the kind of art work you have in mind?"

"Of course." She stood up, slipped on her shoes, pulled down her sweater, and walked toward Rick, who was already on his feet. "Let me take you back to one of my storage rooms." Though there was enough room between the chairs, she brushed him with her hip as she passed. "I'll lead the way." He knew he was expected to notice her tight jeans, and, being a good guest, he obliged.

Rick followed her down a long hallway and they came to a heavy metal door. It was clear that Donatella had planned for Rick to see this room; waiting for them was the butler, major-domo, or whatever title the huge man carried. Dario removed two large keys from his dark coat and inserted them into separate locks before pushing open the door and reaching inside to flip a light switch. He stood aside to let Rick and Donatella enter.

"This room contains pieces which could be described as the business inventory rather than my personal collection." She stepped into the room, adding, "But that doesn't mean I value them less. Everything I own has been chosen with care and love, and is relinquished with no small amount of regret." It was a good line, and Rick wondered how many times she'd used it.

The windowless storage room had an eclectic mixture of art that gleamed under the light of various neon lamps in the ceiling. Against the left wall, paintings hung on rolling wood panels that could be pulled out like large vertical files. The other walls supported shelves of various sizes holding works in stone, metal, and wood. In the center stood a rectangular table covered with a thick felt, so that items could be pulled from their storage spots and examined more closely. After looking around the room Rick glanced down at the spongy carpet which covered the floor. It and the hum of the room's invisible dehumidifier served to soften the sound of Donatella's voice when she spoke.

"The carpet has saved more than one piece of fine art when dropped by a clumsy client. I trust that you will be more careful than they were." Before he could answer she walked to the right corner of the room. "The Etruscan pieces are over here."

Two shelves held stone sculptures in various sizes, some quite large, all with that mixture of Greek and Etruscan styles that only a specialist could sort out. Three bowls were decorated with figures carrying shields and swords, a stone panel depicted a hunter spearing a boar, and a small square of painted ceramic tile showed two women dancing. Rick scanned the shelves quickly.

Without thinking, he said, "I don't see any burial urns."

"No, I don't have any at the moment. Giachi didn't do that many, and they have been snatched up by other collectors."

"Giachi?"

She gave Rick a puzzled look. "Francesco Giachi, of course. The most famous of the 18th century forgers of Etruscan work. Most of the pieces here are authenticated to be from his workshop. Isn't it ironic that forgeries have become so collectible? I wish I had more of them."

Was this a test? Probably not, since she'd kept her eyes on the shelves as she talked. Unlike Dario, who had his eyes glued on Rick. If I make any sudden move, I'm a dead man, he thought. She began to go from one piece to the next, lovingly pointing out some unique feature or how it related to Etruscan daily life. Rick was fascinated. Thank goodness he had read just enough of Beppo's book to appreciate what she was saying and could ask a question or two that made him appear to know what he was talking about. For each of the pieces she noted if it were a copy, or in a few cases if it were original. Apparently there were enough authentic pieces that could be sold with the proper authorization from the government, though exportation required almost insurmountable red tape. Rick nodded noncommittally. She was avoiding prices which would arrive in a later discussion, should they get to that point.

With a coquettish twirl she turned from the shelf and looked at Rick. "They are beautiful, are they not?"

"Yes, so much history in each one. I'm not sure they are the kind of pieces my gallery would be interested in. But if they are, is there…"

"Of course." She raised a finger and looked past him toward the door. Dario had been so silent during her description of the pieces that Rick had almost forgotten the man was there. Now the majordomo stepped forward and passed a folder to Donatella. Without a thank you she passed it to Rick. "There is a sheet on each work in the Etruscan collection in this file. Please take it with you. There is also a price list, though I should note that the prices can change. Shipping and customs paperwork are not included, of course. Nor is the *IVA*."

"Of course." The Value Added Tax percentage on this stuff would be more that what he paid for groceries back in Rome, probably right up there with jewelry and Lamborghinis. He flipped open the file and saw that each sheet had a color photo of the piece with a short explanation. The prices were in Euros. "This will be very helpful. I can fax it back to Santa Fe."

She glanced at Dario who pulled open the heavy door as if it were made of plywood. There was no need for words between these two, they seemed to read each other's minds. As Rick and Donatella walked back down the hallway to the living room he could hear the door locking behind them.

"Now will you accept the offer of a coffee, Riccardo?" From the voice, it appeared to him that Donatella the businesswoman had left the premises. Who would take her place?

Coffee sounded like a good idea, a late-afternoon jolt of caffeine was just what he needed. "*Grazie*, I would love one." Dario had silently come in from the hallway, and once again she gave him a wordless glance, causing his black bulk to disappear through a door. She watched Rick follow the man with his eyes.

"Dario worked for my family for several years when I was young, and was treated very well by my father. When Papa died Dario left Tuscany and worked in the south. A few years ago he reappeared in need of a job and I hired him. He is very loyal."

"Somehow I gathered that."

For the first time she laughed. "Please sit. That chair is not very comfortable; come sit here." She patted the sofa next to her and then kicked off her shoes as she had done earlier, this time crossing her legs and facing him. Rick put the folder on the table and squeezed himself into the opposite side of the sofa.

"So, Riccardo, you have already made the news here in Volterra, and after just a day in the city." She placed her hands on her knees, yoga style.

"I suppose everyone reads the local paper."

"Or watches the news on TV."

"They mentioned me on a newscast?"

"Well, not by name, but the reporter spoke of a visiting American who is here to buy art. It was you, was it not?"

"Guilty as charged." He made a face of mock pain. "Perhaps that's not the phrase to use in this situation."

He was interrupted by the arrival of Dario with a round tray carrying two small porcelain cups and saucers as well as a bowl of sugar and two glasses of mineral water. He placed it on the table in front of the sofa and shuffled out. Donatella added sugar to Rick's cup, at his request, but left her own espresso black.

"The newspaper said that the police are still investigating, and likely will be at it for a while." She settled back into the chair and took a sip. "Don't you think it will be a while?"

Rick didn't want to talk about the case. He didn't know very much of what Conti had found out, though after spending so much time with the inspector, he certainly knew more than Donatella. Given the real reason for his presence in Volterra, the contacts with Conti were something he did not want to broadcast.

"I really wouldn't know."

She had her saucer in the palm of one hand and held the cup by two fingers of the other, gazing over them into Rick's eyes. "We don't get many murders in Volterra, Riccardo. Everyone will be talking about it for weeks."

"Murder? I assumed it was suicide." He couldn't remember if the newspaper story had speculated as to the cause of the fall.

Donatella reached out and put her empty cup on the tray. "This is a small town, we need something other than local politics to talk about. Suicide would not be half as interesting as a murder, now would it? The man was not old, and had a family. Why would he take his own life? The obvious conclusion: murder." Her smile struck Rick as hardly something that should go along with talk of a death.

"I'll stay out of the speculation game."

"Not a game, Riccardo. Especially if you are the murderer." She noticed his reaction and added, "I meant if *one* is the murderer. You don't look like the kind of person who would have done this man in." For her it *was* a game, and she was enjoying playing it with him.

"Or done in anyone else, I hope you meant to say."

She kept the playful expression on her face. "Of course. And more than one person would have been needed to push him over the wall. You probably didn't have time to recruit any accomplices in town, or did you bring some Roman thugs along with you?"

"Just me on this trip." He was starting to feel very uncomfortable. Was it the line of conversation or the woman herself? Erica should have warned him, perhaps if she had gone into more detail about her friend, Rick would have treated this meeting differently. Like meet her at a neutral place in town. Did Erica avoid the details on purpose, perhaps as a test for him? Could Donatella be in on it? Hold on, Montoya, it's true that this is Italy and not Albuquerque, but let's stick with reality here.

"*Ancora un caffè?*"

"No, thank you, Donatella, one was just right. And I really should be getting back, I have some messages to send back to the gallery to let them know what I've been up to. I don't want them to think I'm just drinking wine and eating pasta at their expense."

They rose, and as if on a signal Dario appeared at the doorway. As Rick picked up the folder, he remembered the real reason for the visit.

"Donatella, what you showed me here was very impressive, I hope something will be of interest to our clients in America. May I also mention that some Americans have very specific and—how shall I say?—exceptional tastes. They are always looking for something unique that can be enjoyed purely for its—"

"For its beauty," she interrupted. Unlike Landi, the woman appeared to get the message immediately. "Something to have in a special place and enjoy in privacy." She gestured toward the walls of the room with her hand. "Yes, Riccardo, I think I understand. Let me think about it and call you." She took his arm as she walked him toward the door where Dario was already opening it for them. Rick nodded to him, eliciting an almost imperceptible nod in return, and he and Donatella walked out to the terrace. The sun was starting to drop over the hill west of the villa, taking much of the afternoon's warmth with it. At the edge of the brick he turned to his hostess and extended his hand. She took it and held up her face to let him kiss her on both cheeks. They had only just met, but after all, she was a friend of Erica.

◇◇◇

Rick turned on his lights as he passed through the gate of the villa compound, accelerating without noticing the blue car parked just off the dirt road. Rick was soon back on pavement, wondering if his cell phone would work in this corner of Tuscany to call Erica. It did.

"*Ciao, Ricky.*"

"*Ciao, bella.* I hope I am not interrupting class or something else important."

"What would be more important than talking with you, *caro*? Tell me what you've been doing. Here it is the usual dull

routine. You are having the fun and all I have to look forward
to is a room full of bored students."

Might as well get it over with.

"I saw your friend Donatella."

"Aha. And how is *la bella Donatella*? She did not make any
advances on you, I hope."

"Not that I was aware of." He crossed two fingers on the hand
doing the steering. "She has an impressive collection."

"Are you referring to her art?"

Rick laughed, hoping it didn't seem too forced. "I'm beginning to wonder why you suggested I call her. I thought you two
were friends."

"She is a friend. Not close, but a friend. She does have a
certain reputation, and from my experience at the university,
it is not unwarranted." She paused. "But Ricky, if you saw her
collection, to use your words, you must have visited her villa."

It was time to come clean about Donatella, but how to do
it without getting into too much detail? He had felt guilty
keeping it from her—though likely not guilty enough for her
liking—yet if he told her too much now, it would not go well
with Beppo. While all this was fun, if his translation business
didn't pan out, working undercover was probably not the career
he would pursue.

"Erica, Beppo thought that it might be a good idea to
make contact with Donatella. Professionally, I mean. Perhaps
he thought it would add credibility with the other people I'm
seeing." Stretching the truth?

"Ricky, you don't think your friend Beppo—"

"Erica," he interrupted, "here's the thing. If I'm making contact with dealers, it would seem strange if I didn't call on her,
don't you think? I doubt very much if Beppo thinks she could be
mixed up in this." OK, now he *was* stretching the truth, better
to change the subject. "Something else has come up, which has
nothing to do with my little mission." He told her about the
death of Canopo and his involvement in the case.

"This isn't another attempt by your uncle to get you involved in police work, is it Ricky?" It was an issue that had come up before in Rome. It could have been his mother talking.

"Of course not," he said. "It was pure coincidence that I happened to be with the man just before his death. The police are satisfied I had nothing more to do with him. The commissario I am dealing with for my, uh, work here, is the same one investigating the death of the man." Rick slowed down, he was talking too fast. He also took his foot off the gas pedal and wondered if using a cell phone while driving was illegal in Italy. If so, the police could make a fortune giving out tickets.

"So you and this policeman are old friends by now."

"I wouldn't go that far. He's not happy about my presence in Volterra, and my connection with the murder is not helping things. Fortunately he found out about Uncle Piero, and that seems to have softened him a bit."

"The uncle helping the nephew. That has a long tradition here in Italy."

"True. But Uncle Piero isn't the pope."

"Also true. Ricky, class is about to start, I'll talk with you tomorrow. Be safe, *caro; ciao, ciao.*" The phone clicked and he wondered if there might have been an edge in her voice. Was it his involvement in a murder investigation or the meeting with Donatella?

◇◇◇

He was still thinking about the conversation with Erica when he drove through the city gate and turned into the hotel parking garage. The dashboard clock showed that it was late afternoon, which in Italy meant that much of the day still lay ahead. Many offices worked until six or seven, shops were still open, and most Italians wouldn't even start boiling their pasta water until eight. Best to plug in the lap top and get some translation work finished before dinner. After pulling his coat and Donatella's folder from the back seat, he locked the car door and walked out of the garage to the street, dodging a blue sedan that had just come through the gate. It was getting colder, but he didn't bother putting on the coat since he was steps from the hotel. He felt the warm air welcome him when he pushed open the glass door to the lobby. The woman behind the desk was talking loudly on the phone, as if it were long distance.

"…yes, you should be able to reach him at that cell number, he—" she looked up and saw Rick, waving her hand at him with the clawing motion that Italians use.

"Just a moment, please, he just walked in," she said into the receiver before looking back at Rick. "A call for you, Signor Montoya, you can take it on the house phone." She pointed to a telephone in a small niche on the side wall.

Laying the coat and folder over a chair, Rick walked to the phone.

"This is Riccardo Montoya."

"Ah, yes, Signor Montoya, I was fortunate that you appeared as I was calling. My name is Santo."

The voice was low and smooth, and had a guttural quality that would indicate a person raised somewhere north of the Po River, though Rick was not yet good enough with accents to be more precise than that.

"How can I be of service, Signor Santo?"

"I hope that it is I who can be of service. It is my understanding that you may be in the market for some works of art."

Rick held the phone away from his mouth while he took in a quick breath. *This is it, Beppo's scheme has worked. But who is this guy, and is he for real?*

"Possibly, Signor Santo, but tell me, how did you learn of my presence in Volterra?"

"Besides from the newspapers?" The voice switched to a laugh, which stopped abruptly. "You'll forgive me for making light of a tragedy. Your question is a valid one, but what is more important is that we have made contact."

Rick decided not to push it. Certainly the source of the referral would come out eventually, so at this point the man was just trying to be cautious. Rick couldn't help trying another line of questioning. "Do you do a lot of business with that person?"

"I would rather discuss doing business with you, Signor Montoya, but it would be better if we spoke in person. Would that be possible?"

The guy was good, Rick thought. "Of course," he answered, glancing up at the clock above the hotel reception desk, "when would be convenient for you?"

"I could see you in about forty-five minutes."

"Where are you?"

The man hesitated before answering, and Rick wondered if he was trying to get too much information from the man. But asking him where he was didn't seem that unreasonable.

"I'm not in Volterra, and it will take me some time to get there."

That could mean either that he did not live or work in town, or was outside town at the moment. Rick opted not to ask for a clarification. "I can meet you in the bar of the hotel in an hour, we can talk there."

"If you don't mind, I would prefer somewhere else. Do you know the cathedral?"

"I know where it is, but I haven't seen it yet."

"Ah, it is a jewel of a church, very much underrated. And a perfect place for us to talk without being bothered by anyone. Only old women and tourists are found in our churches at this time of day, even the cathedral, and none of them will be interested in our conversation. I will see you there in one hour."
He hung up.

Rick looked at the phone while he gathered his thoughts, his first one being a question if Santo was really the person Beppo was trying to catch. "Works of art" the man had said. It would be just Rick's luck that there was a misunderstanding, and the man was only an art dealer, like Donatella. Santo could have read about him in the paper and tracked him down at the hotel, a logical place for an American art dealer to stay in Volterra. But then why the cloak and dagger meeting in the church instead of a place like the hotel where business would normally be done? No, this looked like the real thing; the question would be whether he had the real thing to sell. Rick picked up his coat and papers and started toward the elevator, catching the eye of the receptionist. For the first time she gave him what appeared to be a genuine smile before going quickly back to her computer screen. Must be his celebrity status.

◇◇◇

Rick pulled the coat's cloth belt tightly around his middle and tied it in a loose knot. He was glad he'd packed the coat. The weather in Rome hadn't been that cold lately, but here either a front had moved in or it simply got colder in this part of the country. Volterra was way up on this hill, after all. He pulled his small GPS from the coat pocket, switched it on, and read 1694 feet above sea level. He really should have set it to meters now that he was in Italy, but the reading confirmed why there was the chill. Volterra *was* much higher than Rome, which was barely above sea level, and Tuscany was also much farther north. He repocketed the GPS and started up the street toward the cathedral, focusing on the mysterious Signor Santo, and who could have sent the man. It had to be Landi. Who else had he contacted? Well, Donatella, of course, he could be working for her or with her. The only other persons he had seen were Conti, not a suspect, and Zerbino, the same. Polpetto, the exporter, would have been a contender, but Rick hadn't met the guy yet. Unless his secretary with the red glasses could have taken his mention of Etruscan art and run with it. That could explain the difference between their brief encounter in the office and the equally brief meeting on the street. But that would be unlikely, since the boss would want to meet Rick before making any decision to pass his name to someone else.

He took the right fork in the street, passing a small chapel wedged into the triangular corner. Inside he could see a few votive candles flickering weakly in the dim space. The chapel was dedicated to Saint Christopher, the patron saint of travelers, a category Rick fit right into at the moment. It wouldn't hurt to have some extra help on this trip; he should stop in on the way back and say a prayer. That and this visit to the cathedral could also get him some points with his mother, if he wrote about them in the right terms. As he continued up the hill his mind went back to Santo, and something he had been considering since the man had called. Should he call Beppo or Conti before the rendezvous with the man? He had gone back and forth with himself and decided in the end to wait until afterward.

Okay, it was a macho thing: report when there is something to report, don't look like you are afraid of some guy in a church pew. What's he going to do, pull a knife on you in front of the old ladies and tourists? Rick was sure the man wouldn't dare try that on a guy wearing cowboy boots.

He entered a small square in front of the cathedral. On one side was the baptistery, an octagonal structure which had likely taken its design from the Dome of the Rock in Jerusalem, seen by crusaders and recreated in religious buildings around Italy after their return. Rick silently thanked his father, whose interest in architecture had packed such obscure facts into his head, and then faced the cathedral itself. Unlike the baptistery, which stood apart, it was flanked on both sides by other buildings. In case there was any doubt, the large rose window and arched façade made clear its religious vocation. Rick pushed through one of the side doors and found himself in the rear of the church. To his left was a room which looked like a museum, but looking ahead his eye was drawn to the large cross above the altar. Because it was already getting dark outside, he needed little time to adjust to the shadowy ambience. Out of habit he crossed himself, then stood for a few moments in the back looking for Santo. Or someone who could be Santo, since the man had neglected to describe himself.

At least Santo had been correct about those found worshipping in the cathedral at this hour. Three tourists, who looked Scandinavian, were clustered around an ornately carved pulpit halfway up the left side, one reading in a low voice from a guidebook while the others peered at the ivory stone. In the very front row two women sat in silence, their heads bent in prayer. From their black clothing and gray hair, they could have been sisters, but they sat on opposite sides of the row. Rick walked down the right aisle, chose a pew far from both the tourists and the women, and sat down. On, of course, another hard wooden bench. He stretched his legs and noticed some movement at the front of the church, to the left of the altar. It was a short, bearded priest, clad in dark robes. The priest walked to the front of the altar and surveyed the visitors for a moment, his eyes resting on Rick, who clearly did not fit the profile of church goers for this time of day during the week. Rick momentarily entertained the thought that Santo was a priest, which certainly would have been ironic, for the name if nothing else. But the robed figure stepped down and walked briskly to the far side of the church where he took out a key and opened the donation box. Rick heard the clink of a few coins as they were put into a small sack the priest had pulled from his robe.

"May I?" A man slipped into the pew next to Rick, looked up at the altar, and slowly crossed himself. "I hope I have not kept you waiting."

Rick was sitting almost too close to size up the man, and he slid a few inches to one side to put some space between them. Santo was unbuttoning a lined raincoat to reveal a wool turtle-neck sweater, causing Rick to remember poor Canopo, who hated the cold. He glanced down at Santo's wool slacks and dark boots, noticing a few specks of mud on the toes. An art dealer who lived on a farm? Unlikely.

"No, not at all, I just arrived and sat down." Rick now studied the man. There was no facial hair, a few wrinkles on pale skin, and a slightly receding hairline. Probably not a farmer, or he would have had some kind of sun exposure, even at this time of year. Rick guessed an age of around forty, but in good shape.

"The most famous piece of art here is probably the pulpit." Santo nodded toward the group of tourists. Then he turned back toward the altar. "But my favorite is the wood carving there to the right of the high altar. Thirteenth century, unknown artist, a powerful yet crude deposition." Was this an art history class? The dealer seemed to sense Rick's thoughts. "But we are here to discuss Etruscan art, are we not? Let me get right to the heart of it, Signor Montoya. I am not yet convinced that you are a serious buyer." Santo kept his eyes on the wood carving.

The comment surprised Rick, but he couldn't hold back a slight smile. "Is there something I've said or done that would justify a lack of confidence?" Perhaps the answer would reveal Santo's contact.

Santo chuckled. "I suppose not. We have done a check on the gallery you represent, and it exists. The web site shows the styles of art sold there, which is impressive, though not anything that would appeal to me." Rick almost told him that Texans visiting Santa Fe have unique tastes in art, but he kept silent. "I think I just wanted to meet face to face before deciding whether you would be the kind of buyer who…" he searched for the words and found them, "who we normally deal with."

"If I may be frank, Signor Santo, you can be assured that I have the same concerns about the possibility of doing business with you."

"Very true, very true." He nodded his head slowly and stared ahead at the cross before turning to Rick. They might as well have been talking on the phone with the lack of eye contact. "But you should know that I have not been even distantly involved in any suicides or murders." His mouth turned up in an unbecoming grin.

If this little joke was intended to lighten the atmosphere, it didn't work. Rick was annoyed by Santo's *piccolo scherzo*, but let it pass in the interest of moving the process along. "So what's next, Signor Santo?" He put a sharpness into his voice. "I will have to see the works you have for sale, so when will that be? I can't stay in Volterra indefinitely."

Santo shifted his frame on the wooden pew. "Of course, I understand. We will not keep you waiting. I have your phone number and will be in contact."

With that Santo reached over and shook Rick's hand before getting quickly to his feet. He glanced toward the entrance to the church and then walked in the opposite direction, toward the altar. He hesitated for a few seconds in front of his favorite wood carving before crossing to the far left side of the nave and disappearing around a corner. His exit took no more than a minute.

Rick remained in the pew and gathered his thoughts while recorded classical music seeped into the church through hidden speakers. If throwing those last words at Santo hadn't jinxed the transaction, it was mission accomplished. Or at least a good start on accomplishing it. Unfortunately he still didn't know who had put Santo in contact with him, but that would have to come out eventually, the police would see to it. And speaking of the authorities, he'd better let them know right away what just happened. Now, at least, he had something to tell them, and he hadn't been attacked while getting it. But before that, he decided he had to check out the man's favorite work of art in the cathedral. Rick rose from the pew and, like Santo, walked to the front.

The deposition was in the uncomplicated style of the pre-Renaissance, its thin figures carved in a loving but unsophisticated hand, but with colors surprisingly vibrant for art almost eight hundred years old. After reflecting on the work Rick surveyed the corner where Santo had gone and headed for it. As he crossed in front of the altar he checked the two women, still there and still deep in prayer. The tourists had left, but a lone man in the back of the church was getting to his feet while gazing at the cross behind the altar. Rick came to the small side chapel, and next to it a narrow corridor which led to a door. Of course, he thought, when the church was built in the 1200s, the fire marshal would have insisted on another exit. He pushed open the door and found himself in Volterra's vast main square directly across from the police station. How convenient. As he walked across the piazza he dialed Beppo.

◇◇◇

Conti looked up when Rick tapped on his open door. The commissario was in shirt sleeves, the first time Rick had seen him without a suit jacket, studying overlapping papers covering the top of the desk. The points of his collar were showing wear, the downside of being carefully ironed over the years. It seemed to Rick that Conti, or his wife, wanted the man to be presentable, but without the sartorial pretention of the newer generation of policemen. The knot of his tie, slightly larger than was fashionable at the moment in Italy, confirmed the impression. He motioned Rick to the usual seat. After Rick recounted his meeting with Santo, Conti was kind enough not to ask him immediately why he had gone to the cathedral without alerting him beforehand. Instead, Rick brought it up.

"I wasn't sure the man would even show. And simply meeting him didn't seem to be an issue. It was just like my meetings with Landi and the others, but maybe fruitful as well. We'll have to see."

"You have the phone number?" Conti did not seem upset.

"No, Commissario, he called me at the hotel."

Conti made a terse phone call to one of his sergeants while Rick waited. "He will call the hotel to get the number, and then check it. Now, you said you called the ministry. Their reaction?"

"Beppo was pleased, understandably since this whole scheme was his idea. He'll be ready to come to Volterra as soon as there is something more concrete, which would be when I actually see something for sale."

Conti leaned back in his chair, causing a high-pitched squeak. He didn't notice the sound, which had become a part of his office like the furniture and the smell of disinfectant. "It would be wise for your friend not to pack his bags yet, Signor Montoya. There are at least three possibilities here." He held up a thumb, Italian style, beginning the count. "The first, and the one we all wish for, of course, is that you have indeed drawn out the very person the ministry has been hoping to catch."

From Conti's tone, Rick doubted if the man truly wished that outcome. The policeman's skepticism was still evident in his voice and face.

The index finger was added to the thumb of his still upraised hand. "But another is that Santo is simply a legitimate dealer with a penchant for secrecy." Finally the middle finger joined the others, and Conti turned his wrist slowly in the air. "The third is that Santo, if that is really his name, is trying to sell you fakes."

"I will only know that once he has shown me the merchandise."

"Will you?" Conti's eyes searched Rick's face.

"You're correct, of course, Beppo will have to make the final call on authenticity."

"Or we can save him the trip and have it checked by Dr. Zerbino." He waved his hand. "But we are getting well ahead of things, are we not? We must first see if this man reappears, laden with ancient artifacts for our foreign buyer."

Only Rick's respect for his uncle's profession kept him from reacting to Conti's sarcasm. Instead he asked, "Commissario, what do you think will happen?"

"I don't know, Signor Montoya, but if you get another call, I hope you will let me know immediately."

At that moment a policeman entered after making a soft tap on the door.

"Yes, Sergeant."

"The call was made from a public telephone in San Gimignano."

Conti turned to Rick. "Well, Signor Montoya, it appears that your friend Santo may be from the lovely city of towers. And he either can't afford a cell phone or is more secretive than we might have thought."

◇◇◇

LoGuercio stood rigidly in front of Conti's desk, his suit jacket respectfully buttoned. He started to fold his arms over his chest, but immediately realized that it was a gesture which could be taken as confrontational. Instead he let his arms hang, clasping his hands in front.

"Sir, DeMarzo was in a bind when he saw Montoya talking with the other man. He couldn't tail both of them. His instructions had been to stay with the American for his safety, so that's what he did." He paused. "I told him he did the right thing."

Conti exhaled a deep sigh and nodded. "Yes, I suppose he did. If Montoya had told me about the call I could have had someone else there, so we will blame the American. Did DeMarzo get a good look at the man?" LoGuercio relayed the description, which was the same as what Montoya had given Conti.

"Well, Detective, it appears that there may be another contact soon by this Santo, so you should have another man on call ready to back up you and DeMarzo. That is, if Montoya remembers to let us know this time."

◇◇◇

The small table in Rick's room was there for female guests to put on their makeup, but his small lap-top fit perfectly. And the chair, while not heavily cushioned, was comfortable enough. With a bit of evening translation work in mind, he had taken a relatively light meal in the hotel dining room, even passing on wine. Rather than a pasta, he ordered the *acquacotta*, which, as its name—cooked water—indicated, was a light soup with some vegetables added. For *secondo* it had been half a grilled chicken, its crisp skin carrying just the right amount of pepper. After such a repast he deserved something for dessert, a course he usually skipped, but still he stayed with the light fare and ordered *macedonia di frutta*. Nothing cleared the palate, even a lightly seasoned one, like a fruit salad, its competing textures and flavors pulled together by dash of sweet liqueur.

He just finished checking his email when the room phone rang. He hoped Erica would call, but wondered why she wasn't using his *telefonino*. His was charged and lay next to his computer. He picked up the phone and heard a feminine voice, though not the one he expected.

"Ricky, this is Donatella."

"Donatella, how nice of you to call." He said it without thinking.

"And it's good to hear your voice too. I just finished a meeting in town, and thought I'd see if you were free for a drink before I drive back to the villa."

"I, uh, was just—"

"Only to talk business, of course. Erica won't mind, not that she even needs to know."

The woman is a mind reader, Rick thought. "It would be a pleasure. Where shall I meet you?"

"I'm here in the lobby. Don't keep me waiting too long."

He kept her waiting less than five minutes. When he got off the elevator she was sitting in one of the lobby chairs leafing through a magazine. Her coat was open, revealing a long knit dress, its hem covering the tops of calf-length leather boots. Her hair was done up more formally than when he'd seen her at Villa Gloria, and her face showed shadows of color brushed around the cheekbones. The meeting had likely been dinner. When she saw him she put down the magazine, rose to her feet, and brushed back her hair even though it was perfectly in place. They exchanged air kisses.

"So nice of you to stop by, Donatella. Why don't we go into the bar? I trust you have already had dinner."

"I did, but a nightcap is just what I need."

They walked from the brightness of the lobby into a bar whose light was indirect and cozy. A few stools stood empty in front of a bar where a bored bartender looked up from his newspaper. He quickly stubbed out a cigarette while watching the couple walk to one of three empty booths that took up a side wall. Donatella slipped off her coat and tossed it onto the seat. Rick could not decide if her dress was wool, silk, or a blend of the two, not that the fabric content mattered. It clung to her body like a second skin, its long lines broken only by a wide belt that settled at a slight angle over her hips. Before sliding onto the leather she smoothed the dress as if she was used to wearing much shorter attire. When she was seated Rick sat down opposite her. The waiter approached the table, put small paper napkins in front of each of them, and asked what they would like.

"Cognac." Donatella's eyes studied Rick's face.

Rick looked up from her gaze, nodded for the same, and gave the man his room number for the bill. "Do you come into the city often?" he asked, when the barman departed.

"I have friends in Volterra and my work brings me here frequently. I also drive to Florence several times a month and occasionally to Milan." Once again she brushed her hair, sending the light scent of her perfume in his direction. "But I enjoy living alone. Well, alone except for Dario, and Anna, who cooks and cleans."

He was not surprised that Donatella didn't cook or clean house herself. The barman returned and placed two snifters on the table, their brown liquid sloshing slowly. Between them he set a small dish of round truffled canapés, their creamy cheese the color of fine alabaster. After clinking glasses carefully and swirling the cognac, they took small sips.

The liquid burned softly in Rick's throat. "Did you really want to talk business, Donatella?"

She laughed. "If we are to do business we should first get to know each other better, don't you think?" She didn't wait for an answer. "Tell me how you are enjoying our wonderful city. You are enjoying it, Ricky, despite your involvement in that tragic incident?"

He was surprised by the "Ricky." Unless his memory was failing, it had been "Riccardo" at the villa. With Italians he was always called Riccardo—even his mother used it—and with his American friends and Beppo he was Rick. Only Erica used the name Ricky. Could they have talked? It would make sense if Erica had called her friend, especially after she knew Rick had gone to Villa Gloria, but exactly what would they have talked about? He tried to put it out of his mind.

"I haven't seen much, really. The important buildings, yes, but only from the outside."

"Not even the cathedral?"

"Well…" He took another sip of his cognac to quiet his nerves, wondering what was coming next. "Yes, I did get into the cathedral for a few minutes." He hoped her question was innocent and coincidental. It would make sense that any local would mention the cathedral; they are the pride of most cities and Volterra would be no exception.

"The deposition—the wooden carving near the altar—I hope you had a chance to see it up close."

"Yes, I did. A beautiful piece." His memory wasn't totally failing him; he recalled that it was Santo's favorite work in the cathedral.

"And the Rosso in the art museum? I'm sure Erica told you about it, she being the Mannerist professor." There was a hint of playfulness in her voice which Rick chose to ignore.

"I haven't had the time for any museums." He decided not to mention the Etruscan museum. "How did you come to settle in Volterra, Donatella? I had assumed, since you studied in Rome, that you're from Rome."

"My mother is a *romana*, but my father was Tuscan. They separated when I was in the *liceo*, and I went to live with her in Rome. He died a few years later and left me the villa, so after the university I returned here. I suppose I'm a country girl at heart."

A true country girl, Rick thought as he studied her across the table. All she was missing were manure-stained jeans and pieces of straw stuck in her hair.

"But tell me about your real business, Ricky. You said you were doing this buying trip only as a favor to your friends at the gallery." She swirled her drink but didn't sip it.

"Translations and interpreting, English to Italian or vice versa. Sometimes tedious and boring with the written translations, but often I meet interesting people when I do the interpreting. International seminars, visiting dignitaries, that kind of thing."

"It sounds fascinating."

"It can be."

"But your trip here, has it tempted you to go into the art field?"

Not the art field, he thought, but possibly police work. Here he was sitting with a beautiful woman in an ancient Tuscan city, drinking fine cognac, and all his expenses were covered. True, as a deputized art cop he was dutifully trying to get into Donatella's head rather than her bed, but he was having a good time all the same.

"No, I'll leave that to professionals like you. You and Erica." Her expression changed slightly with the mention of her friend.

"And your business, Donatella? From the look of your collection, it seems to be doing well."

She shrugged. "Some months are good, some not. Like anything, the art market fluctuates greatly. The trick is to buy when the market is down and sell when it is up again. Right now it's flat." She took one of the canapés and gave Rick a half smile. "A good time for you to buy." She put it in her mouth and chewed slowly before softly running a paper napkin around her lips.

"And a good time for you to sell, Donatella?"

"Perhaps, but—" She was interrupted by the faint sound of her mobile phone, which she fished out of her coat pocket. After glancing at the number she held up an index finger, the silent message that she needed to take the call. Rick took another drink of his cognac and studied the canapé dish.

She watched Rick with a blank expression while she listened, but only spoke a few words. "*Si…si…capisco…certo…subito.*" She closed the phone and her face returned to its previous smile. "Ricky, I'm sorry, I have to go. Something's come up."

They rose from their seats, and he helped her with her coat. "Nothing wrong, I hope."

"No, no." She took his arm as they walked into the lobby, holding more tightly than when she'd showed him out of the villa. "I hope this won't be the last time I see you."

"I should be able to tell you soon if the gallery is interested, Donatella."

"I wasn't talking about business, Ricky."

He smiled and opened the door to let her step out to the street. The cool air felt fresh and brisk on his face, and thanks to just those few sips of cognac he didn't need a coat. Donatella added to the warmth with a soft kiss on his cheek.

"*Ciao, Ricky, a presto.*"

As she spoke, he noticed a long black car parked a few meters from the hotel entrance. A large figure emerged from the driver's seat and opened the back door. Dario, it appeared, did not worry about illegal parking zones.

Chapter Seven

His mother always said food tastes better when someone else cooks it. That is certainly the case with breakfast, thought Rick, as he pressed the button on the hotel elevator. He could make coffee as well as the next guy, but having it placed in front of him, ready to enjoy, was considerably better than lurching about the kitchen in the morning. And a very small kitchen at that. Find the coffee, find the espresso pot, add the water, add the coffee, light the stove. And then the same routine to heat up the milk. Very complicated. It was probably why Rick usually had his morning *cappuccino* and *cornetto* at a bar on Piazza Navona. But at a hotel, with all the choices, breakfast was even better. What would be on the groaning board this morning? The elevator door opened and he stepped into the lobby.

"Signor Montoya, you have a phone message." Rick detoured to the desk as the woman reached into his key box and took out a piece of paper. "The man just called, I put it through to your room but you must have been in the elevator."

The call was from Dr. Zerbino of the Etruscan museum, the note said, and he was inviting Rick to coffee later that morning. To offer me some stolen funerary urns, he guessed with amusement. He used the house phone to call the museum and recognized the voice of the secretary who had rescued the curator from Rick's clutches the previous day. She knew about Zerbino's message. Yes, could Signor Montoya possibly meet Dr.

Zerbino for coffee later that morning? Excellent. Time and place were confirmed. All very efficient, but with no mention of hot Etruscan artifacts. Rick chose a newspaper from the stack on the desk and resumed his path to the hotel dining room where thick black coffee and a pitcher of hot milk arrived a moment after he was seated, without his asking. Good memory—she would get an extra tip today.

He skimmed the paper while waiting for his *caffè latte* to cool. The death of Canopo had moved from the first page to the *cronica* section where such stories are normally found. There did not appear to be anything new, which didn't keep the reporter from speculating, using the contorted "could have" and "would have" verb tenses that were so popular in Italian journalism. Fortunately there was no mention this day of the unnamed American art dealer.

Rick stirred his coffee and looked at the newspaper without seeing the words. One side of him wanted to push Canopo's death from his mind, but the genes he shared with his uncle would not allow it. Conti had told him little about the case other than the forensic report and being convinced that it was murder. Nothing about suspects, other than the mysterious man on the street to whom Rick unfortunately had paid little attention. Perhaps Conti would share more about the murder when he next saw him, but until then, Rick decided, he should be keeping his focus on Etruscan loot. He took the spoon from the cup and placed it in the saucer.

Waiting for the next call from Santo would not be easy. It was just as well that Rick had this invitation from Zerbino to help pass the time, and of course before it there was his call on Polpetto, the exporter. Unless he was greatly mistaken, Polpetto was now out of the running, but Rick had to continue going through the motions until there was closure to the whole caper. At least it would be fun to see Signora Angelini again, if nothing else to find what personality she would display this time. And what would the exporter himself be like? If the bare outer office was any indication, there could be trouble staying awake. Rick closed the newspaper and paid attention to spreading butter and jam on a crisp breakfast roll. His cell phone, which had been fully charged during the night, lay waiting next to the plate.

◇◇◇

The last of the workers pushed open the tall wooden door, stepped onto the stone street, and walked slowly toward the car. Commissario Conti looked at him as he approached, sensing that the answers would be the same. All the men, starting with Malandro the foreman, had given him the same account for the afternoon of the murder, as well as for the days that led up to it. They could have been coached, though with the surprise visit and his sergeant watching them all inside, he doubted it. But talking with each of them a second time had been worthwhile—at least Conti tried to convince himself of that. If nothing else, he now knew more about the murdered man; not just of the work the man did, but his relationships with the others in Landi's little organization. The reality of Canopo's death was starting to sink in with them, bringing with it a mixture of sorrow and anxiety. Despite the man's Sicilian roots and the Tuscan sense of superiority over southerners, he had won over the men in his shop. As Conti knew from personal experience, that was not an easy feat.

The new arrival instinctively brushed alabaster dust off his work coat and blinked, adjusting his eyes to the sunlight. Conti was glad he'd decided to interview them out on the street, otherwise he would have been the one dusting himself off, as well as trying to get his hearing back to normal. For the final time he pulled the notebook from his coat pocket and leaned back against the warm hood of the police car, fortunately parked in a spot which caught some rays of sun on a day when few were to be seen.

"This won't take very long," he said to the boy who now stood before him. Conti remembered that Nino Reni, barely twenty and the youngest in the shop, had not said much during the first interview, either out of fear or shock. Perhaps this time he would be more helpful. "If I remember correctly, Nino, you've been working for Galleria Landi only two years."

"Yes, Commissario, a bit less than that in fact. Twenty two months. When I finish two years I'll no longer be an apprentice. I'll get paid more."

Already he was more talkative. "Tell me again about the day Canopo died."

The boy tensed up, staring at the ground and clasping his hands tightly together. He's going to stop talking, Conti thought, but then decided that what he saw was emotion rather than a reluctance to speak.

"It was a normal day," he began, after taking two deep breaths. "Orlando was in the shop from eight in the morning until he went to see Signor Landi in the afternoon, except for the lunch break. A shipment of alabaster was delivered in the morning, so he was counting pieces and weighing them."

"Did he seem out of sorts, preoccupied, different in any way than other days?" The answer was not what the policeman expected.

"If someone said he was so worried about something that he took his own life, it's a lie!" Conti's eyes jumped up from his note pad. He watched as the boy looked up and down the street, embarrassed by his outburst. He tried to compose himself, blinking rapidly and rubbing his hands against dirty jeans. "Orlando would never have done that," he said, speaking more softly and slowly. "Never."

"From what I know about Canopo, I would agree with you. Can you think of anyone who would want to do him harm?"

"No. I can think of no one." He stared at the ground. The flash of anger had come and gone quickly, and Nino Reni retreated inside his own grief.

Conti had already come to the conclusion that none of the men was holding anything back, including the boy. He was tired of interviews and frustrated that the case was going nowhere. The door opened and his sergeant emerged, slapping his coat in an attempt to rid it of alabaster dust. His appearance confirmed that Nino was the last one to be re-interviewed.

"That's all, Nino. Thank you for your help."

"You'll find him, won't you Commissario?"

It took a moment before he understood that the boy was talking about Canopo's murderer. Everyone, it seemed, now assumed it was murder. "Yes, yes of course. If you can think of anything that might help, you know where to find me." The boy nodded and turned back to the door, not even glancing at the sergeant as they passed. Conti sighed and stuffed the small notebook back into his coat.

"Did you get anything from them, *Capo?*

Conti shook his head without speaking. The sergeant walked around to the driver's side and got in the car. Conti looked at his watch, opened the passenger door and glanced up the street. "Just a moment, Sergeant," he said through the open door, "this shouldn't take long."

Signora Canopo and her daughter had just turned the far corner and were now walking slowly toward him. The little girl grasped her mother's hand tightly and stared down at the stone like she was counting the cracks between the cobblestones. The woman stared blankly ahead as she walked, but when she noticed Conti she tried to put a smile on her face, but without success. It would be a while before she could smile again. He waited as they approached, watching the mother walk slowly to match the pace set by the girl's short legs.

"Signora, good morning. How have you been?" It was a weak greeting, but he could think of nothing else to say. When he spoke, the girl looked up from the sidewalk, noticing him for the first time. A look of fear took over the small face and she hid behind her mother's dark skirt.

"As well as can be expected, Commissario." She looked down at her daughter, whose face was hidden. "Please excuse Angela. I'm afraid she associates you with…"

"That is understandable, Signora."

"We needed to get out of the house, so I thought we would come by to see Orlando's co-workers. They have been very kind. Is there any news?"

Conti shifted his feet. "We are working through the evidence. These investigations are often slow and tedious." Her face, already grim, became darker. Her lips tightened, and again she looked down at her daughter.

"I know you'll do your best, Commissario," she said as she stroked the girl's hair.

"Thank you, Signora. As soon as I know something I will call."

He suspected that she didn't really want to hear any news of the investigation, knowing it would only make her feel worse.

They shook hands and she walked toward the heavy door, her daughter still clinging tightly and hiding her face. Conti watched as they disappeared inside. An already bad day had been made worse.

◇◇◇

"Signor Montoya, *buon giorno.*"

Claretta Angelini, Polpetto's secretary, stood when Rick was buzzed into the office and reached across the desk to shake his hand firmly. We have a new Claretta, he thought, a third one somewhere between the efficient cold fish of his last office appearance and the bubbly lady on the street. Same glasses, however, but with different matching earrings. Maybe all her earrings were red pendants.

"And a good morning to you, Signora Angelini." Rick retreated to one of the two chairs against the wall. She sat down again, hands clasped together on the desk, examining Rick.

"Signor Polpetto is on the phone and will see you shortly. I hope we will be in the running for your business, Signor Montoya, I'm sure there is competition out there."

Whose side was she on? It was a strange thing to say, and he wasn't sure how to answer. "I've only started making my contacts, Signora, so it is difficult to gauge the competition, if that's what you're getting at."

"I assume you've been to Galleria Landi?" She became more serious, more concerned, and her next statement showed why. "I read in the paper that the man who fell to his death worked for Landi, and since you were the last one to see him—"

"I don't believe my name appeared in print."

"Didn't it? I must have assumed..." Her voice trailed off but she glued her eyes on his face, waiting for a reply.

Rick didn't want to get into the murder case again. "To answer your question, yes, I have been in contact with Landi." Mercifully the phone on her desk rang, and she excused herself to take the call. As she spoke, the phone tapped against her dangly earring. Distracting for her and for the person at the other end of the line. Rick's eyes drifted around the room, shifting his attention from the earring.

This morning the ceiling lamp above him was turned on, but most of the room's light still came from the small window above his head. The only magazine on the table next to him was a worn copy of *Famiglia Cristiana*. Rick picked it up, hoping that reading would forestall further communication with the lovely Claretta. Had he ever seen an issue of the magazine anywhere else but on sale inside the doorways of churches? Not that he was a regular churchgoer, he went just enough to keep his mother happy. These days, when she called from Brazil where Rick's father was stationed, she invariably asked about his attendance at mass. She had even enlisted the family priest at the church in Rome where she, as well as Rick and his sister, had been baptized. The topic of Rick's church attendance was as inevitable as her reminding him about his sister and her family back in Albuquerque, and what a terrible burden it was having one's grandchildren living on another continent. About as burdensome as having a son in his thirties who wasn't even married yet. He was musing on Italian mammas when the inner door opened.

Polpetto was definitely not what Rick expected, despite scrutinizing his photo at the ministry. The man's body almost filled the doorway, and his face radiated a smile that went with his size. He wore a wrinkled blue blazer with a pair of dark brown slacks which had not seen a hot iron since leaving the hangar at the clothing store. No fancy tailor for this guy. He was off the rack, though if ever someone needed to have clothes measured to fit, it would be Polpetto. At least the tie was fashionable, though it barely went with the striped shirt.

"Signor Montoya. Please come in. Signora Angelini has told me that your Italian is fluent so I won't have to expose my terrible English." He crushed Rick's hand in his as he guided him into the office past the secretary's frown. Polpetto noticed her and said, "Let me chat for a moment with Signor Montoya and then you can come in when we are ready to discuss the, uh, business issues." Her expression did not change as the door closed.

Rick was analyzing that little exchange when he was stopped in his tracks. The contrast with the sparse outer room was so dramatic that he and Polpetto could have wandered into another building. Shapes, textures, and colors covered the walls, like a tourist shop in Old Town Albuquerque. It was all drawn together—spatially if not chromatically—by the bright orange carpet that covered the floor. The only uncluttered space was the ceiling, but given his size, Polpetto may have worried about bumping into anything hanging from it. Shelving was so extensive and cluttered that Rick couldn't be sure what color the walls were painted. As his visitor took in the scene, Polpetto maneuvered his way to an old sofa and lifted a stack of magazines to clear a place. After looking around for a moment, he dropped them with a thud on the floor behind his desk, where apparently there was some rare space.

"Please, please." He stretched his hand to the sofa. When Rick sat, Polpetto took his place behind the desk and moved papers to clear his view. "I fear that my habits are not the most organized, despite all of Claretta's efforts."

So now it was 'Claretta.' Had the woman really made any attempt to clean up Polpetto's act? Talk about the Augean stables. Rick managed to keep a serious look on his face.

"We all have our own work styles," Rick shrugged, trying to be as diplomatic as his father, though his father would have had little patience with the disorder of this office. "Thank you for seeing me this morning. I am already impressed by your, uh, collection. Is this the kind of thing you import and export?"

Polpetto's face lit up, if further lighting was possible. "Yes. Or I should say much of it is. No, perhaps most of it isn't. I like to collect things. But I haven't offered you coffee, let me—"

Rick quickly raised his hands. "No, thank you, I just had one. What things do you collect?" Rick again turned his gaze to the rows of shelves. "I see a bit of alabaster."

"Yes indeed." Polpetto's eyes darted to the door and back, as if worried that Claretta could come bursting in any moment. "Those shelves on the right hold mostly alabaster, much of it Etruscan, small pieces of minor value, of course, not museum quality, but I enjoy looking at them. The bronze figures are also Etruscan. Though there may be a copy or two among them; it doesn't matter. The animals are my little menagerie, like a circus. That's why the warriors are on either side; we surely don't want the animals to escape."

Several bronze soldiers bearing shields and spears flanked the various small animals. *They will certainly keep the animals in line,* Rick thought. Time to change the subject. "That shelf there, Signor Polpetto, the stone fragments?"

Polpetto pulled himself from the chair with some difficulty. "I'm glad you noticed, it is one of my favorite collections within the collection." He beamed as he walked to a shelf of fragments from marble tablets, like the ones he frequently saw cemented into the walls of churches in Rome. Their flat surfaces had letters and decorations, some more worn than others, some more elaborate. Polpetto's large hands picked one up as if it were a bird's nest and held it up for Rick to see. Letters cut into the stone next to a fragment of garland.

"Do you read Latin, Signor Montoya?"

"Only the numerals, I'm afraid."

Polpetto gazed at the piece of stone as if seeing it for the first time. "This comes from the burial urn of a likely middle class Roman citizen. Only the last five letters of his name—ULIUS—are found on this fragment, which doesn't narrow it down very much. To think that I can hold in my hands a bit of the life, or rather the death, of someone who lived so long ago is fascinating, is it not?" Polpetto didn't wait for an answer. "All we can do is conjecture about who he was, what he did in his life. Was he a good man? Was he loved, or hated? Did his family have this memorial made to him out of obligation or true affection and grief? We will never know, but the lack of information does not alter the beauty of this stone and its untold story." He carefully returned the slab to the shelf and gave Rick a playfully reproachful look. "But you have not noticed the pieces which may be the most familiar to you." Polpetto pointed over Rick's shoulder with his chin, still beaming. Beaming, Rick decided, was a large part of Polpetto's persona.

Now what? The only collection Rick had as a kid was Matchbox toy cars. Could this guy have a first edition Topolino? But the shelf held a bigger surprise: handwoven baskets of various sizes, which Rick knew had come from the American Southwest. He nodded in appreciation, and his host grinned.

"I saw from your card that you live in Santa Fe, and I have noticed your boots. You must know where these are from." He took one of the baskets from the shelf and passed it to Rick. The weaving was tight, with a faint brown W-shaped design wrapped around it, the only decoration on the otherwise light brown surface.

"I lived in Albuquerque, not Santa Fe."

"Oh, but I thought…Well, this basket is from Zuni Pueblo."

"Of course, I should have recognized it. The design is clearly Zuni, very different from, say, Sandia or Santa Ana." Rick didn't know one basket from another, but he had spent time playing the tables at the Sandia and Santa Ana tribal casinos north of Albuquerque. Polpetto was impressed: first the cowboy boots, and now expertise in indigenous basketry.

"But we are not here to discus basket weaving, are we, Signor Montoya?" The fun was over for poor Polpetto, and his smile drooped with disappointment. "Let me ask Claretta to join us." He opened the door and nodded toward his secretary. Or was she his assistant? Or was she…? The rolling desk chair appeared in the doorway followed by Signorina Angelini, who pushed with one hand and held a pad in the other. She had to provide her own seating. Polpetto returned to the desk and settled into the chair which groaned weakly in protest. He blinked at Rick in anticipation.

"Allow me to explain what interests my gallery." Rick hoped this would be the last time he had to present the speech.

As he listened, Polpetto offered the appropriately serious facial expression and nodded occasionally, while his secretary took careful notes. At one point he rooted through the piles on his desk to unearth a pen and paper himself, scribbled something, and returned the paper to the pile. Would the man ever find it again? That was Polpetto's and Claretta's problem. Rick ended his presentation and relaxed into the sofa, feeling a small object under his right hip. He reached down without being seen and felt what he knew was a round piece of hard candy, fortunately still in its paper wrapper, which he left where it was.

"Perhaps we can be of some help, Signor Montoya," Polpetto was saying. "I do have my contacts in the business, and our company would be able to facilitate the exportation better than anyone in Volterra. I hope that doesn't sound presumptuous, but it is my specialty to get things through customs, in both directions." He beamed at Claretta, who returned his smile.

"I'm sure it is," Rick said.

"If you would give me some time to pull together products that could be of interest, I will get back to you with a proposal."

His manner was very professional, not that Rick had much customs experience by which to judge. It was time to drop the other proposal on Polpetto. Should he raise it with Claretta present? If Santo really was a dud, as Conti hoped, and Landi was not the culprit either, Polpetto and his secretary could be his last chance. But the man didn't come across as one mixed up in illicit artifacts. Claretta, maybe, but not her boss. Still, Rick had to be thorough.

"In addition to those items I mentioned, Signor Polpetto, if you know of any unique piece of art, and I mean ancient art, we have wealthy clients who could be interested. Price is less of a consideration in these transactions, as you can understand." His heart wasn't in it this time, and it probably showed.

Claretta turned the page of her pad and scribbled something. Polpetto stared blankly at Rick for a few seconds and then his face relit.

"Yes, of course. I think I do understand. Let me consider that."

He picked up the pen and started to put it in his shirt pocket, then placed it back on the desk, and finally opened the drawer and found a spot for it there. Rick decided it was time to take his leave, and he was about to get up from the sofa when Polpetto spoke.

"Do you mind if I ask you something, Signor Montoya?" He looked at his secretary and then back at Rick.

"What is it?"

"Well, I suppose everyone in town is wondering about the death of that man, Canopo. And I read in the paper about an American being the last one he spoke to. Was that you?"

So that was it. Polpetto's expression combined curiosity and shame, and curiosity was winning. Claretta's head tipped in Rick's direction, waiting for his reply. She hadn't gotten much out of him in the outer office.

"Yes it was."

"Did the, uh, police question you?"

"Of course, but I couldn't give them anything that was of any help."

"I suppose not." His face again darted to his secretary and then back to Rick. "That afternoon, you didn't see anyone else?" Polpetto didn't say it as if he was expecting an answer, and Rick volunteered none. "A terrible business, and on your first day in Volterra. It doesn't speak well of our city, does it, Signor Montoya?"

"Such things can happen in any city."

"Yes, I suppose no place is immune to murder."

Rick frowned. "Murder? I assumed it was suicide."

"I am no detective, Signor Montoya, but from what I read in the newspapers it made no sense for the man to take his own life. Family, job, and all. Perhaps we all watch too many crime shows on TV, but there must have been something else. My wife agrees," he added, which settled the issue. Rick noticed that Claretta was scowling. "My wife watches a lot of crime shows on TV," Polpetto emphasized. His face returned to its usual brightness. The discussion of Canopo was over. "But I am keeping you too long, you have other appointments. I will be in contact regarding your proposal. Proposals, I should say. Let me see you out."

Polpetto believed that Canopo was murdered. Why would that make sense? It was curious that the man mentioned his wife's opinion. Rick pictured them at breakfast, he preparing to meet with the American art dealer, and she, remembering the news stories, insisting that he ask about the murder. Polpetto would be too embarrassed to bring up such things on his own. Someone must have pushed him to it. And what about Claretta's reaction at the mention of Signora Polpetto?

The three got to their feet, and Rick shook hands with Claretta.

"Signor Polpetto will be out of town tomorrow on other business, but we should be able to have something for you very soon." They were the first words she'd uttered since entering the room.

"Let me help you with your chair," Rick said.

"No, that's kind of you. I can put it back." She rolled the chair to one side, making room for the two men to leave. She caught Polpetto's eye and shifted her glance toward the street.

Polpetto accompanied Rick out of the curio shop that inhabited his office, and through the bare domain of Claretta. He went the extra mile, or at least the extra meters, and took his guest down to street level where he again shook Rick's hand with rough affection. He was still standing in the doorway smiling when Rick reached a bend in the street and glanced back, almost bumping into a man who was intently studying a shop window. He excused himself and continued in the direction of the hotel. There were almost two hours until his meeting for coffee with

Zerbino, enough time to go back and get some work done on his computer. Some of his normal work, that is.

The stones clicked against his heels, and he thought about the case so far. He'd laid the ground work with the three prime suspects, if that was the correct term for them, and either Landi or Donatella must have sent Santo. One thing he didn't want to do was force Beppo to add more names to the list, but if Santo was never heard from again, that might be the next step. Beppo himself believed that these three were the most likely to bear fruit, but had hinted that there were others, including a few outside of Volterra. There was enough to see in this town, Rick thought, most of which he hadn't yet visited. Hell, the laptop could wait, he should do some more sightseeing. And what better venues to see in Italy than churches? He walked past his hotel toward the San Francesco church near the city gate. As he reached the driveway to the hotel garage he heard his phone ringing inside his coat. He recognized the number.

"Beppo, *come stai?*

"*Bene*, Rick, your name came up in a meeting with the minister this morning. I told him that the project is right on schedule. *E' vero?*

This was not the old Beppo, the one he'd again seen at lunch after their meeting at the ministry. They were both creeping closer to middle age, but still hung on to the juvenile banter of high school when it was just the two of them, at least at the start of a conversation. Perhaps someone—the enigmatic Signor Vetri?—was in the room with him. "Of course it's true, Beppo, I am working tirelessly for you and the minister. Relax, you will be the first to hear when Signor Santo contacts me again." That is, if he contacts me again. "I can report that all the first encounters have now taken place, the third one just now with the exporter, Polpetto. Despite the meeting in the cathedral yesterday, I thought I should keep to the original schedule."

"Good idea, Rick." Beppo seemed to lighten up. Slightly. "How was Signor Polpetto?"

"A strange bird that one." Beppo listened to the description of the meeting with the exporter and was laughing at the end. So he must be alone, Rick thought.

"Okay, Rick, I agree that he doesn't appear to be the person to lead a band of thieves, but you never know. It could be a clever façade. We didn't put him on the list on a whim. As I told you in your briefing, he's been involved in some shady dealings in the past, though nothing that could ever be proven."

"I'll keep an open mind, Beppo, but frankly if I had to bet who was involved, I'd put more money on his secretary than on him. He doesn't seem to do anything, except maybe play with his toys, without her being involved."

"Tell me more," Beppo said, and Rick described Claretta and her strange relationship with her boss. "The woman behind the throne," said Beppo, "or at least behind the desk. Of course she may have insisted on being in on the meeting because she is coming on to you. She sounds very much like your type. Remember at school when you dated—"

"Very funny, Beppo. But to get back to my real work up here, at this point Polpetto is last, and Landi is still at the top of my list as the one who put Santo onto me. Donatella is somewhere in the middle."

"Why Landi?"

"Just a second." He waited while a man walked slowly past him, obviously curious about what was being said. "Sorry about that," Rick said when the man was out of ear shot, "A nosey local. Now, Landi. Hard to put my finger on it, but he just seems to fit the profile I have in mind. So much of the stuff he sells in the shop is Etruscan reproductions, why not have a hand in dealing with the real thing? It would be a natural extension of the business, like FIAT going into motorcycles."

Beppo became serious again. "You're probably correct, Rick. I hope it doesn't take too long for this to play out. If you don't hear back from this guy soon we'll have to decide whether to add other names on the list, or admit defeat. As much as I would love to keep you in pasta and wine up there indefinitely, the minister probably won't. He is already getting anxious about the whole idea, despite the good news."

"I've only been here for two days."

"This is your third day, Rick. Worried that you won't get time to try out all the restaurants in town?" There was nothing playful in Beppo's voice, and Rick wished they were face to face to know for sure if there was more to the comment than the usual joking between friends. No doubt Beppo was taking some heat about the idea of sending the American up to do what the police should have handled themselves. Better to let the comment pass.

"Rick, is there anything else happening that I should know? How about your contacts with the local constabulary? You told me yesterday that you had met with Conti on that first day, but you didn't go into great detail. And you went back to see him yesterday after we talked."

"Well, there is something I didn't mention, with the appearance of Santo and all I forgot to tell you. There was an unfortunate accident."

"Accident?"

"Well, not exactly an accident. Conti thinks it was murder… Beppo, are you still there?"

"Yes, Rick, I'm here. What happened?"

Rick told him about his short meeting with Canopo and what took place after it, though Beppo didn't sound extremely bothered by the incident. He asked questions, most about Rick's relationship with Conti, and when they were answered, he returned to the issue at hand.

"If I thought the man's death was related to your work, Rick, I would pull you off immediately. But it appears to be a strange coincidence. Who knows why the man was killed? You said he was from Sicily, so that alone opens various possibilities. Anyway, let's hope that your little trip bears some real fruit, and soon."

"I'm sure we'll hear something before too long," said Rick. "In the meantime, I'm having coffee with your curator friend later this morning. He's warmed up after our initial contact. I may have caught him on a bad day when I dropped in."

"You didn't tell me you had seen Zerbino." The slight edge in Beppo's voice had returned.

"Yesterday. He gave me an abbreviated tour of the museum before leaving to attend to some business."

"Well, I suppose having coffee with Zerbino will be as good a way as any to wait for Santo to turn up with a relic under his arm." There was some background noise that Rick could not identify. Someone coming into the room? "I have to go, Rick. Good luck and stay safe. *Ciao*."

Beppo's last words, though spoken quickly, made Rick feel a bit better about the phone call, and about the advantages of being one's own boss rather than working in an Italian bureaucracy. Beppo was under pressure from his boss and wondering if his idea might have been a big mistake. Rick's unpaid tenure with the ministry would be short and relatively painless, but Beppo was a lifer there.

And what better way was there to support the Italian culture ministry than to soak in some local culture while in an Italian city? The door to the church swung open, and he went from sunlight to semidarkness. The heels of his boots tapped on the stone floor as he walked to the marble bowl attached to a column and dipped his fingers in the holy water. He crossed himself and thought how pleased mother would be.

◇◇◇

Inspector Conti rose from his chair and walked to the window. The scene on the piazza was never the same—something always caught his eye, something he hadn't seen before. Today it was a group of children following a teacher, but one boy was lagging behind in the line, staring past Conti's window up at the ancient tower. The teacher spotted the straggler, called out sharply, and the boy ran to join the class. *Just like Enzo*, Conti thought, and he smiled at the thought of spending more time with his grandson. But if there was anything he would miss from the job it would be this window view.

"Commissario?"

"Yes, Sergeant."

"The detailed forensic report is in on Canopo, he—"

"Let me see it." Conti walked back to his desk and took the folder from the man's outstretched hand. He slowly went through the pages while the sergeant stood in silence in front of the desk.

"*Porca miseria.* This raises more questions than it answers. The dust on his shoes was alabaster from the work shop, we didn't really need to consult with Florence to figure that one out. But as far as the traces of mud, which was the real puzzle, they are not very helpful. 'A red clay which is found in various part of Tuscany.' Thank goodness, we won't have to extend our investigation to Calabria." The sergeant had worked for Conti long enough to know that this was a time to keep quiet. The commissario drummed his fingers on the papers and then looked up as if he noticed for the first time that the other man was there.

"Is LoGuercio around?"

"I think so, sir, would you like to see him?"

"I was just curious." More drumming as he stared at the papers. "Ask him to come in here."

The policeman left and Conti tapped the cover of the file. He was about to return to his window when LoGuercio appeared at the door.

"You wanted to see me, sir?"

Conti almost blurted out another sarcastic reply. "Yes," he said instead. "What has the American been up to?" It was time to take his mind off the murder, even if it meant dealing with this annoying case from Rome. LoGuercio had taken the sergeant's place of honor in front of the desk.

"DeMarzo has been on him most of the time—"

"The question was what he's been doing, not who watched him do it."

"Sorry, sir." LoGuercio tried not to show his annoyance that nobody had warned him of Conti's foul mood. He briefly reviewed Montoya's movements since the previous evening.

"This exporter, or importer, or whatever he is: what do we know about him?"

"I ran a check on him, sir, and nothing turned up. There was a note in the file about the cultural ministry looking into his activities last year, but it didn't specify what they were searching for."

"And of course they wouldn't tell us, we're only the local police. But we know why Montoya went to see him. Go on."

"He runs a small operation, just he and a secretary, he travels out of Italy occasionally with the business, pays his taxes. Well, pays taxes, who knows—"

"Yes, yes, Detective. What does he import and export?"

"He exports alabaster, both the stone itself and things carved from it, some food products like olive oil and honey, some manufactured goods. Coming in, mostly machinery and parts."

"The woman, what's her name...?"

"Polpetto's secretary?" Conti shook his head and rubbed his eyes, as if in pain. "Pardon me, sir, you mean the woman Montoya went to see yesterday. Minotti is her name. Sorry, Commissario."

"Yes, Minotti, the woman from yesterday. I think I've heard of her, and I may have met her at an exhibit opening once."

"Exhibit opening sir?"

Conti tilted his head at the detective. "You are surprised I enjoy something other than police work, LoGuercio?"

"No, of course not, sir." He shifted his weight from one foot to another, recalling an episode in grade school when he'd been called before the headmaster. What he couldn't remember was what he had done that time to get him in trouble.

Conti looked off toward the window. "The exhibit was last year, something at the Etruscan museum. She's very attractive, as I recall."

LoGuercio spoke slowly, choosing his words carefully so as not to make the meeting get any worse. "I wouldn't know, sir. DeMarzo had to park outside the grounds of her villa when Montoya drove in, so he didn't actually see her, or anyone else."

"Of course." Conti resumed drumming his fingers on the desk. "Most importantly, there is no sign that anyone else is keeping an eye on our American friend?"

"No, sir."

A relieved LoGuercio slipped out of the room and Conti eased himself back in his chair. If it weren't for the sudden appearance of this man Santo, he would have been convinced this was a total waste of time and resources. Now he couldn't be sure.

◇◇◇

Rick studied the figures on the wall, a horrific scene of slaughter. King Herod's Massacre of the Innocents was not the most popular theme in religious art, but this artist had devoted an entire panel to the scene. Each of the babies looked strangely alike, as if the painter could only afford to pay for one infant model, or decided to use a relative, perhaps a nephew, at no cost. Like the other depictions of Bible stories in the chapel, this one's figures were dressed in contemporary clothing and armor, no doubt very recognizable to the illiterate twelfth century audience which had viewed it with a mixture of fear and inspiration. Rick returned to the twenty-first century, opening his phone to check its digital clock. Enough sightseeing, it was almost time to meet Zerbino. He walked out of the chapel, turning off the lights with a switch on the wall as the handwritten sign next to it had requested. The honor system was still alive and well in the San Francesco church in Volterra. As he stepped outside, the cell phone rang. It was not a number he recognized, but the voice on the line, while it wasn't Santo, sounded vaguely familiar.

"Signor Montoya?"

"Yes. Who's calling?"

The question was disregarded. "About your need for some Etruscan pieces. We may have something of interest. One of our colleagues will be in contact and take you to where they can be viewed."

"What kind of pieces?"

Apparently the man didn't like questions. "Do not be alarmed when he appears."

The line went dead, and Rick looked again at the number on his phone before scrolling down to see if it matched any of his other calls since his arrival in Volterra. Nothing. He went over what the man had said, which given the length of the phone call was easy to do. There was no mention of Santo, or any reference to Rick's conversation with him in the cathedral. This was probably more of Santo's love for the cloak and dagger. But there was another possibility; what if this were someone else? *Good God,* he thought, how many gangs of grave robbers could there be in this town? But if the call wasn't connected to Santo, who else had his cell number? Better to ask who didn't. He had left it with nearly everyone he'd met, from the police to Donatella, and he'd even told the hotel they could give it out if anyone was trying to reach him. Before walking down the church steps to the street, he made another call. Beppo answered on the first ring.

◇◇◇

Conti carefully placed the phone in its cradle and stared at it, as if it could provide answers to his questions. "Once again it came from a pay phone, this one about two blocks from where we're sitting. I'm still amazed that the telephone company maintains public telephones, given how much Italians love their mobiles. A service to the criminal class, I suppose, for those who don't want to spend their hard-earned Euros on disposable phones." He looked up at Rick, who sat across from him in front of the desk. "You say you recognized the voice?"

"I said it sounded familiar, but I can't remember where I heard it."

"An accent?"

"Vaguely Tuscan, but it was hard to say."

Conti frowned and nodded. "We have television to thank for that. Everyone wants to talk like the news anchors, with no accent at all. When I started out it was easy to tell where someone was from. Now..." He caught Rick's eye. "Do I sound like I'm ready to retire?"

"Perhaps, Commissario."

I can only get a frank answer like that at home, thought Conti.

"And you have given out your phone number to everyone in Volterra, you said. That would include Landi, Signora Minotti, the exporter Polpetto, and various people who work for them, as well as the hotel. And of course the mysterious Signor Santo has it."

"Also Dr. Zerbino, of course."

"Of course. Have you notified the ministry?"

Rick was still pondering his conversation with Beppo. He had expected at least a modicum of pleasure from his friend since it appeared that the plan was now successful, the plan that Beppo had worked so hard to get accepted by the ministry. Instead his voice betrayed concern, though once again it was not easy to detect nuances on a cell phone call. They had discussed who could be behind the call, concluding that it had to be Santo. At the end of the conversation Beppo's message to Rick had been simple: don't take any chances. Exactly what chances he shouldn't take was not clear, but perhaps the news of Canopo's murder was starting to sink in at the ministry.

"Yes, I told Beppo what I just told you." He wondered if the policeman would be annoyed that he wasn't the first to know of the call. Conti's face showed nothing.

"Signor Montoya, if this wasn't connected to Santo, then which of your contacts so far do you think could be behind this phone call? The bait was put out with each of them, now even the exporter, so you must have some hint as to which one has taken the hook."

Rick pondered the question. "Well, as I told Beppo, the most logical would be Landi. He was the top name on the list I had from the ministry, although they didn't tell me exactly why. Signora Minotti is a mysterious character, I must say, but it isn't likely that she could be behind this kind of operation. Polpetto? Well, he's the least likely, in my mind, because he seems more like a character in *opera buffa* than someone running a smuggling ring. And as I found out when I saw him today, his secretary appears to be the brains behind his business."

"Really? Tell me about it."

Rick described the meeting. He omitted any description of the man's office decorations, detailing instead the interplay between Polpetto and Claretta. Conti listened without comment until Rick was finished, then shook his head.

"In the Abruzzi we have words to describe such men, but I don't wish to be judgmental without having met him. Perhaps the ministry made a mistake and should have put her name on their list instead of his."

"Besides Signor Landi, Signora Minotti, and Signor Polpetto, Commissario, there is another possibility that has crossed my mind."

"And what is that?" Conti put his forearms on the desk and clasped his hands.

"That one of the people with whom I dropped the hints told another person, someone they work with, and that person is the one involved in the illicit operation."

"Such as?"

"Someone who works in Landi's shop or at his store. Dario, the man who works for Signora Minotti, looks like he could be in a gangster movie with Al Pacino. Polpetto, of course, only has his secretary, but he may have spoken with other people in town. I did briefly tell his secretary, Claretta, what I was interested in purchasing when I went to the office yesterday, and that was before I heard from Santo."

"That is an interesting theory, Signor Montoya. We both should consider those possibilities." Rick was pleased, since the comment almost gave the impression that Conti considered him a partner in the affair.

"I also have another theory," Conti added, "one that came to me on my last visit to Landi's store." It was Rick's turn to listen attentively. "I have been working on a separate investigation, one which also involves the sale of Etruscan artifacts." Rick's expression changed slightly, and Conti noticed. "No, not the same as your precious burial urns, Signor Montoya, these are *fazuli*, fakes. But it has occurred to me that the dealer in real antiquities you are trying to catch could also be involved in this other activity. After all, there are only so many real pieces that can be dug up, so why not create some good copies to keep one's clients happy?"

Rick remembered Conti's skepticism about the ministry's plan at their first meeting. The old guy was changing his tune now, offering his own ideas about the crime, but Rick would be the last one to rub it in. He was starting to like the man.

"That does seem like a possible scenario, Commissario. But does it help us to figure out which, if any, of these people could be involved?"

Conti pushed up from his desk and walked to the window. Today he wore his jacket, for the autumn chill from the outside was seeping through the ancient stone. Rick pictured the building when winter arrived in earnest. They'd probably be hanging animal skins on the walls and warming themselves over braziers in the middle of the rooms. He turned in his chair to watch Conti and waited for a reply.

"I don't know, I'll have to ponder it a bit more. I'm sure you will also." He turned from the window and faced Rick. "You may want to keep that theory between the two of us. I was thinking out loud, something I don't do normally. You should consider it a compliment."

It was a strange thing to say, and Rick felt uncomfortable in the ensuing moments of silence.

"What happens now, Commissario?"

The policeman spread his hands in a very southern Italian way and shrugged. "What the man on the phone told you, I suppose." He glanced at the large government-issue clock on the wall. "You'd better get to your meeting with Dr. Zerbino. Keep your phone handy. And be careful."

Everyone wants me to be careful.

◇◇◇

Detective LoGuercio tapped on the half-open door.

"You asked to see me, sir?"

"The American was just in here, LoGuercio. But you know that, of course, you are watching the man." He sighed. "Something may be happening with that scheme the Romans cooked up. I'm not sure what would be worse, if the culture cops turn out to be correct, or if the art thieves are not caught." He held up a hand. "I don't need your opinion, if you were thinking of volunteering one. It is now imperative that you watch him carefully. We don't want anything to happen to our precious American art dealer. Is that clear?"

"Yes, sir."

Back in his own office, LoGuercio used the desk phone to make a quick call to DeMarzo, finding out that Montoya had just entered a bar on the main street of town. He briefed the sergeant of the meeting with Conti and emphasized that they must tighten the watch. After ending the call he closed the door to the office, walked to his only window, with its view of the alley, and dialed a number on his cell phone.

Chapter Eight

As would be expected of the man, Zerbino had not chosen one of the many drab neighborhood coffee bars to meet Rick. Instead it was an elegant, brightly-lit place on the main shopping street which, during much of the year, was filled with people eating ice cream. Gelato was a year-round snack food everywhere in Italy, but with the arrival of cold weather in Volterra the flavor options in this shop had been greatly reduced. There were not enough tourists in the city during the fall and winter months to justify keeping more than a dozen basic choices behind the glass counter, leaving the display case only half filled with ice cream. In the extra space, colorful boxes of candy stacked up into small mountains of sweets, surrounded by plates of cakes and cookies, their other specialty.

The fresh baked goods filled the room with warm sweetness deliciously mixed with scents from a shiny espresso machine, reminding Rick why the word in Italian for a fragrant aroma was *profumo*. After taking a few steps into the bar he spotted the curator sitting at a small table reading a newspaper. Zerbino's suit was similar to the one he had worn at the museum, perhaps even the very same, but without the vest. The tie this time was a paisley, with a matching foulard in the jacket pocket. The room's lights gleamed off both the top of his head and the tips of his polished shoes. He looked up as Rick approached, then stood to welcome him, pumping his hand.

"Signor Montoya, so good to see you again. What would you like? Coffee? A grappa?"

"Just coffee thank you, but let me get—"

"No, no, it is my pleasure. Just coffee then?" He hurried to the bar and put in the order while Rick's eyes followed him with mild surprise. This was not the same man he met at the museum. Zerbino returned to their table. Rick shed his overcoat and draped it over a chair next to Zerbino's.

"The day you came to the museum I was involved in some rather delicate issues. I'm sure you know how bureaucracies can be. Sometimes the smallest of conflicts between employees can turn into major battles. It was that way in the university too. So I did not give you the attention you deserved. You must forgive me."

"I understand completely, *dottore*, I remember my days as a graduate student," said Rick. "At American universities we say that faculty politics are vicious because the stakes are so low." It was an old joke, but perhaps new to this guy.

"Oh that's good, that's very good. I must remember it." His head bobbed, and he took out a white handkerchief to wipe perspiration from his bald head. The barman arrived and placed two small cups on the table, along with a bowl of sugar. "So tell me, how is your visit to Volterra progressing? Are you finding the city interesting?"

"A beautiful city, worthy of serious exploring, but as yet I have not had time to see much. I just work."

"Yes, yes, what was it you were involved with? Purchasing art, if I remember correctly? Tell me more about it. Being a museum curator, I suppose we are involved in a similar business, are we not?" He grinned, not sure if he was making a joke or not.

"Our commercial gallery is hardly in the same category as your institution." Rick sipped his coffee. "I'm doing some preliminary market studies on the possibility of future purchases—local art, including alabaster. The gallery owners think that such items could greatly interest their clientele." Rick was almost starting to believe his own BS.

"What clientele do you have at this gallery?"

"It varies, of course, but something exotic, such as art from Tuscany, could appeal to both middle and high end buyers. We have some very affluent clients. Many visit during their traveling seasons." This was not the man to hint about the specialty items he was really seeking. As he spoke, Zerbino studied him carefully.

"Very interesting. I don't know anything about business, of course, my only experience has been with either universities or museums. Our institutions don't concern themselves with profit and loss, but I have always been fascinated by commerce." He surveyed the room and then lowered his voice to continue. "The only commerce that I have been involved with, if you can describe it that way, is with stolen artifacts." Rick tried not to react, and Zerbino continued. "By that I mean keeping our collection from being stolen, of course." He laughed out loud this time, the light from the ceiling lamps casting patterns on his bald head. He returned to his conspiratorial tone. "You may not know this, but art theft is a major problem in this country."

"Naturally I've heard something about that." Rick coughed into his napkin.

"You cannot imagine what museums in Italy have to spend on security devices and guards. It eats up an enormous amount of our budget. I wish I had even half of what we spend on security to improve the collection or renovate the building. And then, after all the expense and time-consuming installation, it doesn't always work. I hope the thieves don't find out about the alarm problems before we can fix them." He stirred his coffee, still without tasting it. "But I don't suppose thievery will go away anytime soon. Certainly not in my lifetime. Another coffee?"

"Not for me." Rick was anxious to change the subject. "*Dottore,* I have been reading a book on the Etruscans to help me appreciate your area, and one of the aspects of their lives which has fascinated me is their reliance on seers to predict the future."

It worked, and Zerbino jumped in quickly. "That is not exactly correct, Signor—" He stopped and smiled at Rick "Can we dispense with the formality of last names? Please call me Arnolfo."

Rick accepted the offer cordially. "Of course."

"As I was saying, Riccardo, to describe the Etruscans as reading entrails or studying lightning in order to see the future is not quite accurate. What they were constantly trying to discover was the will of the gods and what they believed were other mysterious forces in their lives. Overwhelming forces. That is how one famous scholar has described what the Etruscans believed influenced their everyday lives."

"Isn't that the same thing?"

"Not necessarily. If you know your boss' general view of things that doesn't mean you will know exactly how he is going to react to every situation in the future." He chuckled. "There I go talking about bureaucracies again."

"I see your point," said Rick. "The more information one has, the better, whether it's Etruscan, Volterra, or modern Volterra."

Zerbino nodded in agreement. "True…true." He looked down at his coffee as if deciding whether to drink it or not. *Something is going on here*, Rick thought.

"Riccardo, that business with the man falling to his death." He was searching for the right words. "It was terrible, but how unfortunate of you to be found in the middle of it." He looked up to see Rick's reaction, and quickly added, "Well, not in the middle of it as if you were involved, but being there just before he fell, I mean—"

"I understand, Arnolfo. Thank you for your concern." But no thanks for the morbid curiosity.

"What do you think happened? I suppose the police talked to you."

"Of course they did." Zerbino waited for Rick to say more, and he eventually obliged. "I had barely met the man, so I leave the investigation to the police. But I suppose that you, like everyone, believe that it was not suicide?"

"Well, it does seem unlikely, given—"

"His family? That's what everyone thinks, but who can really know what's going on in someone's life, what problems he was facing?"

"I suppose you're right, Riccardo. But with his job at that shop, and probably a good future working there, it just doesn't…" His voice trailed off. "Do you think the police have any idea who could have killed him? If it wasn't suicide, of course."

"Like you, I only know what has been in the papers the last two days. The police interviewed me just once about the case."

"Yes, of course. And the stories have not been very helpful. I mean the papers haven't even speculated on motive. Which they usually do." He pulled the white handkerchief from his lower pocket and mopped his head. The foulard was for decoration only.

Rick watched Zerbino drain his espresso, the first time he had touched it. A tiny drop of coffee fell from the cup to his shirt, fortunately just missing the silk tie. "Arnolfo, I know you are a busy man, and I don't want to keep you from your work. It has been a pleasure to see you again."

Zerbino was staring at Rick, as if he wasn't hearing the words. Finally he snapped out of his reverie. "*Piacere mio, Riccardo.*"

They rose from the seats and pulled on their coats. Zerbino lead the way to the door which he held open for Rick. Out on the street they stopped and shook hands. "If you're going to stay in Volterra for a few more days we must see each other again," said Zerbino. "Perhaps dinner some evening."

"That would be a pleasure, Arnolfo," replied Rick. "Thank you for the coffee."

"You are most welcome, most welcome." He was about to walk off when he turned back to Rick. "And you really must come back to the museum some time for a better tour than I gave you the other day." Before Rick could reply, Zerbino hurried in the direction of his museum.

Strange man, Rick thought. Why the change from barely giving Rick the time of day to wanting the be on a first name basis? Beppo had not come up in their conversation just now, but being a good Italian, Zerbino must have decided that treating Rick well would get back to the Cultural Ministry. At some time he would need a favor in the ministry, so it couldn't hurt to be nice to the visitor. The more cordial he was to Rick the bigger the favor he could ask. But what about the talk of stealing artifacts and museum security? That was eerie. He watched Zerbino disappear around the corner and remembered that Canopo had done the same, on the same street, two days earlier. A lot had happened in those two days.

Beppo would probably find Rick's meeting with Zerbino a nice diversion. Rick pulled out his cell phone, but the call went directly to voice mail. Beppo was probably in a meeting; that's what people in ministries do. He would call back later. Now it was time for lunch, and then back to the hotel to check his email and do some work with his real job; the rent on his Rome apartment would not pay itself. And this time, no touristy diversions. He walked up the street and turned the corner toward the Hotel San Lino. A minute later he was walking through the main piazza, the police station on his right, taking his mind off the translation job awaiting him and bringing it back to the case.

So where was he? It appeared from the mysterious phone calls that something was going to happen, but when would it happen and which of Rick's contacts would turn out to be the guilty party? The same possibilities turned over in his head. Landi the most likely. Landi had said, after all, that he would be in contact with Rick about some special items of interest. He had expected Landi himself to call, of course. Rick also recalled the face of the girl working at Galleria Landi. Did she show only grief, or was there fear as well?

Polpetto simply seemed too *buffo* to be a serious contender in the crime department, though his business was murky at best, especially with that secretary involved. Not that Rick understood import export. In addition, he hadn't even seen the man prior to Santo turning up. But there was something from the visit to

Polpetto's office that stuck in Rick's mind: the way the man had held that Etruscan fragment in his hand.

That left Donatella, and again Rick could not picture a friend of Erica being involved in something so unsavory as tomb robbing. The sexy leader of a gang of thugs, with her loyal major domo keeping everyone in line? It could make a good movie script, but no more than that. A better plot line would be the museum curator. Rick smiled at that thought and then remembered his latest conversation with Conti. Conti thought there might be a connection with another case he was working on, and Rick suggested looking for a second layer of suspects. Both ideas had one thing in common, that perhaps they should be moving beyond Beppo's initial list.

Rick looked up to see his destination, whose menu was propped on an easel outside the door. Crime thoughts were wiped from his mind, substituted by visions of warm plates of food. This was Tuscany, with a chill in the air, so it was time for some Tuscan soup. He pulled his hands out of his coat pockets and rubbed them together.

◇◇◇

"I understand your reluctance." Conti carefully chose his words. "But you will have to agree that Signora Canopo is burdened enough with her grief that she does not need to be bothered." On hearing this, the bank manager shifted nervously in his chair, looking across the clean surface of the desk at the policeman.

"Yes, the poor woman is going through a terrible time, but you must understand, Commissario, that this is highly irregular. Surely you don't believe that the man's bank records could help with your investigation."

Why the hell do you think I'm here? Conti wanted to say, but instead he chose to be soothing. "We try to be as complete as possible. No stone unturned, as it were." Getting a judge to sign off on this would take forever, and what he'd just said about the widow was true, she didn't need to be involved in this. Was the man going to help him or not? Conti contained a smile as the man reached into a drawer and took out some papers.

"Very well. Signor Canopo had three accounts with us. One was a normal checking account, with his wife as co-signatory on it. You know that of course."

Not specifically, but he let the comment go with only a nod, and the manager continued.

"The other was a savings account that I know they were using to build up for a home purchase. They started it several years ago when their daughter was born. I remember when they came in to open it."

"And the third?"

"That one is a bit more curious." He shifted the papers in front of him on the desk. "Canopo came in one day by himself and opened this one, his wife did not sign any of the documents. It is also a checking account, but separate from the other. Of course the widow will have access to it now. After doing the required paperwork." Conti ignored implied criticism delivered with emphasis on the word "required." "She likely knows about it," the manager added.

Conti raised an eyebrow. "When did he open this third account?"

"About a year ago." He checked the papers. "No, I'm sorry, eight months ago. Every few weeks he made deposits. No withdrawals have been made on the account since it was created."

"Do you have copies of the checks deposited?"

The man again consulted the paper again and gave Conti a sheepish look. "No checks, it was always cash."

◇◇◇

"The phone's ringing, I have to go."

Detective LoGuercio snapped the cell phone closed and walked quickly to pick up the telephone that sat on one corner of his bare desk.

"LoGuercio."

"Detective, this is Sergeant DeMarzo."

"Yes, DeMarzo, no problems with the American, I hope."

"No, sir, none at all. On the contrary, he has settled into his hotel for the afternoon. He told the woman at the front desk—"

"Woman at the front desk?"

"Yes, sir, I've gotten to know her well and she told me that when Montoya picked up his key just now he asked if the room was made up, since he was planning to work there on his computer for a few hours."

"That should make it easy for you, DeMarzo."

"Yes, sir, it's why I was calling. My wife was going to pack something for me this morning, but the baby spilled her food on the floor, then my mother-in-law called, and—"

"Do I really need all this domestic information, DeMarzo?" LoGuercio was a bachelor, and ate his breakfast at a bar near the police station. Nothing ever spilled on the floor.

"Yes, sir. I mean no, sir. What I meant to say is that I haven't had anything to eat since breakfast, so I wondered if I could get a quick *panino*. There's a small bar just down the street from the hotel, and—"

"Of course, go ahead, since he's holed up in his room."

"Thank you, sir, it will only take a few minutes, then I'll return to the lobby of the hotel. There is no other way out for him than through it."

◇◇◇

Rick stood up, watched the leaves blowing around the empty swimming pool outside his window, and slipped on his wool overcoat. He was a good translator, but for some of the more knotty phrases he still needed his English-Italian dictionary, at least to be sure that there wasn't some nuance he might have missed. He hadn't yet found an online edition he trusted. There was nothing like paper and ink, even in the electronic age. But sure enough, he'd left the thick book in the trunk of the rental car, parked in the back of the garage next to the hotel.

Putting his computer on sleep, he descended to the main floor, walking quickly past the front desk and out to the street. He pulled his collar around his neck when he felt the wind coming down from the main square, a river of cold flowing past him and out of the city through the stone gate. Reaching the end of the hotel façade, he turned right and started up the ramp into the garage, squinting to adjust to the gloomy space. Two small bulbs hung from wires in the cement ceiling, enough barely to make out the various cars parked on either side. He walked to the end of the row, found his rental, and reached into the left coat pocket for the keys. He found his GPS and shifted to the right pocket, pulling out the keys. The trunk popped open easily, and fortunately its small light helped him find the dictionary wedged into one corner near the jack. He slammed the trunk shut and headed back toward the street. The cold wind was now hitting him directly in the face, and he lowered his head.

As he turned up the street a dark red Opel drove up from the right and braked directly in front of him. Rick froze in his tracks, clutching his dictionary as if it were his wallet. The driver's side window lowered slowly, and Rick saw a dark-haired man dressed in a leather jacket. He wore sunglasses and had a stubbled face which in Italy could be either fashionable or sloppy. The man looked vaguely familiar, but then his was the type of face Rick passed a dozen times a day on the street. He looked Rick up and down, the gaze pausing briefly on the boots and the dictionary.

"Signor Montoya, I think you are expecting me. Get in please, I have something to show you."

This really is happening, thought Rick. He looked down at the book in his hand and toyed with the idea of leaving it at the hotel desk, but decided he didn't want to miss this chance. It was what he was here for. He walked around the car, opened the door and ducked in, tossing the dictionary into the back seat.

"My dictionary," he explained, as the car surged ahead in first gear.

The man threw him a strange look and turned his eyes to the street. "I don't think you'll need it."

Sergeant DeMarzo was smiling down at his sandwich on the counter next to the glass of mineral water. Yellow cheese oozed out the sides, its golden color contrasting nicely with the dark grill marks on the toasted bread. It had been a long time since his morning *cornetto*, and with the baby carrying on he probably hadn't digested it very well. Just as DeMarzo picked the sandwich up and opened his mouth, the red car sped past the front of the bar and started up the hill into the center of the city.

Rick looked over at the man. "Where are we going?"

"You'll see."

"What is it you're going to show me?"

"You'll see that too."

The driver stared straight ahead and Rick decided he wouldn't get much out of him, at least not during the drive. There would likely be someone at the other end, wherever that would be. One thing for sure, this was not the voice of the man who had called him outside the church. The car turned onto a narrow street which ran around the outside of the main piazza, passing the building which housed Polpetto's office, while the driver kept his eyes tightly on the road. Just ahead a small boy stepped out of a doorway, causing the driver to honk and curse under his breath. At the corner the car turned onto a bigger street, though still not wide enough for two lanes of traffic. It dropped steeply down to one of the city gates, and suddenly they were outside the walls. The views changed from solid gray stone to trees swaying in the wind. The road went past rows of small houses, the spaces between them widening as they drove farther from the city itself. After a few minutes the scenery was mostly woods and fields, with an occasional house tucked back off the road. Leaves of tall trees further reduced the waning afternoon light. Fifteen minutes later the car slowed suddenly and pulled off the pavement onto a dirt road. The maneuver was so fast that Rick barely had time to look around. I am not going to remember any of this, he thought. The Opel rolled to a stop at a clearing and the man turned off the engine and got out of the car. Rick opened his own door and stepped to the ground.

They walked to the front of the car and looked down into a deep ravine. In New Mexico it would have been called an arroyo, though here in Tuscany there was considerably more vegetation than in the American Southwest. Rick glanced around and noticed other tire marks in the soft earth around where the car was parked. The clearing was small, bordered on two sides by trees which rustled softly, their leaves holding on as long as they could before the cold dropped them into a dry carpet on the ground. The man stood silently and then pointed down into the ravine.

"Down there is where we are going. Follow me carefully, I wouldn't want our American buyer to break a leg." His laugh had the cackle of a heavy smoker. Rick thought it better not to mention his rock-climbing experience.

There was a path, though it would have taken Rick a while to find it himself. It started steeply and then ran parallel to the ravine edge before cutting back in the other direction. As they descended the trees closed in on them, making the path even harder to see. The man had shed his sunglasses and now he pulled a dark metal flashlight from his coat, but didn't turn it on until they reached the bottom of the ravine. Here the ground was somewhat clear, probably due to water which ran through the ravine during rain storms, tearing up any plants that tried to grow. After walking about fifty feet the man climbed up one side of the gully and stopped, pointing his flashlight at some bushes. Rick wondered what was going on, but then noticed that the bushes seemed out of place, their color slightly differ-ent from the rest of the vegetation. The man stepped forward and pulled them aside, revealing wooden planks crudely nailed together to form a door. He slid the door to one side and bent down to squeeze into the small opening.

Rick followed, but once inside he could see only the circle of light formed by the flashlight moving around the floor. He stood still and watched as his guide found what he was looking for with the flashlight, a wooden table directly ahead of them. The man walked to the table and the sound of a switch brought a pale light to the cave. Under the table was a row of automobile batteries that connected by ground wires to four pole lamps light-ing the low ceiling. Rick noted that it was flat and even, carved by human hands rather than formed by nature. Rick lowered his eyes, immediately noticing the reason for their descent into the cave. Along the far wall were three large rectangular niches, each about four feet wide and three feet tall. One was empty. In the other two were Etruscan burial urns which looked strikingly like the one Rick had seen in Beppo's office.

◇◇◇

Detective LoGuercio stared at the papers on the desk in front of him but read nothing. His thoughts were on choices—his own. Most Italians took government jobs for secure employment, decent pay, and a steady pension after retiring as young as possible, but he had joined the police in search of excitement. He soon found that the excitement came in brief spurts between long days filled with boredom and routine, regulations and forms. Palermo had its edgy side, as would be expected, but he never felt truly challenged. Then came the assignment to Volterra, and shortly after, the offer. Again he asked himself it had been a mistake to accept. He tried to get his mind back to the file in front of him when the phone rang.

"LoGuercio."

"This is DeMarzo, sir. I…I can't locate the American."

LoGuercio leaned forward in his chair. "That's impossible, you called me only fifteen minutes ago to say he was locked in his room with his computer. What happened?"

The sergeant spoke in short bursts, gasping for breath. "I finished my sandwich quickly and walked to the hotel, ready to sit in the lobby to wait for him. When I got there the girl at the desk, she's the one—"

"Yes, yes, the one who's been helping you, go on."

"Yes, sir, well she told me that Montoya had left the hotel a few minutes earlier with his coat on. He didn't drop his room key, he just walked out the door."

"Did she see which way he went?"

"No, she doesn't have a clear view of the street. I rushed outside and covered a few hundred meters of the street in both directions. Nothing."

"His car?"

"Still in the hotel garage."

LoGuercio looked up at the yellow ceiling of his office, trying to decide what to tell the man to do. "I'll put men on the gates of the city. You start walking around the main streets near you to see if he appears. If not, go back to the hotel and stay there, he will have to return some time. Call me immediately if he turns up. He can't have gone very far. If you're lucky he just went out to buy a newspaper or some shaving cream."

"Or something for his computer."

Like a new hard drive. "I doubt that."

He hung up, breathing heavily. You wanted excitement? Now you have it. Where would Montoya have gone, especially after telling the desk he was going to stay in his room? If it wasn't just a quick decision to play tourist, someone must have called him. Who? The more pressing question going through LoGuercio's head was something else. How long should he wait before telling Conti?

◇◇◇

"*Ecco*," said Rick, trying to stay as calm as he could. He walked over to the first urn while the man leaned against the table, the flashlight now back in his pocket. As he watched Rick he pulled out a cigarette and lit it, the smoke adding to the stale odor of the cave. The urn was at chest height so that Rick could reach out and run his fingers over the stone decoration. The surface was relatively clean, like it had been recently rubbed with a cloth. Particles of dust clogged the tiny recesses of the design, and given its intricacy, there were many nooks for dust to have collected over the centuries. At first Rick thought it to be a battle scene, but then he noticed a large bear on the left side of the panel, reared up and facing the spears of the hunters. Would the dead man have really killed a bear? An Etruscan Davey Crockett? Rick was not aware that any bears lived in this part of the peninsula, but perhaps the man had traveled further north for sport or as a soldier. Or it may have been the depiction of some legend or myth. Whatever it portrayed, it made an exciting bit of bas-relief theater, drama about which the toga-wearing Etruscan sculpted on the lid seemed blissfully blasé. He reclined in the typical banquet position, as if saying "Yes, I killed that bear in my lifetime, now I can brag about it to everyone in the afterlife. What does a dead guy have to do to get some more wine around here?" Rick moved to the next niche.

The theme on this one was clearly classical, even if the figure on top had the same relaxed demeanor as his neighbor. It depicted a chariot carrying a man clad in a flowing robe followed by another man on foot wearing light armor. The chariot, with ornate decorations on its side and wheels, was pulled by four strong horses. Above the scene loomed a winged figure, a deity of some sort, looking straight into the face of the charioteer. Contrasting the flowing lines of robes, wings, and horseflesh, regular stone blocks of a temple ran across the top of the urn and bent around the sides. Rick was so intent on studying the stone that he almost jumped when the man spoke.

"Do you think you can find some rich client who would be interested in such a piece?" He tapped ashes on the dirt floor.

Rick hoped the man didn't notice how quickly he was breathing. "It depends on price, of course, but these urns are certainly unique." He tried to shift into his role as buyer, wondering what he should be asking. "What about delivery?"

"We have shipped them to other countries before, always hidden with legitimate goods, and there's never been a problem. Customs officials in most countries are overworked and underpaid. I trust that is also the case in America." He took another pull on the cigarette. "We will require half payment to close the deal, and the other half after delivery. Bank account numbers will be given to you. I trust those terms will be agreeable?"

"You haven't mentioned price."

"No, I haven't. That will be the subject of another meeting. We thought you would want to talk with your people in America before we get to that point."

"Yes, I think I would." Rick turned back to the urn, rubbing it and picking up a trace of dust on his fingers. "When will that next meeting be?"

"Very soon."

"With you?"

"Probably not."

Likely with Santo again, but Rick guessed that his present companion did not want to get into such specifics as names, just as Santo had pointedly avoided them. He was about to return to the urns when he noticed, for the first time, a wide plank the size of a door, leaning against the opposite side of the room. Wires from the batteries ran under it.

"Is there another room? Do you have more pieces in there?"

The man had been slouching against the table, but now he pulled himself to full height and raised his right hand, the burning cigarette between two of the fingers. "We have not yet completely excavated the area."

So I guess I won't see that room, Rick thought. While the man stared at him, sending the message that it was time to leave, Rick tried to think what else he should be asking. What would the Commissario ask? What would Beppo need to know? He admitted that he was more intimidated by Conti than his high school buddy. He was still trying to get his head around the concept of Beppo Rinaldi as an art cop.

The man stubbed out his cigarette on the floor and pulled the flashlight from his pocket. "I think you have seen enough, Signor Montoya, to make a decision. Go out first, and I will turn off the lights and follow." Rick did as he was told.

By the time they climbed the path up to the car the darkness had arrived in earnest, and along with it a drop in temperatures. Rick put his hands in his coat pockets, looking across the hood of the Opel at the man who had put away the flashlight and was pulling out the keys.

"I need to make a visit to the bushes," said Rick. "Too much wine with lunch and much too cold in that ravine."

The man's throaty laugh turned into a cigarette cough as Rick walked behind a clump of trees. When he emerged again the man was sitting in the Opel with the engine running. The car went into reverse and made a wide turn to put it back on the narrow trail, emerging from the trees a few seconds later at the edge of the pavement. The return drive was just as twisting, and perhaps even more confusing to Rick thanks to the darkness. It was also filled with smoke, until Rick finally opened his window and leaned his head toward the fresh air. After twenty minutes of silence, the man pulled to a stop and Rick realized he was at the entrance to a large parking lot, behind which loomed the walls of the city.

"You can get out here." He pointed to the right with his chin. "Take that stairway."

Rick climbed out and closed the door, leaning over to say something through the open window, but before he could speak the man put the car into gear and sped off. Rick watched it drive away and realized that he had forgotten to get his dictionary from the back seat. He also had not checked the license plate. Wondering which was more bone-headed, he walked toward the stairway and realized he was in the parking lot where the American couple had watched the deadly fall of Canopo.

Had it really been just three days since his arrival in Volterra?

◇◇◇

When Commissario Conti stopped pacing, LoGuercio knew what was coming.

"How long's it been now."

The detective once more looked at his watch. "An hour and ten minutes, sir."

"Tell me again what happened and what you did after he disappeared."

Feeling like a suspect, LoGuercio slowly recounted his conversations with DeMarzo, how the man took a break to have a bite to eat, how the woman at the front desk told DeMarzo that Montoya had left the hotel through the front door a few minutes earlier, and how he, LoGuercio, had sent out various men to search for the American. Conti was looking out the window when he spoke again.

"So if he turned right after he got to the street, he could have gone out through the gate and left the city. How unfortunate that we don't still have guards with swords and spears at all the gates of the city, like the Etruscans and Romans did, checking everyone who comes in and out. There's a church there, San Francesco, just before the gate, did you check it?"

"Yes, sir."

Conti continued to stare out the window. "And if he turned left up the hill, once he got to the fork in the street he could have come up here to the piazza or bent to the right, toward the cathedral and the baptistery. You sent men there too, I suppose. He might have decided to do some sightseeing or was having another meeting with the mystery man."

"I did, there was no sign of him."

"Most likely he got into a car, and—"

"But not his own, sir."

"Yes, yes, LoGuercio, I got that, his car is still in the garage. He got into someone's car and now could be half way to Pisa. Perhaps my *capo* at the Questura in Pisa could start looking for him there. Should I call him?"

LoGuercio prudently decided not to answer.

"Why don't you get back to your office to continue coordinating the search, such as it is."

"Yes, sir, I will let you know the moment he appears."

"You do that."

LoGuercio made his escape while Conti stood at the window watching a tall man crossing the piazza, his shadow handed off from one street light to the other as he walked. Going home after a day at the office, no doubt, something Conti wished he could do. He heard a rap on the door behind him. Perhaps LoGuercio had some news. He turned to see Rick standing in the doorway, and felt a strong sense of relief. Was it because the man was the nephew of a fellow policeman, or was he starting to like this American? He pushed the question out of his mind, and decided he would wait a bit to tell LoGuercio. Let him stew.

"Signor Montoya, you have reappeared."

Rick looked puzzled. Suddenly he remembered the rather unspecific assurance from Beppo during his briefings in Rome. The police in Volterra will be looking after you, his friend had

said. It had not occurred to Rick that he had been under surveillance these three days, but now it made perfect sense. He
would have to think back on his movements since his arrival to
remember any strange people who could have been following
him.

"So you were expecting me to stay in my room."

Conti shrugged. "Never mind that, take off your coat and
tell me where you've been. Since you have come here instead
of the hotel, you likely were not making the rounds of tourist
sites. There must be something to tell."

Rick shed his coat and recounted in detail what had happened from the pick up outside the hotel garage until the drop
off at the parking lot below the north wall of the city. Conti
did not interrupt the description, but when Rick finished the
questions began.

"You're sure this wasn't the man who called you."

"Absolutely. He has a smoker's voice which the caller did not."

"So at least two people are involved in this. Three, assuming
Santo is involved, and four if Landi is behind Santo."

"My thoughts exactly, Commissario."

"The car. Describe it."

Rick was dreading this one. "A dark red Opel, four doors,
late model, clean inside and out. I'm afraid I didn't take note of
the license plate."

Conti's reaction was relatively benign. "Your uncle would
not be pleased."

"I suppose you're right, Commissario. Another thing. He
drove off before I could get my English-Italian dictionary from
the back seat."

"Of course, the dictionary. It will help them deal with the
American customs officials the man mentioned." He gave Rick a
tiny smile. "Do not despair. I'm sure the ministry will reimburse
you so you can buy another." He rose from the chair and walked
to his favorite window. "So you say you drove out of a gate on
the north side of the city, and then started on a route with many
twists and turns through a forest." He stared out the window as

he spoke. "I know that area. I could easily get lost there myself. God knows where this cave is."

"Not just God, Commissario."

Conti turned and gave Rick a cold look. He was not in the mood for humor, at least not someone else's humor. "*Non capisco.*"

"Well," said Rick, "when we got back up to the car I told the man that I needed to answer the call of nature." Conti's eyebrow raised. "When I went behind the bushes, I took out this." Rick reached into the pocket of the jacket that was draped over the chair next to him.

"A mobile phone?"

"No sir, it is a global positioning device. I turned it on and froze it on the coordinates at that spot. May I?" He reached across the desk for a pen and paper, laid the GPS down next to them, and copied some numbers. "There." He passed Conti the paper. "The ravine is at this longitude and latitude. If you have a computer with internet access, I can locate it exactly."

Conti looked at the numbers as he picked up his desk phone. "Martino, you are the computer expert. I have something for you."

Five minutes later the uniformed policeman returned to Conti's office and spread out a map on the table at the opposite side of the room. "It's right here sir, about fifteen kilometers from the center of town, just off the road to Ulignano." He placed another sheet in front Conti and Rick. "This is a satellite picture of the area, but unfortunately the resolution doesn't bring it in that clearly."

Conti shook his head in silent commentary on his personal relationship with technology. "Thank you, Martino, that was just what I needed." Unaccustomed to such comments from his boss, the young policeman grinned and started to leave the room when Conti added, "Oh, could you tell Detective LoGuercio that our man is here with me and that I'll talk to him later?" He exchanged glances with Rick and then turned back to Martino. "He'll know what I mean."

After the policeman was gone Conti gathered the maps and returned to the chair at the desk. Rick took to his regular assigned seat in front of it. After looking down at the map for a few moments, the policeman finally spoke. "Signor Montoya, it appears that you have been successful. Unless this is an elaborate hoax, and the urns you saw were fakes, the ministry was correct in sending you on this mission. As I told you when we first met, I was skeptical, to say the least, but I must now admit that I was wrong."

Rick almost felt sorry for the man. Or perhaps he was feeling sorry for himself since this adventure, which he had been enjoying, was about to come to an end.

"At this point," Conti continued, "we must bring in the ministry directly." He consulted a pad on his desk and dialed a number. They both waited while a phone in Rome rang.

"Dr. Rinaldi. Commissario Conti. I have good news, I hope."

A long conversation ensued between Conti and Beppo, while Rick sat silent. Toward the end Rick got on the line briefly to accept the congratulations of his friend and get Beppo's promise that their next dinner was on him. It was agreed that Conti and a contingent of police would make a predawn visit to the cave and set a trap for those who would eventually have to show up. Beppo would leave Rome early enough to arrive in Volterra by midmorning. He would examine the urns for authenticity and see what was in the other rooms of the cave. Most importantly for Rick, the undercover work was done. When Conti finally hung up the phone the two looked at each other in silence before the commissario finally spoke.

"Let me ask you the same question that I posed on your last visit to this office. Which one do you think it is, Signor Montoya?"

He was expecting the question; he'd been asking it to himself since the drop off at the edge of the parking lot. Conti eased back in his chair with the usual creak and watched Rick's face.

"I am still leaning toward Landi. The exporter, Polpetto, doesn't seem organized enough to run an operation like this.

And as I said, our Signor Santo appeared before I even spoke to Polpetto. So unless it is his secretary who really runs his business, Polpetto is almost certainly ruled out. And even though he is a large man, he doesn't seem muscular enough, emotionally, to be *capo* of a group of criminals that must include the man who took me to the cave. Though it's true that my driver did talk about experience with customs offices, which could link him with the exporter." Rick stopped talking for a moment and rubbed his forehead. "But something has stuck in my head about Polpetto. Perhaps it's of no significance." Conti kept silent and waited for Rick to continue. "It was the way he looked at a small fragment from an Etruscan tomb, a piece from his office shelf."

He looked at the policeman, whose expression was neutral, and shook his head. "But no, Landi seems most likely. I saw him dealing with his men in the workshop, and that was not the most wholesome of groups. And *la bella* Donatella? She's somewhere in the middle. Her relationship with her *maggiordomo* raised questions in my mind, and I could picture her ordering around other men like she did Dario. And she is a successful business-woman. There would be no reason to rule her out of a criminal activity, other than pure male chauvinism." Rick again waited for Conti's reaction.

The commissario smiled slightly and creaked his chair into a more upright position. "I was at Landi's workshop in con-nection with the Canopo investigation, and I agree with your point about him and his workers. I also have a suspicion about Landi's involvement with fake artifacts, because of some items I saw in his shop. If he's involved in that trade, trafficking the real thing would be the logical next level for him. I don't know Polpetto except from what you have described to me. And my only contact with Signora Minotti was a casual one. We met at an exhibit opening. None of the three have has any issues with this office, so if they are up to anything they must be very good at it."

Or your office is not very good at your own business, thought Rick. "Is there anything new on the Canopo case, Commissario? If you don't mind me asking."

Conti frowned, but it was unclear to Rick if the man was annoyed with the question, annoyed with the subject being changed, or was just deciding what he wanted to tell Rick. Or deciding if he wanted to tell him anything.

"Nothing which helps prove anything one way or the other. I continue to believe that he did not take his own life, and the autopsy does not contradict murder. I don't have a motive, but I'm sure he was engaged in some activity outside of his position with Landi, his bank accounts show it. I must assume that whatever he was doing, it would not be viewed favorably by us here in the building."

"Doing something on the side for Landi?"

"Or someone else."

"And that something could have been dealing in stolen Etruscan artifacts."

"And that is another good reason, Signor Montoya, for you to be retiring from this case and leaving it completely to the professionals. Retiring with honor, of course."

Rick was getting used to the Commissario's ironic half-smile. He wanted to probe more about the murder, but interpreted Conti's last comment to mean that their conversation was at an end.

After Rick left the office, Conti picked up his phone, pressed one of its buttons, and said a few words. A sergeant appeared almost instantly, pad and pen in hand.

"Yes, sir?"

As Conti talked the man scribbled. "Put out a search for a dark red late-model four door Opel. If we're lucky there will be a large dictionary in the back seat. I know that's not much to go on, there must be hundreds of red Opels in the province, but do what you can. Run a license check on all that you find to get the owners' names, but don't approach any of them, at least not yet."

The sergeant hurried out the door as Conti rested his head in his hands. After a moment he got to his feet and went to the window, rubbing his eyes to squeeze out the fatigue. It was now completely dark outside, but a few lights were on inside the buildings around the square. As he watched, a woman came

out of the tourist office and locked its door behind her before
shuffling across the square, holding her coat tightly around her
neck. Conti checked his watch and wondered how many card
games his brother-in-law had played by now in that bar on the
main square of San Giorgio.

◇◇◇

As Rick left the piazza and walked down the hill toward the hotel,
his thoughts were of Erica. That, at least, was the positive side
of this quick end to his undercover work; he would be with her
tomorrow in Rome. Where would they go for dinner? Certainly
not a Tuscan place, he'd had his fill of those dishes the last few
days. Perhaps something simple, like da Lucia in Trastevere where
they serve the best *spaghetti alla gricia* in the city. He would need
a reservation. At this time of year it was only the tables inside and
their dining room was about as big as Conti's office.

As he pondered major decisions of life in Italy he came to the
small triangular chapel on the corner and remembered his promise to himself to make a visit. The room was about half the size
of his hotel room, and considerably darker. He crossed himself,
slipped a coin into the small metal box near the entrance, and
took one of the cards with a picture of Saint Christopher. He
would not be a traveler for long, he thought, as he tucked it into
his coat pocket. The patron saint of travelers and a GPS. What
more could a tourist need? Leaving the chapel he stepped onto
Via San Lino, like his hotel named after the city's most famous
native son. Perhaps not that famous; everyone knows who the
first pope was, but how many remember the second? Rick was
thinking about Pope Linus when he heard the muffled ring of
his cell phone. He smiled when he saw the number.

"I was just thinking of you, *cara*."

"I'll bet you were, Ricky."

"No, Erica, really. I was thinking how wonderful it will be
to see you, and now, how soon we'll be together."

"Really? Why is that? I mean, why is it going to be soon?"

Rick decided he probably should not go into any detail on
the phone. Silly to think that anyone could be listening, but

just the same…or was he trying to impress her. "I'll tell you all about it when I see you, but it appears that my business here is ended, and ended successfully."

"That's great, Ricky." He was pleased to hear the enthusiasm in her voice. If only it would last until he got back to Rome tomorrow. "I suppose that you'll be dining tonight with one of the lovely ladies of Volterra."

Rick grinned as he strode toward the hotel door. "I'm not a very fast worker, *cara*, it will once again be a lonely meal for me tonight, probably on the thin gruel they serve in the hotel." Was he laying in on too thick? Not a chance, these Italian ladies love it. "The only sweet part of it will be thinking about being with you soon. I'm almost to the hotel now, and when I get to my room I'll start packing my bag."

"I can't wait to see you too." Rick heard another voice but couldn't make out what was said. "Ricky, I'll call you back, I have to deal with something here. *Ciao*." The line went dead and Rick looked at the phone as if it would tell him what was going on. It was not like her to break off a call, especially when she was in an upbeat mood. He put the cell phone back into his pocket, pushed open the glass door of the hotel and started across the lobby to get his room key. A woman was standing at the desk talking with the receptionist, her back to Rick. She wore a fashionably long coat, red denim slacks, and brown boots gleaming like they just came out of the shoe store window. The desk clerk spotted Rick and said something to the woman, causing her to turn and watch him approach the desk, her head tilted slightly, a hint of a smile on her face.

"I guess I don't need to call you back now, Ricky."

◇◇◇

"You have to tell me *something*, Ricky, anything. I came all the way up here, after all."

"I was under the impression that you came here to see me." The meal, like the afternoon, had started well, and Rick did not want it to unravel. With Erica things could unravel quickly.

"Of course I came up here to see you, but…*insomma*."

It was the all-purpose Italian phrase to indicate frustration, and the way Erica had said it also made it irrefutable. He knew that when an Italian lays an *insomma* on you, about all you can do is hold up your hands and sigh, and that's what Rick did. "When it's over, which should be very soon, you will know all there is to know."

He poured her more wine, a smooth Vernaccia with a slight hint of wood from its aging barrel, trying to nudge her off the topic. They were in what the woman at the hotel desk considered the best restaurant in town. "If you insist on eating somewhere other than our dining room," she had added.

Her recommendation was proving to be a good one. It was a relatively new place, open only a year, which is an instant by Italian culinary measurement. The atmosphere was what one would expect, an ancient building completely modernized but maintaining its rustic feel. There was nothing rustic about the food, however. It followed the rule of thumb for high end *ristoranti* in Italy: the more words describing each dish on the menu the smaller the portions and the higher the prices. The first course Erica had ordered consisted of a few ribbons of fresh pasta tossed with even fewer crustaceans and some sprigs of something green. Rick's *pasta e ceci* soup was tasty, but he finished it in what seemed like seconds. At least the bread was plentiful, and it was fresh and warm. Rick pulled a crusty piece from the basket.

"Erica, I appreciate your patience on this."

"What patience?"

"Okay, let me rephrase that. I would appreciate *having* your patience. Let's talk about something else, can we? How are your classes going?"

"That's the last thing I want to talk about, Ricky. I came up here to get away from all that." Her eyes indicated, to his relief, that she'd decided to ease up, at least for the moment. He understood her frustration, and in fact he was anxious to tell her everything. She went on. "What are we going to do tomorrow? Tell me what you've seen already in Volterra and we can decide."

He was actually thinking more of the evening than the next day, but he told her what little of the city, at least the tourist part of the city, he had seen in the last three days. He omitted his meeting with Santo in the cathedral, and the visit to the cave. "You haven't even scratched the surface of this place, Ricky, and like all Italian cities it has layers upon layers."

That seemed like an apt description of this case, Rick thought, surprised that he was still thinking about it. "So, *cara*, what would you have in mind to educate the rude American on his first trip to Volterra?"

The second course arrived. For Erica it was a piece of grilled fish carefully centered on a thin crisp slice of potato and drizzled with a lemony sauce. Put before Rick was a slice of beef whose pink texture contrasted with the three green strips of asparagus next to it. He had seen larger pieces of steak put in doggy bags back in Albuquerque, but he kept his thoughts to himself.

"The cathedral is a good one, there is a famous wood deposition near the main altar, and the carving on the podium is worth seeing."

"I think I've heard of that," he said as he stared at the plate and recalled Donatella's similar comments about the deposition. Pulling his mind back to the meal, he wondered if the flavor of the meat would make up for the portion. He carefully sliced off a small bite. "You've been reading up, or did you remember the cathedral deposition from your last trip here?"

"I did consult my Touring Club Toscana guidebook," she replied. "It's an old edition, but the sites here haven't changed much. It's Italy, after all."

Only the portions in the restaurants have gotten smaller, Rick thought. He carefully cut another very thin piece of his meat to make it last, and put it in his mouth. The taste was as good as any steak he had eaten. It was not for nothing that Tuscany was called the Texas of Italy, and Volterra was on the northern edge of the Maremma, Tuscan cowboy country. He glanced around the room as he chewed. No Stetsons. There were only a few empty tables left, the word was out that this was the place to eat, and the clientele appeared to be predominately local. Not that there were many tourists in town at this time of year. Rick chuckled as he watched one of the waiters leading a man and woman to a table at the opposite end of the room. She held the man's arm tightly with a look somewhere between affectionate and coquettish.

"What is funny, Ricky?" Erica was also not rushing to consume her fish.

"The couple that just came in, at the far table." He made a slight movement with his chin, and Erica turned her head slightly in that direction. "They are two of the people I met this week, and it appears the guy's secretary may be more than just an employee. This must be the night of his wife's favorite crime show, and she preferred to eat in. Oops. He's spotted me, and here he comes." They watched as the large man carefully worked his way across the room, forcing a few chairs to be pulled in as he walked. Rick stood when he reached their table.

"Signor Polpetto, so good to see you again."

"*Piacere mio*, Signor Montoya."

"This is my friend Erica Pedana, visiting from Rome."

Polpetto bowed formally and shook Erica's hand. "I hope you will enjoy our city, Signorina, including this excellent restaurant. I see you have chosen the *coda di rospo*, one of their specialties." Erica murmured praise for the dish. "I will let you get back to your meal." He turned to Rick. "This is not the time for business, Signor Montoya. Let me say that I am still putting together some possibilities for your gallery, and I'll be in Florence tomorrow to gather more information. But Claretta and I are curious—did you ever find those special items you were seeking?"

Rick could get nothing from the thin smile on the man's face.

"I believe so," he finally answered.

"Good, good. Well, it was a pleasure to see you, and to meet you, Signorina."

Polpetto shook their hands again and walked carefully through the tables, trying to keep his bulk from bumping into any of the other diners. He sat down and bent his head to say something to the secretary, who wore her usual glasses with matching earrings. She placed her hand on Polpetto's, listened carefully, and looked across the room, giving Rick a nodding smile. He could not help noticing something new: bright red lipstick. Evening wear.

"What a strange man," said Erica after she returned to her plate. "Will he be on the list when you eventually give me a complete report on all this?"

"Yes, of course." Strangely, Rick's thoughts were not on the case, but rather on something else which had crossed his mind about Polpetto's appearance in the restaurant. Erica's next comment startled him; she was thinking the exactly same thing.

"I hope he manages to get enough to eat in this place."

Chapter Nine

Rick was back to his normal morning routine. Well, almost normal. He had just returned to the breakfast table after taking a call at the front desk. He poured Erica another cup of coffee, adding a touch of hot milk, just the way she liked it.

"That was Zerbino, the curator of the museum. He invited me to come by this morning when the museum's closed. Said he felt badly about giving me short shrift the other day. I accepted, but didn't mention your presence. Why don't you come with me? He certainly wouldn't mind."

Erica brushed away some of the crumbs from her half-eaten *cornetto* and stirred her cup with a small spoon. "I've been to that museum, Ricky, and to be honest, I'm not very keen on the Etruscans. My Etruscan course was taught by a professor who was constantly looking at me in a way that I didn't appreciate."

"I do, but I certainly wouldn't blame—"

"Ricky." He'd forgotten. No joking until after the coffee does its work.

"Sorry. But Zerbino seems like a nice guy, and I assume all Etruscan scholars are not dirty old men. He'll be giving a private tour of the museum." He rooted through the basket in the middle of the table to find another piece of the soft white bread. Still hungry, he was tempted to order the eggs and bacon that he had seen on the table of some English tourists. He resisted, taking a slice of bread and pulling the top off a small plastic cup of Nutella. He carefully spread the chocolate on the bread. Nutella, the great rejuvenator.

"Thank you, Ricky, but I'll pass on the Etruscans. I have some work to do anyway, a thesis I have to review before next week, and I'd rather get it over with. And by the time I'm finished reading it you'll be back, and I can take you to the Civic Museum to see Rosso's Deposition. The best painting in the city, bar none. It will win you over to Mannerism."

He gently took her hand. "You have already won me over, Erica. I cannot conceive of any student who would not be completely captivated by the field, with you teaching it to them."

She pulled her hand back and used it to lift her coffee cup to her lips. "Sure, *caro*. Have some more Nutella."

◇◇◇

Inspector Conti sat in the front passenger seat of the unmarked police car as it curved through in the wooded area north of the city. His men had arrived before dawn and hidden themselves and their vehicles, but so far nobody had shown up for work at the cave. Perhaps this was a day off for everyone, or the grave looters union had negotiated a very favorable work schedule. It would be good, Conti supposed, to get this business cleared up so he could devote all his resources to the Canopo murder investigation. He might even assign LoGuercio to the case, despite his losing track of the American last night.

"Take off your hat, sergeant, in case we come across someone going to the same place we are. We don't want to scare them off."

The driver removed his blue service cap and tossed it in the seat behind him.

"It should be just around this bend, Commissario, according to the directions they gave me this morning. There will be a small road leading off—there it is."

The car slowed and left the pavement, turning into a break among the trees, a path barely wide enough for the vehicle. After a hundred meters of ruts and bumps they entered the clearing.

"Are you sure this is the right place, Sergeant?" As he spoke Conti saw various policemen emerging from the trees, weapons in hand, and answered his own question. "Never mind, it is."

Conti stepped onto the dirt of the clearing, noticing that in addition to the men coming out of the woods, two had appeared behind him on the path into the clearing. One of the men strode quickly over to the car.

"Commissario, good morning. We have our vehicles down the highway a few hundred meters, but there is room over there to hide yours. If anyone appears, once they are into this clearing we can block their exit. But I'm beginning to think that we have come on their rest day."

As his car was driven behind the bushes, Conti looked around and saw that the area was just as the American had described. He walked over to the ravine and peered down, his eyes searching for the cave entrance.

"It's over there, sir," said the policeman, pointing his hand. "You can see that the bushes have a slightly different color, the leaves are a bit lighter." Conti nodded. "I can lead you down there when you are ready, sir. We've already taken pictures of the footprints inside, so you can step anywhere without a problem."

Conti had to admit to himself that he was curious to see this cave. The only part of the case that irked him was that it was Montoya who had broken it open, just as the culture cops in Rome had planned. He didn't mind being wrong, except when it was another public safety arm that turned out to be right. Well, these rivalries would soon be a thing of the past for him, replaced by more wholesome ones on the card tables and bocce courts at San Giorgio. He was about to ask the sergeant to lead him to the cave when he realized that he had forgotten to call off the tail on Montoya. Cursing softly to himself, he opened his cell phone and dialed.

"LoGuercio?…Where?…That's fine, but you can pull back, the case has been resolved. I'll explain later, go back to the station."

So Montoya was at the museum. That was certainly as good a place as any for the man to spend the morning. Conti didn't think there would be any immediate repercussions from the raid of the cave, but it was just as well that Montoya was in a public building where nothing could happen to him. He pocketed his phone and signaled to the sergeant that he was ready to descend into the ravine.

As they traversed down the narrow path, Conti wondered if it had been used by wild boar hunters, or even by the boars themselves. Fortunately poaching was not something under his purview, there was another corps of law enforcement which dealt with hunting and fishing. Which was just as well since he enjoyed a bit of fresh *cinghiale* out of season as much as the next person. Indeed, the Tuscan specialty would be a dish he would miss when he moved back home to San Giorgio. Close to the cave opening the sergeant cleared away the loose brush and moved the boards aside. He pulled a flashlight from his pocket and turned to Conti.

"I'll go in first, sir, and turn on the lamps. They have them on batteries."

Conti waited until he saw the glow of light through the opening, then bent over with some difficulty to enter the cave. He was definitely getting too old for this kind of activity. When he straightened up, not without more difficulty, he was inside the room that Rick had described, its walls and ceiling spread with a yellow glow from the lamps. He immediately walked over to the niches in the wall and studied the urns. Like all Italians, Conti had been taught about the Etruscans in grade school, but despite living in the heart of their ancient territory now for several years, he'd never gotten around to learning much more. Police work was like that. So it was no use examining the urns, verification of their authenticity would be something for the damn art cops. He turned to the sergeant.

"What's in the next room? The American didn't get into it."

"I think you'll find it interesting, Commissario," said the policeman as he lead the way. The wooden plank that Montoya had described had been pushed to one side, revealing another doorway, about as low as the entrance to the cave itself. Being careful not to trip on the wires, Conti bent again and found himself in another room, this one slightly larger than the first, and well lit. When he looked around, his mouth dipped to a frown.

What the devil is this?

◇◇◇

Rick was about to ring the bell at the side of the museum door, as Zerbino had instructed, when he remembered the cell phone issue with the building's security system. He pulled his out, did the needful, and returned it to his pocket before pressing the bell with his thumb. If it was working, it must ring well inside the building, since Rick heard nothing. When he was starting to wonder how long he should wait he saw the large figure of Zerbino through the glass, a key chain swinging from his hand like a prison guard. Even on his morning off the man was dressed like he was about to give a lecture to a group of university scholars. After some fumbling with the lock the door was opened, and the two men shook hands.

"Riccardo, so good to see you again. Come in, come in."

"This is really very kind of you, Arnolfo." Their heels clicked on the empty marble floor. Unlike their last visit, when Rick had squeezed through various groups of giggling school kids, the building was pleasantly quiet. The collection appeared even more ancient in the silence, causing Rick to lower his voice, as if they were in a church. Zerbino, however, was lively, if not bubbling, as he talked about the museum.

"I can't tell you how exciting it was for me when I won this position. Becoming the curator of such a collection is the dream of any Etruscanologist." They were in a room displaying metal Etruscan artifacts of daily life: utensils and goblets, pins and other jewelry. Zerbino was in his element, pointing out how certain objects changed their design with fashion, how ideas were borrowed from the Greeks, and the extent to which the Romans were influenced by Etruscan design. Rick was fascinated by the running commentary and could not help contrasting this tour with the first one when Zerbino seemed merely to be going through the motions. They moved through various other rooms and found themselves in the first of those displaying the museum's famous collection of funerary urns. Zerbino looked around the shelves and his voice became more serious.

"These wonderful pieces, Riccardo, remind me of one of the scourges of our profession; the trafficking in ancient art. It has been going on for centuries." He paused and turned to face Rick. "And it continues today." Rick remembered Commissario Conti's comment about consulting Zerbino in the early days of the case. Perhaps he was going to boast about supporting the valiant efforts of the police. The curator walked slowly around the room, looking at the urns in silence. Suddenly he stopped and turned, looking at his guest. His face had changed.

"You can imagine that for me, as someone who is so involved in preserving these beautiful objects, it was a great shock to find someone in my very midst who is involved in that insidious trade."

Rick stood in silence, digesting the man's words and attempting to make sense of them. Was it possible that Zerbino knew about Rick's undercover job? Conti had been so careful in telling Rick to keep anything from Zerbino, it was unlikely that the man could have found out, unless it was from someone else in the *commissariato*. Rick suddenly thought of another possibility. With all the hints I've been dropping around the city about wanting to buy special Etruscan objects, Zerbino could have gotten wind of them from someone and actually thinks I'm a trafficker. And now the outraged Etruscanologist is confronting the unscrupulous criminal, ready to make a citizen's arrest. He's certainly large enough to do it.

"I don't understand, Arnolfo, what are you getting at?"

Zerbino's mouth turned to a leering smile as he looked directly at Rick. "Your activities here in Volterra have not gone unnoticed. Need I say more?"

◇◇◇

The second room of the cave held two crude tables made of long planks, each supported by wooden sawhorses, and each holding a set of Etruscan urns. Industrial pole lamps, like the ones in the other room, directed their light to the surfaces of the two tables. Spread on them were chisels, hammers, rulers, and other tools. Conti walked to one of the tables and examined its two urns, realizing immediately that they were similar. No, not similar, virtually the same, or at the very least close to being the same. The design was identical, a winged god surrounded by warriors who were led by a man with a long sword. Certain details of the one, in front of which most of the tools lay, were still a bit rough, but someone looking quickly at them would have had trouble telling them apart. The copy would probably be a perfect one, detectible by only the most learned of Etruscan scholars. Conti was trying to put it all together in his mind when he noticed a dirty folder on the far side of the table. Inside was a photograph of the urn he had just examined. The photograph was enclosed in a protective plastic sheet on which a label had been attached to the bottom. The label had the logo of the Etruscan museum and what Conti guessed to be a catalog number. He held up the photograph and compared the urn pictured with the one on the table. The only difference was that the urn in the photo was sitting on a shelf in the *Museo Etrusco Guarnacci.*

Conti turned and walked quickly out of the room, almost colliding with the top of the doorway. Cursing, he bent down and nearly ran through the other room toward the cave entrance where he did collide, but this time with a policeman whose head was down to enter the cave.

"*Mi scusi, Commissario,*" said the man as he picked himself off the floor, brushing his hands of the mud that had stuck to them when he fell. "I was bringing you an urgent message," he added, hoping it could deflect some of his boss' anger.

"Make it quick, I'm in a hurry."

The man read from a piece of paper he took from his jacket pocket. "A call from the station. They found the red Opel. A meter maid spotted it after she had seen our notice on the bulletin board this morning."

"She is to be complimented. Are they sure it's the right one?"

"There was an English-Italian dictionary in the back seat."

"Excellent. Where is it?"

Again the policeman glanced at the paper. "Via della Porta Marconi, a side street that doesn't get much traffic. Near the Etruscan museum. In fact it was just off the street itself, parked in one of the spaces reserved for the museum." He looked up from the paper and saw Conti staring down at his hands.

"Let me see, corporal."

"But it just has what I—"

He grabbed the man's hand. "No, not the paper, let me see your hands." Conti looked at the upturned palms and then bent down to the ground and picked up some of the clay from the cave floor in his fingers. "This could be even worse than I thought."

Conti was out of the cave before the young policeman could find any words to answer. As the commissario stepped outside he pulled out his cell phone, punched the buttons and then stared at the small screen when he heard the voice of one of the policeman above.

"There is no signal down there, Commissario," the man shouted, "you'll have to come up here."

Conti cursed and started up the path, tripping a few times as he hurriedly made his way, so that when he got to the top and pulled out his phone again he was nearly out of breath.

"*Rispondi, Montoya, per l'amore di dio, rispondi,*" he gasped into the buzzing phone.

He gave up and tried another number.

"LoGuercio, where are you?…No, I want you to go back. Here's what you should do."

◇◇◇

"There must be some misunderstanding, Arnolfo, I'm in Volterra to buy alabaster and other Etruscan reproductions."

"Of course you are." The grin stayed on Zerbino's face as he raised his eyes to look past Rick toward the back of the room. "Ah, I thought you would never get here," he said, still looking past Rick, who now turned around to follow Zerbino's eyes. "Perfect timing, we are about to talk business," said Zerbino as he turned back to Rick. "Riccardo, I think you have met Signor Malandro."

It took a moment to place the man who was taking his place next to Zerbino. Rick looked at the face whose mouth now mirrored the half smile of the curator and remembered. When he had seen it the first time, the face was covered by the shadow of a stubbled beard and a film of alabaster dust. Without the chin stubble and dusty blue coat, Rick decided, the guy almost looked presentable. He even wore a relatively clean shirt. But why was the foreman of Landi's workshop here? What did he have to do with Zerbino and the museum? Rick tried to put the pieces together, but nothing fit. It was all too confusing. Malandro works for Zerbino? We're going to talk business? What the hell is going on here?

"Signor Malandro overheard you talking to Landi about artifacts. He was convinced that you could be a serious buyer, and I value his judgment. When you and I met for coffee I got the same impression. That is why I went ahead with your visit to the cave."

Rick sighed. "Driven by your other, uh, colleague, Arnolfo?"

"I have many colleagues, Riccardo. The more of them one has, the more information one can accumulate, and information is the key to any successful business. Would you believe that the man who drove you to the cave works at the Volterra Chamber of Commerce?" He threw a smile at Malandro, which was reciprocated. "Passing information on, sometimes correct and sometimes wrong, can also be very helpful. Especially for keeping the police off our trail so they can spend their time sticking their noses into the business of others." Zerbino and Malandro again exchanged grins.

He should have been scared, or at least worried, but instead a calm came over Rick as he arranged his thoughts. All right, Montoya, this was why Beppo sent you up here, and Beppo knew what he was doing. He knew you could handle it. Relax. This will be easy. Talk, play the part, get your ass safely out of the museum and then contact Conti. Remember how disappointed you were last night when Beppo and Conti jerked you off the case? Now you can *finire con bellezza*, as Italians say. Finish this with class.

"How nice that you are involved in this enterprise, Arnolfo, it now takes on a certain—what is the word?—a certain seriousness." He noticed a suspicious look from Malandro and added: "Not that your other partners did not deal with me in a completely professional manner, of course. But let us go to the crux of the matter, an issue which concerns me greatly. Your little cave was impressive, but how do I know that it is the real thing?" His steady voice surprised even himself. "I've yet to be convinced that I have seen even a single genuine piece of Etruscan art. I can't have you sending copies back to America, as good as they may be."

The two Italians again smiled at each other, it was getting to be a big part of their routine. Then Zerbino laughed and stretched his arms wide. "Look around you, Riccardo, you are surrounded by genuine pieces of Etruscan art."

Rick's eyes went from one wall to the other and then back to Zerbino. "I hardly think we can just pull something off a shelf, Arnolfo. How do the pieces in this museum help me?"

Zerbino rubbed his hands together, ready for the question and relishing the opportunity to answer it. "Riccardo, there are hundreds of urns in these rooms. I am the curator of the museum and even I don't know the exact number." He pointed to one on a top shelf. "Do you see this wonderful piece? Notice the intricate carving of the battle scene. What beautiful work, don't you think?" He glanced at Malandro whose half smile had turned full. "The original is in a private collection in Berlin, if I remember correctly." Zerbino pointed to another shelf. "And that one up there, it is somewhere in the Middle East." He paused to see the look on Rick's face. "But you, Riccardo, you will have an advantage over those buyers. You can actually choose the exact piece you want to purchase. It will be like going into a fine jewelry store and pointing to the necklace you wish."

He was enjoying the whole scene, striding from one side of the room to another, pointing at the shelves like he was once more lecturing to a class. "The process is quite simple. You pick the one you want and it will be removed from display, replaced by a small card indicating that the urn is under restoration. Then my friend here and his staff will work their magic. A few weeks after that, a piece of authentic Etruscan history is in your gallery in America. And at the same time, what everyone assumes is the lovingly restored urn returns to its place of honor on this shelf."

Rick nodded, impressed, despite himself. "So everyone is happy, the buyer has his stolen art and the seller has made a profit. Your business plan is brilliant, Arnolfo."

Zerbino positively glowed. He raised his index finger in the air. "Ah, but don't forget about our precious museum patrons, those tourists and school children who can't tell the difference between an Etruscan pot and one made by your Navajos. Those patrons, my friend, are also very happy, now able to admire a professionally restored burial urn. Look at the wonderful restoration Malandro did on this piece. Why it's almost like new." Malandro bent to an abbreviated bow.

"What about serious scholars?" asked Rick. "They must come from all over Italy to see this collection."

Zerbino walked from the shelves to where Rick stood in the middle of the room. "Not just from Italy, my friend, but from around the world. Another advantage of my position, Riccardo, is that I control which pieces are available for close professional observation. With so many urns it is not a problem. And even scholars are usually drawn only to the most famous pieces in our collection. I'm afraid I can't let you select one of those for your buyers. You must forgive me." Zerbino was pleased at the little joke.

Rick's mind was churning, but he kept himself on the business at hand. "Arnolfo, you have convinced me of authenticity. The only other major issue to discuss, before I call my people in New Mexico, is price."

Rick watched the expression on Zerbino's face go from the wide smile to a worried frown. *What could this be about?* he wondered. Surely the man was expecting the question, was he changing hats from the friendly salesman into that of the tough negotiator? Then Rick understood. Zerbino was not frowning at him, but rather a something directly behind him. Or someone. As he began to turn to see what it was, Rick heard a new and unfamiliar voice from the back of the room.

"Dr. Zerbino, I regret to inform you that the American is working for the police."

The man standing at the doorway was dressed in a well-cut dark suit, light blue shirt and simple striped tie. He did not strike Rick as the kind of man who would be involved in a criminal activity, but then neither had Zerbino on first meeting. It was not the dress and demeanor of the man that concerned Rick, it was the large pistol which he held up stiffly in his two hands, giving the clear impression that he knew how to use it. And had likely used it before.

The curator spoke first. "I don't understand," he stammered, while removing the large white handkerchief from his pocket and wiping his bald head. Zerbino was clearly as bewildered as he was angry. The smiles and laughs were gone. He glared into Rick's face and took short breaths to contain his indignation.

The man with the gun spoke again. His words were cold and deliberate.

"Just what I said, Dr. Zerbino, he has been hired by the art police in Rome to flush out traffickers of Etruscan artifacts. And it appears he has been successful." Hints of delight appeared in the man's eyes.

Rick, Malandro, and Zerbino stared at the gun. Rick could only guess what part in the gang the man played, but what was clear was that the police had been infiltrated. Unless the leak had come all the way from Rome. Could someone in the ministry be involved, feeding information to the very criminals Beppo was trying to catch? His adventure had suddenly turned dangerous, and now there was no policeman following him to step in and save his skin. Ironically Conti had probably called off the tail right when he really needed one. Whoever this guy was, he had now exposed the undercover work to the very person the ministry was trying to trap. Worse yet, Rick was now in the trap himself. Zerbino's voice cut through Rick's thoughts.

"Who are you?" The curator's weak voice almost cracked.

What the…? But it took Rick only a few seconds to understand the meaning of Zerbino's question, and when he did he took a deep, relieved breath. Perhaps his relief was a defense mechanism to deal with the situation and he was really frightened. He would leave the self-analysis to another time, alone with his uncle and a bottle of wine. At this point, all that was coming to mind was that he owed his skin to Conti. And this guy, whoever he was, might just be invited to a four course dinner, even at the place with the high prices and small portions.

"My name is LoGuercio. Detective LoGuercio. You'll forgive me for not showing you my identification card, but my hands are otherwise occupied." The policeman moved the barrel of his gun slightly, and Rick was now relieved to see that it had in fact been pointed at the space between Zerbino and Malandro, and not at him. "Signor Montoya, come over here please. You two, raise your hands, if you would. I doubt if you are armed, but I must be cautious."

Zerbino and Malandro stood together stiffly and did as they were told. Rick moved carefully away from them and approached LoGuercio, who now slowly took his left hand off the pistol and reached into his pocket for his cell phone. Still keeping his eyes on the two men, and the gun pointed directly at them, he pressed one of the buttons with his free thumb and put the phone to his ear.

"Commissario Conti?"

...be hard to convince a judge of that, Dr. Zerbino. You ...itted that he worked for you, and the clay from your ...on his shoes when he died. What other explanation ...ere be?"

...ry simple one. But when he was killed, as much as I ...o help you with your investigation, I could not reveal ...bvious reasons."

...on." Conti was not buying it. Nor was Rick.

...mention of murder had evaporated the little self-...nce that Zerbino had left. He talked rapidly. "You see, ...ssario, one of Canopo's duties was infiltrating similar ...l operations in Volterra, and he did it very well. I wanted ...o an eye on the competition, because if the police—I ...of course, if you—started investigating other dealers, ...uld have stumbled onto our work. Then I realized that I ...actually push the authorities toward other crime, and that ...keep you busy and happy. And away from our business. ...ill have to forgive me." He studied Conti's face and got no ...on. "But I fear that the other group of criminals may have ...d out about Canopo's double dealing, and they were not as ...tant about the use of violence as I would be."

...What is the group you are talking about?"

...erbino shrugged and pointed at the shelves. "They are not ...lved in anything of this quality. It is the usual fakes and ...ery, poor copies which fool most of the people who buy ...al artifacts. But very lucrative, I am sure." He looked from ...urns to Conti. "But of course, I forgot that you have seen ...ir work." Conti frowned. "The shed, Commissario?"

..."So it was you who left the tip with us about the shed."

..."Not I exactly, but it was done on my orders. And it was suc-...ssful, I dare say. I suspect it set back their work considerably, ...d kept you busy."

..."Who is in this other group of traffickers?" It was LoGuercio ...ho asked the question, surprising Rick. Apparently his work ...cornering Zerbino had given him the right to interrogate the ...an. Remembering the deferential manner all the policemen

Chapter Ten

Suddenly their ear drums split open. It was as if they were standing in the middle of a siren factory on testing day. The harsh sound of the alarms caromed off the museum's cement walls, trying to blast out the doorways, but met by more of the same howling coming from the other rooms. Flashing lights added to the atmosphere of a prison escape. The noise and flashes came from small fixtures that Rick had not noticed, wedged high in the corners of each room. Fortunately, LoGuercio did not drop his pistol, but when his eyes instinctively darted around the room Malandro bolted for the door and was out before the policeman could recover. Zerbino remained frozen in place.

"Turn off the phone!" Rick shouted. LoGuercio stared at him and then understood, mashing the buttons. As suddenly as they started, the sounds stopped.

"I don't think he'll get very far, Signor Montoya, I have men around the outside of the building. And Commissario Conti should be on his way."

As if on cue, Conti strode into the room, out of breath, with two uniformed policeman in tow. The man's usually rumpled suit was slightly stained on the knees with dirt. *No doubt the steep path down to the cave,* Rick thought.

Conti surveyed the scene. "Who is the man we just stopped trying to run out of here? He looked vaguely familiar."

"Malandro, Commissario," answered Rick, "He's the foreman at Landi's workshop."

"Of course. He looks almost presentable. Is Landi mixed up in this? If so, it's even more complicated than I thought." He saw that Rick was about to answer and raised a hand to stop him. He was in charge now. "And what was all that noise?" He looked at Zerbino, who had lowered his arms to his sides, and smiled. "Your alarm system? Don't tell me, Dr. Zerbino, that someone was trying to steal your precious Etruscan urns. I hope you were able to stop them, it would truly be a shame to lose even a single one of them."

Though it was intended for Zerbino, the sarcasm was not lost on Rick. So Conti knew about Zerbino's scheme; something he saw at the cave tipped him off. Then he understood. Of course, the work on the copies, that was what was going on in the other room of the cave, the part he wasn't allowed to see yesterday. The conversation now between Conti and Zerbino should prove interesting. LoGuercio, it appeared, had the same feeling of anticipation. He was looking at his boss as he lifted the tail of his jacket to holster the pistol behind his back.

"Welcome to my museum, Commissario, but I would have preferred that your visit had been under different circumstances." Zerbino held out his hands, palms up, and then clasped them together over his chest. He seemed smaller than he had been before LoGuercio had appeared, as if the air had gone out of him. "I suppose it would be futile to deny what has been going on, since I just finished explaining it all to your intrepid under-cover man here. The temptation of riches and so many urns. Who would miss a few of them? And the collectors have such a deep appreciation of their beauty."

"Every piece is a precious part of the patrimony of Italy," said Rick. Since he was working for the Ministry of Culture, he felt an obligation to stand up for their mission.

"The patrimony of Italy?" Zerbino returned to his professorial manner in responding to Rick, regaining a few inches of height. "And what is Italy, my dear Signor Montoya? A recent invention of the latest inhabitants of this peninsula, nothing more. This idea that the past belongs on an altar to be worshipped is

something unknown to the E
who roamed these lands over th
of value be locked behind glas
bidder? So you see, Commissa
ancient tradition."

Conti shook his head slowly.
for crime," said Conti, "but that
It's brilliant people like you, *d*
name." He smiled at his own hum
of artifacts to the art police, who
My interest right now is in other c

"Then I suppose I will be hand
from Rome?" asked Zerbino.

"I wouldn't exactly call them co
staying with us. Murder is considered
will take precedence over trafficking i

Zerbino's eyes widened and he too
understand."

"Canopo," said Conti. "He worked
"Yes, yes, he did, but I had nothing–
"Nothing to do with his death? What
Canopo? Was he having second thoughts
in your little criminal operation? Were y
to the police? Or did he want to get more
profits? It must have been something very
killed. Or did you do it yourself?"

Glistening beads were appearing again
despite the cool temperature in the room.
into his pocket for his handkerchief, but wh
policemen instantly put their hands on their
a defensive gesture and used his bare hand to

"Violence? *O dio*, not me, Commissario. Ho
consider such a thing? Canopo worked for me
one of my most trusted and valued assistants.
great loss to my…to my work."

at the station had shown with the commissario, Rick found it a bit strange. But Conti appeared not to be concerned with his subordinate, and he looked back at Zerbino for the answer to the question.

"As much as I would love to help you, there is little I know other than the names of three of their members who were Canopo's contacts. At least the names they gave him, which were likely not their real ones. The one thing I must say about that organization, they value secrecy."

"The more you can remember the better," said Conti. "The judge may look more favorably on your own case if your memory improves." To help make the point, Conti signaled to one of the policeman to handcuff the museum curator.

Zerbino smiled for the first time since Conti's arrival. "I was expecting you to say that. I will do my best to recall as many details as I can." As a sergeant was putting handcuffs on Zerbino he turned back to Conti. "Commissario, there is one detail I do remember."

"Yes?"

"The men that Canopo dealt with never mentioned the name of the leader of their organization, as I said." He looked down at the handcuffs and back at Conti. "But he told me that once, only once, one of them slipped and referred to the boss in the third person."

"And what use is that?" asked Conti.

"He used the pronoun 'she,' Commissario. Could that help?"

◇◇◇

Rick had argued for a straight shot to Donatella's villa, but Conti made the decision to talk to Polpetto's secretary first. If what Polpetto had told Rick the previous evening was correct, only Claretta Angelini would be covering the office, and it would not take long to get her story. Then, if need be, they would make the long drive to Villa Gloria. Rick didn't tell Conti that he hoped a visit to the villa would not be necessary. Less than five minutes after leaving the museum, two police cars came to a stop in front of the exporter's office. Conti and Rick got out of the back seat and LoGuercio exited the front. They huddled with the three uniformed policeman in the follow car.

"You are sure, Signor Montoya, that there is no other way out of the second floor office?"

"I didn't see any other door, Commissario. The only way in and out of the office was through the hallway."

Conti turned to the others. "Detective, take one of the men with you and check out the downstairs while Montoya and I go up to the office. Have the other two stay here on the street." He looked back at Rick. "Are you sure she will let you in?"

"I have no reason to believe she won't."

Conti nodded silently and Rick pressed the button below Polpetto's name. The door buzzed open almost immediately. They looked at each other and Rick pushed open the door to let Conti enter. They climbed the steps while LoGuercio and the other policeman began to reconnoiter the area behind the stairwell. The office door did not open as quickly as the one from the street, Rick and Conti waited several seconds after their knock before they heard the welcoming buzz and click. When Rick pushed open the door, Claretta was standing behind the desk straightening her skirt. On seeing him she smiled broadly. She had lipstick on, bright red like last night, to match the glasses as well as the earrings.

"Signor Montoya, I did not expect to—" The smile remained, but the gaunt figure of Conti behind Rick brought a questioning look to her face. "You have brought someone with you. I am afraid that Signor Polpetto is in Firenze today, if you need to speak to him…"

"We would like to speak to you, Signora Angelini." Conti's somber voice had its effect on the woman. She stiffened and made no movement to sit down.

"And you are?"

Conti took a small leather case from his pocket and opened it for her inspection. "Commissario Conti, Signora. I have some questions to ask you. About your dealings in the arts market, such as they are."

Fear tightened her face now, and she clasped her hands tightly while looking at Rick for support. Was this simply the usual reaction to a sudden encounter with the police, he wondered, or could she actually be the leader of the forgery gang?

"I don't understand, Commissario. What has Signor Montoya told you?" She looked again at Rick, now lit with anger. "And why would he be talking to you?"

Conti ignored her questions and continued. "We have reason to believe that this office, and specifically you, Signora, have been involved in some activities that cross the line between legitimate business and illegal activity. It would make your situation much more favorable if you told me about it now. But if not, we can take you to my office."

"Tell you about what?"

The movement of her head toward the door to Polpetto's office was almost imperceptible, but Rick spotted it. So, apparently, did Conti; he pushed back his coat and took a small revolver from its holster. Claretta was staring at the gun when the door to Polpetto's office opened to reveal the man Rick had last seen in the cathedral. And, to Rick's relief, he was unarmed. Claretta threw her arms around Santo, pushed her cheek against his chest, and began to sob.

"Silvio," she said with difficulty, "this is a policeman, and he said—"

"I could hear," Santo answered while looking at Conti. "You can put your gun away, Commissario, we are not common criminals."

Rick was now more convinced than ever that they in fact *were* criminals, but he watched Conti shrug and holster the pistol.

"I have men in the hall and outside the building, and they are armed more than I. But you have not told me who you are."

"This is Signor Santo," said Rick. "The man I met in the cathedral."

Conti smiled. "Ah yes, the person who was going to offer some questionable art work to the American dealer."

Rick watched the reaction of Claretta to Conti's words. Forget ordering a murder to maintain group discipline, he thought, this woman didn't appear capable of leading a girl scout troop. If anyone was in charge, it had to be Santo, but even he didn't act the part.

"You were right, Silvio," she sobbed, looking up at Santo, "Polpetto found out. We never should have done it." A thin black streak of teary eye liner crept down her cheek.

Rick saw that Conti was frowning. *The policeman is confused*, he thought, *and so am I*. Polpetto must be part of all this, so what could the man have found out? Had she ordered the murder, and now she thinks her boss learned of the crime? Once again he asked himself what the hell was going on.

"Commissario," said Santo, his arm around Claretta, "what we did was unethical, perhaps even immoral, but it was hardly criminal. And surely it doesn't warrant coming in here with guns." Conti was still frowning, and Rick remained silent. "I am a reputable art dealer, but I suppose my reputation will now be ruined. I—"

"It was my fault, Silvio, it was my idea."

Santo continued to face Conti while his arms protected the woman. "She had nothing to do with it, it was my decision completely. Polpetto did not need any more business, but having an international client could have helped me, helped us, get the boost we needed."

"So that's why you wanted to meet me in the cathedral."

He looked at Rick like he was being offered a life preserver. "Yes, of course, Signor Montoya, you'll understand since you are in the art business, you know it can be vicious. So I didn't want to risk it getting back to Polpetto." He stroked Claretta's face, almost knocking off her red glasses. "I had some very good pieces I was going to show you tomorrow. I don't suppose that you might still—"

"What kind of pieces?" asked Conti. "Some good forgeries?"

The question appeared to bother Santo more than having a gun aimed at him. "Certainly not! I may have been unethical in trying to take some business from Polpetto, but the art work I sell is authentic and of the highest quality."

Conti looked at Rick and shook his head sadly.

Two minutes later, on the street outside the office, Conti had finished giving instructions to the policemen before getting back into the cars.

"Commissario," said Rick, pulling out his cell phone. "This trip to the villa is going to take us some time. I should call my friend to tell her I'm going to be late getting back to the hotel. Since your men were following me, I trust you know about her arrival in Volterra yesterday?" Conti flicked his wrist to indicate that time should not be wasted on a long conversation.

◇◇◇

Erica spoke in a low voice so that Dario wouldn't hear. "You'll excuse me for saying so, Donatella, but what a strange man he is. Though he does seem to be a very careful driver."

They were walking slowly between a row of Roman columns and a low stone wall. Other than a small group of Japanese tourists clustered together a few hundred feet away, listening intently to their guide, they were the only visitors to the ruins on this morning. The weather may have had something to do with it; clouds were rolling in from the west, covering the archeological area, as well as the rest of the city, with a gray shroud. Both women wore thick-soled boots, perfect footwear for the combination of dirt and stone that was their path. Long wool coats protected them from the cold, and they both kept their hands in the pockets as they walked. Neither wore a hat. Even on the ski slopes Italian women preferred to let their hair, and hair style, be seen. Everything in their attire was casual yet practical, though the line between casual and chic in Italy was often a fine one.

"He isn't just a driver, Erica, he does a bit of everything for me in the business. When I need some problem resolved, I usually turn to him."

"The way he's following us he seems to think he's also your bodyguard."

"I suppose so. Is that yours?" Erica didn't understand the question at first, then fumbled in her purse to pull out a cell phone.

"Yes, Ricky. Did you call the hotel? I didn't answer in the room because I'm not there." She smiled at Donatella. "Donatella came by and picked me up, so we are catching up on each other's lives while doing some sightseeing. And it was a wonderful excuse not to do my work. What? We're at the amphitheater. You haven't? Why don't you join us? *Benissimo*. Yes, I'm being careful, and her assistant is here watching over us. See you in a few minutes." She closed the phone and returned it to the purse. "That was Ricky, he—"

"He's done at the museum and is going to join us. Got that." She took Erica's arm and leaned close to her ear. "I suppose we should talk about him before he gets here."

Erica laughed softly. "I believe we've done enough of that already, don't you think?"

Donatella did not match the laugh of her friend, and kept her eyes on the path while she formed a reply. "My contact with Ricky was strictly business, Erica, you know that."

"Thank goodness for that, *cara*." They walked several steps in silence before Erica spoke again. "Let's leave Ricky for another day. You haven't said much about your business, except it's expanding. It must be going well."

They turned to walk behind what had been the amphitheater's stage, its outline now formed by broken walls and paving stones. At the far side of the stage a double tier of Corinthian columns was all that was left of the original decorations that ran the length of the structure. It had been a marvelous backdrop for those sitting in the arc of stone seats. Drama, comedy, Roman, Greek, all performed here. The two women made their way between what had once been the walls of the changing rooms to emerge onto the stage itself. High above them rose the north walls of the city.

"Business is going well, though there have been some setbacks, especially one recently, but that is the nature of any business. The problem that caused it was taken care of, and now we should be doing quite well. And I hope to do some business with Ricky. You won't mind that I bring it up with him when he arrives."

"No, of course not."

Donatella looked up at the tiers of stone seats above them. "Isn't this a magnificent place, Erica? You Romans build things to last, don't you? One can imagine what it was like to be an actor in those times, the seats filled with the cheering public when you performed well."

"No different than being an actor now, I suppose. Without a microphone, of course."

While the two women strolled across the grass of the stage, Dario leaned his large frame against the stone and glanced back over the ruins. The Japanese tourists had moved to an excavation area that was covered with a corrugated plastic roof to protect it from the elements, a cover which could be put to use soon, given the gathering clouds. Two men in suits had come through the gate and were walking slowly toward the amphitheater. The taller one, his hat pulled well down over his head in anticipation of the weather, held up his arms like pointers, talking and gesturing toward parts of the structure as they walked. The other, younger and more stylishly dressed, looked where the first man directed, and listened intently, nodding in appreciation for the history lesson. Dario glanced at Donatella and then looked back at the two men, tracking their movement with a steady eye. They stopped, the one still gesturing as he talked. The two women were now seated a few rows up from the stage where they could see the ruins spread out below them. Something caught Erica's eye.

"There's Ricky. He has someone with him."

Dario had taken his eyes off the other two men and watched the new arrivals, relaxing somewhat when he recognized Rick. Donatella gave him an almost imperceptible nod, and he leaned back against the stone, returning his attention to the first two men. The taller one with the hat was now using his hands like a movie director to frame the view of the amphitheater while he talked and walked steadily toward the stage.

Rick kissed Erica on both cheeks and stiffly shook hands with Donatella.

"Donatella, Erica, let me introduce Paolo LoGuercio, who I met at the museum. He has just arrived in Volterra and had not visited the amphitheater either, so I invited him along. I didn't think you'd mind."

The detective bowed his head slightly.

"So you are new to Volterra," said Donatella while looking at LoGuercio with more than neighborly interest. "What brings you to our lovely city? Tourism, I suppose?"

If Donatella was expecting a smile from LoGuercio, she didn't get one. "No, I was recently transferred here with my work. A nice change from the south, I have to say."

This perked up Donatella even more. "Ah, so you are here to stay." She took in his tailored suit and silk tie. "Where do you work?"

"I am with the police, Signora Minotti."

Donatella stiffened, but quickly regained her composure. Her reaction was not lost on Dario, who began stepping rapidly toward them. While LoGuercio kept his attention on Donatella, Rick surveyed the ruins, assessing the situation. He saw that Conti had pushed his hat back and was now trotting briskly along the path, the other plainclothes policeman at his side. They were almost to the stage. Dario's eyes darted between the two groups of men and began running toward his boss, his eyes narrowing.

"You know my name?"

"Yes, Signora," answered LoGuercio. "And when you are finished with the tour of the amphitheater, if you would be so kind, we would appreciate your presence in my office. We have some questions. It should not take long."

Rick turned just in time to see Dario's dark figure lunging toward them at a speed unimaginable for such a large man.

It all happened very fast.

Erica gave a short cry of pain as Dario's thick fingers grabbed her arm and pressed the gun into the small of her back. "You will not move, any of you, or Signora Erica will be shot." He spoke with the calm of someone who had used a pistol before, and the other four men did not move from where they stood. "Signora Minotti and I will walk from here to the car, with our friend here, and you will remain where you are." To emphasize his point he twisted the barrel of the gun again, causing Erica to wince.

"Dario," said Donatella, in a barely audible voice, "let her go. There must be some misunderstanding." She turned to the others, not hiding the look of fear on her face. "He is very protective, he's been like that since I was a child."

"Put the gun down, you know you won't be able to get away." Conti tried unsuccessfully to use a soothing voice. Dario's eyes swept from one policeman to another, but the hand on the gun did not move.

"Dario, don't do this, it isn't worth it." Donatella again, her face now almost white. She spoke in short gasps.

Dario kept his eyes on the other men as he spit out the words. "Not worth it? Not worth it? You have never seen the inside of an Italian prison, Signora. If you had, you would not say that. Come, we have no time to lose." But Donatella remained frozen in place, like the stones that ringed the theater.

"This will only make your situation worse, Dario." Conti kept his eyes locked on the gun in Erica's back as he spoke. "Give me the gun now or your time in prison will be considerably longer. And it will not help Signora Minotti."

Dario glanced at Donatella and his eyes narrowed even more, if that was possible. Conti was smart, thought Rick; play on Dario's loyalty to his boss. Donatella's next words did not help matters.

"Commissario, I never thought there would be violence. I swear it."

The look on Erica's face showed that she was finally making sense of the confusion, understanding that this was not about stolen artifacts after all. It was about murder. She stared at her friend in disbelief.

If Dario was disappointed with Donatella's lack of loyalty, he didn't show it. The expression on his face had not changed since he had pulled out his gun, and it did not change now. Nor did his voice, still cold and raspy.

"Then we will leave you out of it," he answered to Donatella. He cast her a glare full of venom before returning his attention to his hostage. "Come, Signora, you will be my ticket out of here." Erica cried out again as the barrel jabbed into her back, causing LoGuercio instinctively to move toward her. He caught himself and stopped immediately.

"You will not arrest me," said Dario. "No one will." He spit on the ground just short of LoGuercio's polished shoe.

"Don't try to stop him, detective." Conti's words were quiet but firm.

Dario and Erica had to maneuver through two stone steps and a narrow drainage ditch before reaching the flat grass of the stage. Rick's fists hung stiff and tight as Dario shoved Erica, the gun digging into her body. Conti hurriedly raised his hands toward the gate. Rick realized he was signaling to his men on the street to stand off and let Dario and Erica pass. If they got to the car, anything could happen.

As she was forced down the steps Erica's left shoe slipped on the smooth stone. She screamed and collapsed to the ground, extending her arms to break the fall. Dario stumbled, feet tangled with hers, lurching him backward until his head smacked the flat stone of the step. He shook his head and recovered quickly, raising his gun while pushing himself up with the other elbow, his widened eyes assessing his situation. His reflexes were quick, but not as quick as those of LoGuercio. When Erica and Dario tumbled, the detective dropped to one knee, drew the pistol from his belt, and fired, all one smooth motion. Blood spurted from Dario's neck, a mortal wound. He blinked at the LoGuercio's gun barrel in disbelief before sinking back on the rock, his head turned toward Donatella. She had crumpled to her knees and was sobbing as his blood pooled slowly on the stone.

Oddly, Rick thought of police training. The drop and shoot was one polished act, no doubt practiced until it was expert and natural. LoGuercio might have won honors in shooting competitions. Did they only teach them to shoot to kill and not shoot to wound? He would have to ask Uncle Piero.

Erica pushed slowly to her knees, rubbing her skinned hands. She avoided looking at the crumpled body next to her. She stood, wrapping herself in Rick's arms. "Is he—"

LoGuercio, standing over Dario, answered. "Yes, Signora, he's dead. He could have shot you. Or any of us. If he had reached the car—"

"We all saw what happened, LoGuercio." Conti's face filled with concern. He turned to Donatella, who locked her hands over her mouth as she stared at the body.

If this were the States, thought Rick, Conti would read Donatella her Miranda rights. But instead the commissario opened his cell phone and called for an ambulance.

Chapter Eleven

Erica was right. The huge painting was as spectacular as she said it would be, almost enough for him to drop his distaste for her beloved Mannerists. The scene had been painted hundreds of times, but Rosso Fiorentino's take on Christ's descent from the cross was so striking that Rick understood why it was considered his finest work. Though Erica spoke in hushed tones in keeping with the darkened ambiance of the museum, he could hear the passion in her voice. He'd heard it before, less than a week earlier, when she had urged him to take on this assignment. Help save the country's artistic patrimony, she had said. Now he heard it again.

The visit to the museum was doing more than give Rick another opportunity to hear Erica's passion for art. They needed to take their minds off what they'd seen among the cold stones of the amphitheater. Unspoken, but understood. They would have to talk about the ugliness eventually—they both knew that—but at this moment they worked to keep their minds and eyes focused on beauty.

He and Beppo listened while she talked about Rosso. The artist had been a bit of a kook, even more than other Mannerist painters, and Rick could see that there was an element of the bizarre in this canvas. But despite the quirkiness of his style, Rosso had created a masterpiece in his version of the deposition. The only face in the painting not contorted in sadness or pain was that of crucified Christ himself, as the other men struggled to bring his body down from the cross. That one face showed only dreamlike tranquility. His peace contrasted with the turmoil of the others, especially the grief of his mother, barely visible in the shadows while comforted by three women in bright robes. Erica sat between Rick and Beppo on the wooden bench, silent after going through her long explanation of the work.

"Your minicourse on Rosso was excellent," Rick said, "but I'm not sure one needs it to appreciate this work."

Beppo reached behind Erica and rapped Rick lightly on the back of the head, something they used to do to each other in school. "What Rick means, Erica, is that he loved your explanation. I know I did. I must have missed the Mannerism seminar at the university. Perhaps I could audit your course in Rome."

"That's sweet of you, Beppo, but I understand what Ricky is saying. The best paintings, after all, are those that pull you in even if you know nothing about the subject or the artist. Not that I'm trying to talk myself out of a job."

"You can always get work with the police," said Beppo, "after your experience on this case today." They continued to study the large work of art on the wall in front of them. Unseen by Beppo, Rick squeezed Erica's hand, as if to say that it was time to return to reality.

"I don't think I'm cut out for police work, Beppo." She managed a tight smile. "And remember, it was Ricky who uncovered your gang of relic thieves."

"But," added Rick, "Beppo was the one who dreamed up and designed the whole scheme. I trust he will be advancing at the ministry." He leaned forward on the bench and looked past Erica at his friend. "Is there a better office in that building?"

"Only the minister's."

Rick returned his gaze to Rosso's painting. "I don't suppose he'll want to give it to you, Beppo." More staring, more silence. "The museum can't top this one. Let's go to lunch."

"I am taking you both to a late lunch," said Beppo, jumping to his feet.

"You mean the ministry is inviting us?" Rick grinned at Erica.

"No, no. Beppo Rinaldi himself. I will do it with great pleasure, after all that the two of you went through this morning. I have already made a reservation at a place which comes highly recommended on the *Via dei Prigioni*. It seemed appropriate considering the various people who will end up in prison after today." They walked out of the darkened room toward the entrance. The weather had cleared, allowing some sun to push through patchy clouds as the trio stepped onto the street's stones.

Rustic was again how the restaurant décor would be characterized in most circles, though given the age of the town, almost every building in the center fell into that category. The room's white walls changed to brick and joined above the diners' heads in rounded vaults, giving the impression that they were eating in what had been a storage room. That is exactly what the space had been, centuries earlier, but those same centuries had obscured the exact details as to what had been stored and sold here. It was probably just as well they didn't know. And the three Roman diners weren't curious; after the usual quick arrival of bread, wine and mineral water to the table, their attention was now on the menu. It was Tuscan fare, as would be expected.

"Shall we split a *fiorentina*?" asked Beppo, "I haven't had a good steak since my last visit to Florence."

"I could go for that," said Rick, "the steak I had last night only whetted my appetite for red meat."

Erica quickly agreed, so the second course was set; now for the all-important pasta decision. Erica opted for soup, a simple tomato, but the two men needed something more substantial. For Rick it was *pici*, a freshly rolled and cut Tuscan pasta, but with a meat sauce instead of the traditional garlic and bread crumbs. Beppo opted for *paglia e fieno*, cream sauce tossed with a mix of spinach and semolina *fettuccini* which really looked like hay and straw. Decisions made and wineglasses clinked, conversation turned back to what could not be avoided. Rick began.

"Erica, you have to tell us, was your stumble an accident, or did you fall on purpose so you could trip Dario?" He wondered if he'd made a mistake to bring it up, but he needn't have worried.

She smiled and sipped from her wine, a smooth white. "How could you think it was anything but an accidental fall, Ricky?" The normal Erica, full of mystery, had returned.

"That answers my question. *Sei brava.*" He tapped her wine glass with his. "But let the record show that I was about to fall upon Dario and wrestle his gun away. I can never hold myself back when there is a damsel in distress, especially one—"

"Ricky, we shouldn't be joking about it," interrupted Erica. "I will never forget the look on poor Donatella's face."

"She was just as guilty of Canopo's murder as Dario," said Beppo softly. "It was she who ordered him to do something to the man."

"But I can't believe she really thought Dario would kill him. Scare him, yes, murder him no." She took another drink of wine, more than a sip.

"That may be her defense," said Beppo, "but with the murder and her whole operation of fake antiquities, she should be spending quite of bit of time behind bars."

Rick thought it was time to shift the talk away from Erica's friend. Or more accurately, former friend. "I have to say that I'm relieved that Polpetto is free of illegal activity. I kind of liked the guy."

"You just feel bad that he was being betrayed by his secretary," said Erica. "That's just the reaction I would expect from a man." She shook her head slowly with dramatic disgust.

At least she didn't say "a man like you," thought Rick. It was something.

"By betrayal are you two referring to Claretta trying to send business to her boyfriend?" asked Beppo. "Or just that she had a boyfriend?"

"I meant both, I guess," answered Rick as he pulled a bread stick from the basket.

"You two seem to have overlooked," added Erica, "that Polpetto was cheating on his wife himself."

"Significant," Beppo said, "that the woman in our midst brings up that minor detail."

"So," said Rick, "if we hang poor Polpetto with that peccadillo, the only one of our original group of suspects without sin is apparently Signor Landi. And he was the one I always suspected to be the main culprit. I will not quit my day job to become a detective."

"Good," said Erica and Beppo simultaneously, followed by general laughter.

"But one thing about Landi," said Beppo, once they all had regained their composure. "He has to work on his hiring skills. Two of his employees, Canopo and Malandro, were secretly working for Zerbino."

"Good point," said Rick. "That couldn't have helped productivity." He refreshed all their wine glasses and held up the empty bottle to the waiter who was passing their table at that moment. "*Subito*," was the man's reply as he whisked the bottle from the raised hand. Rick approved the service. "Give this guy a good tip, Beppo. But something else has been nagging me since we left the amphitheater. What about the interplay between Dario and the detective? At first I thought that Dario's reaction to LoGuercio was because of his revulsion to arrest, and being taken in by a rookie cop would be especially grating."

"LoGuercio is relatively new," said Beppo as he pulled another piece of crusty bread from the basket, "but the way you described it to me, Dario was reacting to the person who was going to arrest his boss. He couldn't have been pleased by that possibility."

"That was my sense," said Erica. "I don't know much about criminals, but his loyalty to Donatella seemed far beyond the usual relationship of someone to his boss. I felt it from the moment they picked me up in the car."

"I got that feeling too when I visited her villa, but the interplay this morning still seemed a bit strange. It was as if Dario knew LoGuercio."

"And the cop shot him to keep him quiet?"

"I didn't want to say that, Beppo, but now that you bring it up, it did cross my mind. Conti had a funny look on his face when LoGuercio shot the man."

"We all did, Ricky" said Erica. "Did you see that other cop with Conti? I thought he was going to faint."

"Yes, I guess you're right, it's just that—"

He was interrupted by the arrival of the first courses. Starting with Erica's soup, they were placed in front of the three diners, and after the traditional wishes of *buon appetito*, cheese was sprinkled on the pasta and utensils were lifted. Following the initial tastes Beppo continued the conversation.

"I can assure you, Rick, that LoGuercio did not know Dario. He only arrived here a few weeks ago from Sicily. I find it surprising that someone who is the nephew of a prominent policeman would conclude that a professional was involved in crime himself."

Both Rick and Erica glanced at Beppo, but were reassured by the look on his face.

"You're right, Beppo," Rick answered, "I've been reading too many seedy crime novels. These *pici* are excellent, would anyone want a taste?" The wine and food were having a relaxing effect on the trio, especially with Rick and Erica. "But, Beppo, how do you know so much about detective LoGuercio?" The answer was not what Rick expected.

"He works for me." Beppo grinned as he twirled some *paglia e fieno* on his fork and took in Rick's stunned face. "This should not go beyond this room, since Conti doesn't know, but we arranged to have LoGuercio work on the case when he was transferred up here."

"And to keep an eye on dear Ricky?" Erica patted Rick's hand, just as his mother used to do when he was a kid.

"Well, let's say, Erica, that we felt better with someone from outside the city working on the inside, and it turned out to be a good decision. LoGuercio kept me informed of what Rick was up to. Conti's decision to put him in charge of tailing our friend here was coincidental, of course, but very helpful."

Rick shook his head and frowned. "No wonder you didn't seem that concerned when I was checking in with you. You knew everything already. But in this town Conti is going to find out, and he won't be happy. He's pretty grouchy normally, and this won't make his day."

"He may not ever find out, Rick, he's retiring at the end of the week and moving to the Abruzzi."

"Good news for the police force here," said Erica. "But possibly not for his wife."

At that moment all eyes turned to the wheeled cart that had been pushed to the side of the table by their waiter. The platter on it held their *fiorentina*, grilled to perfection and oozing juices. The waiter paused for effect and then picked up a carving knife and fork to begin his work. It was the biggest piece of steak they had ever seen, but they would do their best.

Chapter Twelve

Before taking another drink, Commissario Piero Fontana held up the glass and studied his nephew through the almost clear liquid. The wine was a Greco di Tufo, a smooth white which had been the perfect foil to the grilled fish they just enjoyed. The waiters had cleared the dishes, brushed away any stray crumbs, and now patiently hovered offstage. Rushing the clientele was never allowed, and certainly not with these two regulars.

As always, Rick had the impression that Uncle Piero had been sewn into his tailored suit that morning. The jacket was unbuttoned now as the policeman leaned back with the satisfaction that comes from a good meal. A light blue shirt—embroidered with *pf* initials in the place of a pocket—framed a print tie that Rick did not remember seeing before. Perhaps, he thought, the reason Piero had never married was he didn't want to split his wardrobe money with anyone.

"This experience in Volterra has changed you, Riccardo. I can see it in your face." He took only a small taste of the wine, knowing it was the end of the bottle.

Rick nodded. "I suppose it did, *Zio*. But I don't know which part of it changed me the most."

"What do you mean?"

"Well, the whole undercover operation, if that's the word for it, was fascinating, exhilarating, even fun."

Piero smiled proudly. He had never made a secret of his disappointment that his nephew did not go into police work.

"Witnessing a man shot like that," Rick said, "even though he deserved it, probably aged me a few years. I would imagine that you had that reaction the first time."

The policeman nodded while rubbing a beard that was somewhere between a five o'clock shadow and a nearly full growth. "Yes, yes I did. What else about the experience has changed you?"

"This may sound strange, but I think I've become more Italian."

"And this may sound equally strange, Riccardo, but I'm not sure if that is a good thing or a bad thing. Tell me what you mean."

Rick twisted the stem of his wine glass while forming his reply. "The way I find myself thinking about people, for example. Not as trusting? More cynical? Canopo risking his future for some extra money and paying with his life. Zerbino going against everything his profession stood for. And Donatella. She appeared to be just a good businesswoman, and look what she was up to. And…"

Piero tilted his head as he looked at his nephew. "And Erica?"

Somehow he wasn't surprised that his uncle had brought up Erica. "Not in the same category as those others, of course, but something is stuck in the back of my mind." Piero waited for him to continue. "Maybe it's silly, but she's never said if she'd called Donatella before arriving in Volterra."

"You didn't ask her?"

Rick drained his wineglass. "No."

"Why not?"

Once again, Rick hesitated before replying. "I've asked myself that a few times and concluded that I'm afraid of what she would answer."

Piero leaned forward and put his palms on the table. "You're more cynical, less trusting of people, and you want to avoid confrontations with women. No doubt about it, you are Italian." He raised his glass and tapped its rim with Rick's. "*Benvenuto paisano.*" Rick forced a smile. "But let's go back to the first part," his uncle continued, "about the thrill of doing police work."

"I thought you might focus on that, *Zio*."

"The news of your exploits in Volterra has reached even the offices of the *polizia* here in Rome."

"You of course have had nothing to do with spreading the news."

Piero put his hand over a wounded heart. "I am forbidden to be proud of my nephew?" Rick grinned, but did not answer. His uncle continued. "Your skills were just what were needed in this case, and—you never know—they could be of value to the authorities again."

Rick was about to take a sip of his wine but stopped and put the glass down. "What do you mean by that?"

"Well, someone in the office was of the opinion that a person with your multicultural background could be helpful in certain cases. I naturally assured them that you would consider it your civic duty to assist the police when asked."

"*Zio*, don't tell me that—"

Piero held up his hands and stared down at the table, as if his nephew was focused on trifles and it was time to discuss serious issues. "*Bene*," he said, "we have established that you went to Volterra more American than Italian and perhaps returned the opposite. But, *caro* Riccardo, I would urge that you hold tight to your American passport to keep you from sliding completely into the cynicism you see around you. It's your American side that endears you to me, and, I'm sure, to everyone you've met in Rome." He put the spread fingers of his hands together over his chest in a gesture that was second nature for Romans. "But for the moment let's both be very Italian and return to the important business at hand. How shall we finish this meal in true style?"

Once again, Rick thought, I must *finire con bellezza*. But this time it would be easier. "How about the cheese board, *Signor Commissario*? We haven't had it in a while."

"A splendid idea. But that will mean red wine. A nice Dolcetto d'Alba, perhaps. We are celebrating, after all." He called over the waiter and gave him the order before settling back into the chair. "And what are your plans now, Riccardo?"

"My interpreting schedule is full through the holidays. I may try to do some skiing in January; a friend from college wants me to join him in the Dolomites. I'll need a break from my work by then."

Piero smiled. "Like the break you took in Tuscany."

The waiter returned with a bottle of red wine, and Piero began to study its label as if it contained the missing clue to an unsolved murder.

Author's Note

While this story and all its characters are pure fiction, Volterra is a real and thriving Tuscan city which proudly displays its rich history through the museums, churches, and public areas mentioned in this book. I have tried to describe them accurately and in the positive light which they deserve. Volterra is the ideal stop for the traveler who wants to see all the famous periods of Italian history in one place. Etruscan, Roman, Middle Ages, Renaissance—it has everything.

The *Museo Etrusco Guarnacci*, on the east side of the historic center, boasts the finest and largest collection of Etruscan burial urns in the world, as well as numerous other period artifacts including the haunting sculpture known as the Shadow of the Evening. A short walk away is the *Pinacoteca e Museo Civico,* whose collection includes, among many fine paintings, Rosso Fiorentino's Deposition. Painted in 1521, this huge canvas is considered by many Mannerist scholars as Rosso's most important work. A few hundred meters from the museum is the Roman theater that can be viewed from high on the wall or entered from below. One of the best-preserved Roman ruins of its period, it dates to the first century BC. Volterra's jewel, as with so many Italian cities, is its main square, the *Piazza dei Priori*, the heart of civic life since ancient times. Among the stone buildings on it is the somber city hall, still performing its original function, whose façade always impresses visitors. Just behind the piazza, the city's cathedral sits squeezed between other more mundane buildings, belying its impressive interior and beautiful works of art.

Along with traditional sightseeing, the alabaster around which this book is centered continues to bring tourists to Volterra. It is easy to visit workshops, and carved pieces of the stone are sold in shops everywhere. Visitors will also find artisans who specialize in Etruscan revival jewelry, something that fits easier into suitcases than alabaster.

Of course there's the food, and no discussion of Italian cities can omit cooking. Western Tuscany, like every part of the region, has its culinary specialties including dishes featuring one of my favorite ingredients, wild boar, that can garnish pasta or stand alone as a main course. Set yourself up with a plate of it on a restaurant patio, add a glass of the local Montescudaio wine, and you'll know that the real reason we love visiting Italy may not be the history and art.

I hope this book convinces readers that for anyone coming to Italy, especially if they find themselves in Tuscany, Volterra is not to be missed. And if a bed for the night is needed, they might consider the Hotel San Lino, named for the pope, which really was a convent in a previous life.